STAINED FATE
STAINED SERIES

JORJOR BATTLE

Stained Fate
Copyright © 2024 by JorJor Battle
All rights reserved.
Published: Jordan Battle 2024

With an exception to book quotes in book reviews, no parts of this book may be reproduced in any form without written consent from the author. Any further questions can be directed to: Jorjorb1015@gmail.com
This book is a work of fiction, and any names, places, characters, businesses, places, or events are fictitious or used fictitiously and part of the author's imagination. Any real-life similarities are purely coincidental and not meant to be done by the author.

First Edition
Cover Designer: AS Book Desing
Editor: Maddi Leatherman (EJL Editiing)

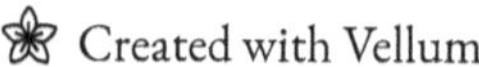 Created with Vellum

*For my girls who thought they were fated to be alone—
you're not*

TRIGGER WARNINGS

This is an new adult romance book that contains darker themes readers should be aware of. The themes include sexual content, death, familial abuse, mentions of trafficking, and self-hate.

I

WILLOW

GETTING HOME IS THE BEST FEELING IN THE world. Besides finding a book that absolutely shatters you, getting home from work is the next best way to rejuvenate my soul. Unlocking my door, I step inside and take my heels off at the door. Nola, my orange cat, comes scampering across the matted carpet floor, straight past me to the kitchen, where I assume her empty food bowl is. Nola and I are big girls—it's probably why she tolerates me. She is my first and probably last cat.

I understand Nola eats all her food by the time I get home. Instead of leaving her bowl empty for the rest of the day as I probably should, I refill it. Nola is a stray turned house pet, and food is a luxury I will let her indulge in whenever my little cutie wants. I hear her scratch against her ceramic bowl as I drop my purse on the counter and reach for the teapot sitting empty on the stovetop. I need my evening cup of tea before I do anything else, and this old-fashioned pot will take at least twenty minutes to boil.

Nothing calms me down like a pot of hot water and a bag of tea leaves. Letting my cardigan slide off my shoulders, I set it over one of my dining chairs and grab Nola a cup of food. Nola rubs against my legs as I walk towards her bowl. I know deep down that the food in my hands is the only reason she's giving me any sort of attention. Yet I can't help eating it up and mumbling in a baby voice about how much of a good girl she is. Nola pounces on her food as if she hasn't eaten all day.

Seeing her content, I go to my room; my fingers pull at my work clothes. The itch for soft cotton t-shirts starts at the cuff of my blouse and spreads to the entirety of my back.

My room, similar to the rest of my apartment, has boring white walls and dirty matted carpets. When I first breezed through town, I wasn't sure I was staying, but here I am five years later and loving this little town in Michigan. Rainfall Avenue was the town name—a popstar's fan was naming the new town, and I honestly can't blame her for picking a street name for a town. Rainfall Avenue is made up of two sides, split almost directly in half. There is a human side and a paranormal side. Humans typically stay in their half of town, though not all do. I think it's because of natural instinct. The same way I sense prey on their side of town, I assume they sense predators on ours, which makes the sensible humans stay away.

Now that paranormals are growing, both in species and size, we're taking over other towns, cities, and probably countries at this point. Shifters mainly stay in Rainfall Avenue; it's referenced as the shifter side purely due to our population. While there are witches, vampires, and fairies that may stay in Rainfall Avenue, the four seasons that Michigan goes through make it hard on other species.

Vampires are sensitive to light, and the bright sun of the summer months irritates them. They often have winter homes where they go May through September. Fairies do fairly well since they control the elements, but they prefer the high heat of summer. They are largely located down south, and witches stick with fairies since they are alike in abilities.

Shifter's bodies can acclimate to environmental changes similar to regular animals, and evolution is much faster in us than in humans. Our bodies will change—such as the thickness of our skin—based on the consistent experiences that our bodies' face.

I wonder if it's time to move into something more permanent. The idea of settling down was only a dream of mine, not something I thought would ever happen, especially since I lost my soul mate. I dreamed of a place to share with him, with room for more bookshelves and the kids we'd have one day. We were going to have the picture-perfect family. But as the Moon Goddess must have decided, just because I want something doesn't mean I'm destined for it.

Nola jumps on the dresser as I open my drawer with pajamas. Nothing beats changing into coordinated pajamas before bed. I never thought I'd ever come to appreciate a nice pair of pajamas, as I do now. I pick up a silk orange set, and an itch crawls its way up my arms and around my shoulders. Scrunching my face, I turn back to the drawer, pulling it all the way out. Something isn't right. I stare blanketly at the drawer. What is wrong? Something is off.

My pajamas aren't folded correctly. In fact, the drawer is a mess. My eyes trail over the mused drawer. There's no shame in a messy drawer, but I had organizers and rows of color coordinated clothes and this is not it. These are messily rummaged through, and the ones that are folded aren't folded the way I fold them.

Letting the pair in my hands fall to the ground, I open another drawer, noticing my leggings are folded incorrectly, too. I fold my leggings in half and then roll them; these are folded twice and then rolled. Would I do that subconsciously? I mean, I watch TV while doing laundry. Maybe I was distracted? No, because even when I am distracted, I'd still follow my usual patterns, and I don't leave my drawers messy either.

Oh my goodness. Someone else must have been through my stuff. I pull open another drawer, pulling out socks and underwear. The socks were fine; I guess they weren't as interesting as my underwear? My underwear was obviously messed with. The tight rows of perfectly folded underwear are loose and strewn about.

My breathing becomes labored as I pace, noticing all the things that were misplaced or messed with. My clothes, a lamp on the opposite nightstand, wrinkled bed sheets, certain books are out of place. Everything is an easy fix, sure, but no one had been here since my best friend Flora spent the night over a month ago. My room was perfect before I left for work this morning. This had to have happened today, between the hours of eight and six. Someone was in my apartment uninvited.

I can hear the teapot on the stove screaming to let me know the water is done, but I can't move. I'm frozen in the middle of my room, the rough carpet scratching my feet. I blink slowly, my hands holding my head up and tangling in my curls.

Someone was here.

Someone was here, uninvited. Someone broke into my dingy apartment. To do what? To steal what? Searching around again, I only notice a few bras missing. I only know that because I own exactly three regular bras, and now I only own one. The rest of the bras I own are sports bras. I prefer to be comfortable. "Who was here?" I ask out loud to Nola.

Nola is still sitting on the dresser, licking her butt as I try to talk to her. "I buy you food, change your litter box, and give you love, yet you can't tell me who broke into my apartment?" I yell in fear, which takes her by surprise and hurts my heart as she skitters away. Attempting to swallow my building panic is nearly impossible, but I have no idea what else to do.

I finally rush to turn off the stove, but my hands are too shaky to make myself a cup of tea. What if I am being delusional? What if this was me? The panic is starting to win my internal war; I snatch my phone from my pocket nearly tearing my dress pants to text... to text who? Who could I possibly ask for help? I've made two friends since moving here. They're the only two people I would be comfortable enough to ask for help, but I can't call them. What if this is more than a bra snatcher? What if the person who did this is targeting me? I couldn't endanger them. I have to deal with this alone.

What if the person comes back? What if they are still here? No, I would have heard them. It would be hard to get past my enhanced shifter hearing. I can't smell anything out of the ordinary either, not that smell is reliable anymore with today's technology. They could be using scent blockers. It's too easy to get them, and in pill form, it's even harder to trace. Should I shift and let my bear check the place out? No, I'd never get my deposit back. She's too big—she'll destroy the place.

It's fine. Whoever it was isn't here. I would know, right? I'm not completely stupid.

Oh my goodness, I have to leave. I can't stay here. I grab Nola, holding her tightly in my arms as I make my way towards the door, but I stop again. My hand pauses on the door handle, and I let out a forced breath as I stare straight at the dirty white door.

Where would I go?

I don't have family here. Shoot, I don't have a family anywhere since I left them back in Kaler City. I have Flora; she'd take me in, right? Were we close enough friends to help each other out with these kinds of things? I would help her in a heartbeat, but I couldn't put that burden on her. No. She has her own stalker to deal with. What if they are after me now? Oh, what if it was... what if—oh my goodness, I can't bring this to Flora. I have to stay. I have to tough it out alone.

I triple-check the lock on the door before going to each window in my apartment and checking the locks on them. Nothing is broken. But the back window in the living room is unlocked. Dread crawls around my neck as I stare at the lock on the window. Did I leave this unlocked? Was it left unlocked after the intruder left?

Slamming the window shut, I lock it, then unlock it, and lock it again. This apartment is secure, and I am home. The intruder won't be dumb enough to break into a shifter's home while they are home. I hope they aren't dumb enough. I have no idea who I could be dealing with. Who would do this to me? Why?

I turn on all the lights. Every single one of them. It screams I am home, and I'm not quite sure if that is stupid or smart, but I will be able to see. I mean, I would be able to see regardless, since I share my body with a bear who has exceptional night vision.

I'm not sure what to do; all I can process is the silence eating at my skin, making my movements tight and stiff. Going back to the front door, I pull one of my dining chairs over and prop it under the knob, providing an extra lock on the door.

I let out a breath as I step away from the front door. I'm safe. I'm okay.

Maybe settling into my normal routine will help ease the haunting sensation covering my skin. You know what? A cup of tea—yup, a cup of tea will settle me right down. But first, I need a shower with so much steam it covers the mirrors and water that is piping hot.

I run to the bathroom. Locking the door behind me, I wash my face and then step into a much-needed scalding-hot shower. Maybe I'll sweat out my panic? Oh my goodness, I forgot I don't have an untouched pair of underwear in my drawer. I can't trust that a pair has gone untouched.

You know what? It's okay. I'll have to go without. It's probably better to go without sometimes, right? Maybe? Gosh, I don't need to justify anything; I need to forget everything and move on. It could be nothing, could be all in my head.

I let the steam cover me and the mirror as I wash my body. My bathroom is my safe place, with no windows, one door with a lock on it, and four solid walls. I can breathe in here. I try to distract my mind by thinking about the book I'm reading right now, but I'm seriously failing. My billionaire cowboy lover fell to the back burner as the echoing ring of my phone nearly makes me jump out of my skin.

Peeking through the shower curtain, I see it is an unknown number coming through. I don't want to answer it, not that that is anything new. I never want to answer the phone. How I work as a personal assistant who is always having to make calls is beyond me. Still, the phone rings, and I have no idea who is on the other line. My eyes are stuck on the unfamiliar number on my phone. Could it be the person that broke in, wanting to scare me more? I shouldn't answer, but my gut is telling me to. Would the person who broke in really be calling me? With a racing heart, I step out of the shower and press the green button with wet fingers.

"Hello?" I answer as I pull a fluffy towel around my body. I sit on the lid of the toilet seat, confused by the silence on the other end. I'm about to hang up—maybe it was a prank call? But a familiar voice fills the line. One I never thought I'd hear again.

"Willow?" The voice is low, questioning, and feminine.

"Layla?" I ask as I wrap the towel closer around my body. Is she in trouble?

"You answered?" Layla mumbles as if she's called my number before. Maybe she has, and since she doesn't have caller ID, I never answered, or maybe she thought I would have caller ID and was avoiding her. Who knows?

"Layla, are you okay?" I ask. I haven't spoken to Layla in five years. It has been five long years since the man I was going to mate, Milo Barrow, was killed. Layla was his little sister and, commonly, our third wheel. She is someone who I once thought of as family. Layla never calls me, though, even before I broke off contact with the Barrow family. Layla was a young teen at the time and a huge texter. Which confuses me even more as to why she is calling me out of the blue.

"Did you kill Milo?" Layla asks, her voice coming out hushed and rushed and even then, the words dropped like heavy weights on my chest. I cut the shower off as silence fills our conversation. The phone has suddenly gained ten pounds, and I'm having a hard time holding it up to my ear, but I persist.

"What?" Fresh hurt and old memories rush into my mind. How could I kill my mate? My one true love. What would make Layla think I killed her brother? "Why would you even think that of me—"

"Willow, don't play with me right now."

"I could never—I could never hurt Milo," I say, balking at the very real conversation I'm having right now. "How did you even get my number?" When I went no contact, I truly went no contact. I moved out of town, changed my number, and deleted my social media—everything. I didn't want to remember Milo and anyone who was part of my time with him. I had an impossible time moving on with my life. I didn't have friends for a while, let alone date. I mean, how could I? I had found my soul mate, and he slipped right through my fingers. Milo was my one chance at love, and he is dead. He was my everything; we were getting ready for our mating ceremony, for Pete's sake. How could Layla believe I killed him? If anything, his death killed me.

"Then why did you disappear?" Her voice rings through the speaker, and I drop my phone. It clunks on the ground. I'm sure it's cracked, and I leave the bathroom. I can't do this. Not today, not ever. How dare she ask me, accuse me, of killing the one person I am destined to love and be with for the rest of my life? I can't do this. I can't take this right now. I don't bother picking my phone up, let alone ending the call. Like a zombie, I crawl into bed—no clothes, no lotion, no bonnet—and close my eyes, praying this day will end already.

2

WILLOW

THE DAY AFTER MY BREAK-IN ISN'T ANY EASIER than last night was. Here I am, sitting in my car at the grocery store parking lot, freaking out about going inside. I'm gnawing on my bottom lip, and my fingers are shaking slightly. I hate leaving the house, and after having an intruder in my apartment, this has only intensified. I awoke this morning and found that I didn't have a single tea bag in my whole apartment. *Did my intruder steal my tea bags too?* I had to rush to get ready so I could make it to the store before work, and now I don't want to get out of the car.

I hate grocery stores with a passion. I walk in there and get distracted. Each extra minute I spend in the grocery store has me hearing the swoosh of money flying out of my bank account.

I only need one thing. I need tea bags, and I refuse to go another morning without them. I have no choice but to go into the too-loud, too-bright, and too-crowded store.

This store is on the shifter side of town, and because of that, it's open twenty-four hours a day and is always busy since paranormals don't need as much, or any, sleep.

Tracing the stitching along my steering wheel, I stare at the gaudy lettering of the store name. I count the minutes that it should take to walk in and grab my tea. Five if there are long lines, three if I use self-checkout. Sighing, I get out of my car. The quicker I go in, the sooner I'll be at work and can forget this ever happened. I huff at the thought of everything that has happened in the last twenty-four hours. Having my home broken into and then running out of tea bags? I mean, there is only so much a girl can take.

Dread doesn't cover my body as it normally does when I think about the break-in, but it sure does find a cozy little spot at the base of my neck. I haven't loved being in my apartment for a while, and the break-in solidified the urge to move. I don't want to move to a new town, though I should, but at least to a new apartment. Nothing about my apartment screams home anymore. Maybe I should have grown closer connections with my neighbors or kept in contact with my family, so I would have somewhere else to go when I needed change.

I snicker as I think about my family—in reality, I'm not sure they would have my back. *Come on, Willow, don't be stupid.* They'd cast me out before I even made it to their front door. They showed me how much I meant to them, and they couldn't be bothered to show an ounce of empathy to a woman who lost her mate. That kind of love was never extended to me.

Maybe I would've gotten it from Layla and I probably

would've gotten it from Milo too, had he not died. Those two were the only good things I had when I lived in Kaler City. I first met Milo, my soul mate, in high school. It's rare to find your fated mate so young; in fact, we'd never heard of someone finding their mates in high school before. What were the chances I did?

Our creator, the Moon Goddess, created each paranormal species in her light. When she created us, she gave each of us a blessing, a person who would be our perfect match in love, our soul mates. Typically, each paranormal gets one mate; rarely will someone have more than one, but polyamorous mates have happened before. Every person has one person in the world that is destined for them, and I had found mine in high school.

Little did I know, while Milo was destined to spend the rest of his life with me, I was destined to live a life alone —and for that, I could nearly curse the Moon Goddess. How could she bring this fate upon me? What evil have I done to deserve this?

She's supposed to give us light and hope, and yet she's taken mine away. What hope is left for me in a life where I'm destined to be alone?

It's rare for someone to not find their mate—it's one perk of living such long lives, but living beyond a mate's death is rare. Typically, you die with your mate. You're together even in death. But I didn't die, and I have no idea why.

Were we wrong about the Moon Goddess, or am I an exception?

And Layla—how could she have called me last night to accuse me of killing my mate? Did she really mean that?

I'm surprised she hasn't called me back since I hung up on her... maybe I should call her and give her a chance to explain. My cracked phone weighs heavy in my hand as her last question races through my mind. Why did I leave her?

Why did I leave the one person left who loved me? She was a kid back then, mourning her brother. I was so wrapped up in my grief that I didn't think about how I'd be leaving her behind.

The memory of her lip gloss and tear-stained face brings me to a halt like a bear claw to the eye. I remember us hugging each other when the news finally broke. She cried nearly as hard as I did. I remember petting her hair and holding her tight as if it was only us left in the world, and then in the next moment, I was gone. I should've stayed but I... but I couldn't stay in Kaler City anymore.

I hadn't even put her number as a contact in my phone. Going back to my recent calls list, I see her number and our three-minute conversation. Clicking on the number, I try not to give myself too much time to back out.

"Willow?"

"Layla, we need to talk," I say as she answers the phone. I stood in the middle of the parking lot, stuck in my thoughts. It's no wonder someone broke into my apartment if I am such a ditz in public like this. I'm an easy target. I scan the parking lot. It's probably safer to go inside. Much safer since I have no idea what's going on in my life right now.

Walking into the store, I wait for her to respond, wanting to hear her voice again, even if she's yelling at me. I miss the cub. I bite my lip, realizing I miss her a lot.

"Willow, I know I scared you yesterday, but—"

"Scared me? Layla, you accused me of killing my mate."

"I know. I just—it's nasty, and I shouldn't have said that. I know you didn't kill Milo, but I thought that if I angered you enough, in the heat of it, you'd give me your address so we could talk."

"You could've simply asked me," I say, in awe that she'd think I wouldn't want her to find me.

"How? I had a hell of a time getting your phone number, let alone finding out where you live. You left me, Willow. You didn't want me—I got you had a lot going on, but I needed you. I still need you."

She needed me? Layla needs me? "Why do you need me, Layla? What's wrong?"

"I'm just—I need a place to stay for a few, please," she begs.

"Of course, you can stay with me as long as you don't think I killed your brother," I say, waiting for her to confirm she doesn't really think that.

"I don't. I swear I don't."

"I'm about thirty minutes away from Kaler City. Can you get here?" I ask before giving her my apartment address.

"I can get there. Thanks, Willow. You have no idea how much I need this," she says before hanging up. I pause my pacing in between the cash registers and the bathroom and slide my phone back into my purse.

I should ask more questions. I should question the heck out of her. Is she even old enough to move out of her parent's house? What do her parents think about this? But even after all these years, I trust Layla is, well, Layla. She may not be the little fifteen-year-old following Milo and me around the mall or eating the food we were trying to prepare instead of helping us in the kitchen anymore. But she's still Milo's little sister, and she's still practically *my* sister.

I couldn't let her hang out to dry again. Not knowingly. Not this time. Whatever she needs, I can help her with.

I beeline to the aisle where my beloved bags of tea leaves are. I try to keep my eyes focused on the target and not let the chocolates and cakes in the next aisle distract me. My bear—my lovely, sweets-loving bear I share my body with—is itching for me to turn my head to the left and take five steps to surround myself with desserts. I don't disagree with the animal in me. Cake slices did pair nicely with tea, but I need to focus. I am here for one thing and one thing only.

I don't break my stride until the yellow box holding rows of my desired good glares at me from its display at the end of the aisle. Walking up to the display table, I observe the boxes. I never pick the first box in a row or a box that is damaged. If I am paying full price for something, it better be in the best condition possible.

I can't help myself. I run my hand over the boxes, picking them up one by one and inspecting each box. I take my sweet time—my earlier need to rush is long gone as I become consumed with picking the right box. I can't deny my eyes from tracking to the desserts peeking at me from the next aisle. I can hear the dings and swooshes of my bank account, and I play with the possibility of being broke forever. Those cakes do sound good right about now, but now I'm only wasting time.

Finally, picking the perfect box, I twist on my heel and head towards the self-checkout. I'm going to be a good girl and deny me and my bear by not stopping by the sweet treats. I am going to pay for this box and go to work. That is the plan until, of course, the toe of my heel catches on the table leg of the tea display. Yellow boxes go flying. Wind and embarrassment caress my face as I make my way down, falling face-first towards the floor. At least, I was headed towards the ground until a strong hand wraps around my arm and yanks me up, straight into a chest.

"Are you okay?" a smoky voice asks as I crash into the chest of whoever saved me from having to deal with bruises on my soul and on my physical body.

Glancing over my shoulder, I see the mess I made and all the attention I am drawing. Gosh. How embarrassing. Gulping, I stare at the man I am currently standing incredibly close to. Only my squished arms separate our bodies.

"Umm, yeah. Thanks," I mutter, taking a step back. I focus my attention on the yellow boxes littered on the floor. Only a few fell off the table, but my heated cheeks don't know the difference. Bending at my waist, I pick up the fallen boxes, making sure to keep the one I selected separate from the now damaged boxes. The mysterious hero bends to pick up the boxes too. As much as I want to tell him he doesn't have to help me, my embarrassment wouldn't let any more words out of my throat. Constricted by too much emotion, I hold back the mountain building in my throat as I turn to clean up my mess. I'm hyperaware of his presence. Not because I'm scared, but because I'm—I'm not sure why. I finally look up at his face, and shock colors my face.

"Eddie Enchanted?" I ask, even though I know exactly who he is.

"Willow, how nice to see your sweet behind again. Tripping over tea boxes?" My mysterious hero is Eddie Enchanted. The same man who saved me from falling in this same store a couple of months ago. The same man who I tried to keep as much distance from while working alongside his Pack to save my best friend. The same man who made me question everything I thought I knew about, well, good smelling shifters.

Scents can be signs of mates for shifters. Milo smelled of lemons. Fresh and tasty, and I loved the way he smelled. I'd walk close to him just to catch a whiff of his scent. It was perfect on a hot summer day. Eddie though, Eddie's scent is different.

I first met Eddie in this grocery store months ago, and I could smell him distinctly. His scent came to me before I saw him. Enticing me. My instinct was to follow his delicious scent around the whole store, and that's when I ran into a freezer door and he pulled me back, steadying me and lighting my skin on fire.

That's when I knew I had to stay away from him. Away from temptation.

His braids fall in his face as his lean and muscled body bends down to pick up a box that went flying off the table. Our hands brush, and I can't stop the smile that takes over my face. Now I feel like a schoolgirl who ran into her crush, but I don't have crushes. I can't have crushes. I had my chance at love. I had a soul mate. I shouldn't be flushing at the sight of him.

I need to get out of here and find a new grocery store to go to from now on. What if I see him here again? I shouldn't want to. I can't betray my mate. Oh, my goddess, I can't.

After making such a mess here, how could I show my face again? Bringing the box I was going to get to my chest, I give the best smile I can muster up to my hero of the hour. His brown eyes pierce into mine. I'm sure my face is beat red, and even though I have a darker skin complexion, nothing could hide the heat radiating from my face. "Thanks, really, for your help."

"No problem, sweetcakes," he says. He is smiling at me, and gosh, did it make me blush about ten times harder. Eddie Enchanted is handsome. Of course, he had to be, or else this moment wouldn't have been embarrassing enough. Eddie Enchanted is most definitely attractive. In fact, he may be too attractive. Milo was handsome too; he had deep dark skin since he loved the sun—maybe more than he loved me sometimes—and narrow eyes and thick lips. But Eddie has those corded forearms. Gosh, those forearms do something for me, I—no, no. I nothing. I'm not supposed to be looking, let alone drooling. Eddie has glasses, *naturally* he is automatically handsome. Glasses plus his smooth brown skin and braided hair that reaches his eyebrows. It's not abnormal to think another man is attractive... right?

I mean, why did Eddie wear glasses? Paranormals don't need enhancements like glasses or hearing aids since the magic that created us would fix impairments; at least, that's what we've been told. So, it's not my fault I think he's attractive. He makes himself good-looking on purpose —there's no shame in finding that he succeeds in his purpose.

He is dressed in business attire too. Goddess. Slacks and a loosely tucked in button-up shirt. His voice is deep and heavy, covering me with shivers in the best way. In a pleasant way—a way where I want to keep him talking but know I don't have the social skills to keep him going. And he smells good. Too good. Like tobacco and vanilla. Gosh, I want to smell him again. I scrunch my face and dive my nose closer. Yeah, that smell is definitely him.

"Willow?" My eyes shoot up to his as I snap out of my daze. Oh my goodness, am I out here smelling men? Has it really been that long since my mate died that I'm desperately smelling other men?

"I'm—I've got to go to work," I mutter. I nod my head in thanks before turning on my heel again, this time without tripping. I speed to the front of the store, paying for my tea bags and getting the heck out of here.

3

WILLOW

GETTING TO WORK IS SUCH A SIGH OF RELIEF. I can breathe normally now that I've swiped into the building. Walking into the small cafeteria, I pour hot water in my mug and drop a tea bag inside. Once I had made it to my car, I'd stuffed a few little tea bags in my purse in case I had run out at work, too.

Now that my tea craving is settled, I finally make it to my desk. I put my purse and work bag down by my desk as I crack open my planner. I'm a personal assistant to Flora Enchanted, CEO and head designer of her company Danity Rebels. We create all sorts of accessories, ranging from shoes to jewelry, for paranormals in the United States. Our designs are shifter focused with accessories designed to handle shifting into a multitude of animals.

Flora comes up with the hit new designs. I make sure she gets to all her meetings on time, send emails, get lunch on days we're not having lunch at Clothes Before Bros, and whatever else she needs. Working for Flora has been the best job I've ever had. She took a chance on me, hiring me when all I had to sleep on was a plate on the floor since I had only took what could fit in my car and left Kaler City.

I love my job; taking care of people is what I do best, and what better job to do that than a personal assistant?

Flora Enchanted comes around a corner, and her sudden presence makes me jump in my seat. Am I going to be a jumpy mess all the time now? My eyes search around the room for anything else to focus on. One breath in, one breath out as she gets closer. I pray she didn't notice my jumpiness, and if she did, I hope she won't say anything.

"Hey, darling, glad to see you come in today." Flora nods her head towards her office, signaling I should follow. I nervously laugh as I grab my planner and follow. My hands sweat as I follow. Does she know? About the break-in? About my feelings for Eddie. Is it written across my forehead? I wipe my forehead as if there is writing there. I'm overly aware of everything I do now that I'm keeping a secret from her. I can't help but think of the little tells I may be giving to cue her into something being wrong.

Nothing's wrong. I'm fine. I'm completely fine. Nothing out of the ordinary happened last night that she, of all people, should be worried about.

"I'm slightly off my rocker today," I mumble, trying to brush off my tardiness as a small blush covers my cheeks. What's up with all the blushing today? So much for being completely fine.

"I'm not mad you're late—I mean, I just got here myself, but is everything okay? You're never late," she asks, sliding her long box braids over her shoulders. Opening her laptop, she reads over her version of today's plans.

Off the bat, she's asking if I am okay. I wasn't ready for these questions, and I'm sure I'll blow if she digs, I need to do better at acting like everything is normal.

"I had to stop at the store for tea bags this morning—nothing serious."

"Didn't you go grocery shopping recently?"

I knew it. I knew I wouldn't have let my stash get low. I couldn't function without a morning cup of tea. There is no way I would've let myself run out of tea bags. The intruder must have taken them along with my bras, but why?

"I must have been drinking more than I thought." I brush it off. "I have your first meeting in thirty minutes with the design team to confirm the next line of hat designs. Are you ready?"

"Yeah, don't let me forget my black book." She giggles as she holds the book with all her designs up in the air. She's forgotten her designs before, and it's my job to make sure they make it there.

"Of course." I smile, glancing over the rest of her plans for the day. She types away on her computer, and my eyes don't stray from my planner. My mind, though, is not in the room with us. In fact, it's still at the grocery store smelling that tobacco and vanilla scent I can't push past.

My day moves along, as if it's moving on without me. We jump from meeting to meeting till the clock strikes one. Lunch time. The one meeting Flora and I love most is our lunch meeting with our third, Luxe Wildflower. Lunch with the girls is routine—the one thing I can count on every week. Luxe Wildflower, Flora Enchanted, and I met at Luxe's current place of employment, Clothes Before Bros, a retail shop in downtown Rainfall Avenue. It is a cute little clothing boutique, and the backroom is where the lunch is taking place.

Flora drives us over to lunch, rambling on about her designs, a conversation I love to be a part of anytime except right now. After we arrive, I pull a rolling chair to the round table in the center of the room and sit with my best friends of five years. Five years since I moved from Kaler City, five years since I met the first people I'd genuinely call friends. My salami sandwich lies open on the table.

Even with our weekly lunches, we weren't always this close. We respect that each of us has a past, and it wasn't something we ask each other about. We didn't ask about family, and we didn't ask about our shifter animals.

That's one thing shifters keep a secret with the Black Shifter Market and cage fighting being at an all-time high. The Black Shifter Market is an underground market selling captive shifters for twisted, sick people, and some of those same twisted, sick people also run the cage fighting bids. The employees of these markets are called collectors who collect shifters off the street for the highest bidder's pleasure. Stronger animals such as predators are often hunted for the cage fighting bids, often forced through drugs and guns to fight for their lives for the entertainment of others.

To keep ourselves safe and away from collectors, shifters have become secretive about their animals. Collectors study all the ways to best any animal and, unfortunately, are good at what they do. When we thought these guys were after Flora a few months ago, we had to trust each other and join forces with the Enchanted Pack, Flora's mate's Pack, to help protect her. As it turns out, it wasn't the collectors after her, but someone much closer.

We used to be secretive with each other until recently—when Flora was kidnapped, I shifted during the rescue mission, and my bear killed one of her kidnappers.

I shouldn't have shifted. But I did, and I realized then that these girls meant more to me than I had thought. My bear is pretty possessive, and family, true family, is hard to come by. She must have deemed these girls as true family sometime over the last five years and wasn't too happy to see Flora in danger. That was the first time, and hopefully last time, we kill anyone ever. We're not killers. I'm not a killer.

I'm not a killer.

I couldn't hurt a fly.

Until now?

The mental torment I've been putting myself through ends now, and I will handle the break-in, whatever is going on with Layla, and whatever else comes. I'm capable. What choice do I have?

"Any hot stuff I should be aware of while I'm here? What's been selling fast?" Flora asks, glancing over the clothing racks that surround the room.

"Nope, my manager has been getting last season's designs for a discount," Luxe shrugs, smiling down at her phone. "Maybe there's something you'll like, Willow."

"Whatever," I mutter shyly, walking to the closest clothing rack. I'm not a fashionista like Flora or an it-girl like Luxe. I dress comfortably. It doesn't help that my body temperature runs ten degrees hotter as a bear shifter, either. I live in thin fabrics and layers.

"How's mated life?" Luxe asks, wiggling her eyebrows at Flora. Flora was recently mated to Dylan Enchanted, making her a member of the Enchanted Pack. That Pack is the most diverse Pack I've ever come across, filled with a couple of different types of shifters and now a vampire. They are Pack of six men, and with one of them finding their mate and a stray vamp named Remi on their rescue mission, there are two women.

"Wish I would've given him my mark the first night I met him." The smile on Flora's face almost sells this little statement of hers, but we know what really went down between the two.

"You could hardly stand him when you first met," I say. Flora's happiness in having her mate should've made my heart heavy. I should've been jealous, or miserable at the mere mention of mates and others being happy about finding and living with theirs. But the pain that I once felt isn't as crushing anymore. The pain isn't really there, to be honest. I never thought I'd be at a moment in my life where I pretend to be sad. But it is the right thing to do, and that—now that hurts.

Milo plays like a distant memory in my head, and the guilt from that weighs me down more than my love for him.

Will I ever get over this guilt and move on? Flora and Luxe go on rambling about who knows what, and I'm staring at my sandwich with a fake smile. Maybe... I don't have to be alone anymore? I may never have another lover, but I don't have to be alone in all aspects of my life.

We have always been good about not prying or digging into each other's secrets, but these are my friends. The best friends I've ever made. I've killed for these girls, and they still know little about me; maybe that should change? Should they know I've already found my mate? That he died? That he was murdered the night before our mating ceremony, and now I am destined to be alone forever?

I take a deep breath and move my gaze to the two. They are waving their hands, in exaggeration, smiling, laughing, and having a great time. Did I want to ruin this with my doom and gloom? No, I don't. Maybe I shouldn't. There's a time and place for everything, and maybe this isn't it.

No, I'm gonna do it.

"I haven't shared something—something I would need to share," I say, trying to push my negative thoughts aside. My hair covers my face, and my skin is getting clammy. I shouldn't be nervous. These are my friends. My best friends. Best friends are supposed to be there for you, and make you smile; it's about time I treat the people I call friends like genuine friends.

The words *my mate is dead* are close to slipping from my lips. I wish they finally would. It's getting harder to breathe, and I'm not sure what I'm scared of. Is it admitting the fact that he's dead, or is it finally sharing something monumental in my life?

"I—" I try again, yet it won't come out. My face is flushed. The rush of air in my chest finally makes its way up my throat, and I am going to get the words out this time. I can do it.

"My mate is dead."

It didn't even sound right coming from my lips. It didn't have the same heart-shattering impact it had before. He was supposed to be my world, my reason for breathing, and yet, after five years, I can talk about him as if I am talking about a distant relative. What is holding me back? The silence in the room edges me to continue. To fill the crushing impatient silence closing my vocal cords. I have to move fast, or I will lose my momentum.

"We were planning our mating ceremony. He was my match made by the Moon Goddess, and we were to be mated." Not all shifters do the whole mating ceremony and celebrations with friends, but bear shifters do. I've dreamed of my mating ceremony since I was little. The beautiful dress in the forest and family and friends surrounding us, partying. Then at the end of the celebration, when it's just my mate and I giving each other our biting marks, it was always my dream. It's the signal to the start of my life. But now I'm twenty-five, and my mate is dead. "The night before our ceremony, he went missing. Later assumed dead."

Luxe and Flora share a look, and I instantly become insecure.

Maybe he got cold feet. Maybe it wasn't meant to be. Maybe he's in hiding, is what everyone would say.

We had all the signs of being mates: we were in love, we clicked, our scents were more than appealing, we were destined for each other. We were soul mates. I knew it. It was as clear as day.

I take another deep breath, forcing my words to continue revealing truths I thought I'd never speak out loud again. "I think he was murdered. We were in love and spent everyday together. I loved him. There's no way he would've left without an explanation, at the least," I try to explain, running my sweaty hands over my thighs over and over again. Gosh, when did it get hot in here? "And there's this situation with Layla."

"Who's Layla?" Flora softly asks. She puts a comforting hand on my arm, and while I appreciate the thought, I'm more worried I'll get Flora's hand all sweaty from all the heat radiating from my body.

"His little sister, she contacted me the other day." My sandwich held the eye contact I should have been giving them, but I couldn't meet their eyes. Not yet. I can't see their pitying faces or worry lines. I can't see the two people I've grown closest to thinking I am desperate or stupid or wrong.

"How long has it been since you've last talked to her?" Luxe asks. I can hear her twiddle with her water bottle. The steel against her fingertips dampens the silence, eating away at my nervous state.

"Five years," I mutter. I finally meet their eyes. Switching between the two. They remain relaxed, their faces neutral, and I can't decide if that is worse than pity. It is then when Luxe's face breaks into a smile, completely throwing me off guard with her next question.

"Is your name really Willow?" Luxe asks jokingly. I want to laugh; I want to be normal. I want to laugh so badly, but I can't. A sharp, pained laugh comes from me. My skin itches with the need to run and to keep the rest of my story to myself.

"Layla thought I killed him," I utter, holding the

connection of Flora's hand and Luxe's eyes as I say the words I've found to have hated the most.

"You did tear Cassandra into pieces, literally," Flora says. She tries to wear a light-hearted expression, but the event still has a hold on her. Flora was kidnapped. Her kidnappers were trying to replace their deceased daughter with Flora Cassandra was the mother, and while I *am not* a stone-cold killer, I learned my bear definitely is.

Cassandra Bray is the first person I've ever killed. Her life is gone because of me. No matter how evil she was, she is dead because of me.

But Flora is safe because I killed Cassandra.

I'm *not* a bad person.

"I didn't kill Milo. He was family, not threatening my family."

"So, this Layla person called to accuse you of killing your soon-to-be mate," Luxe says, her eyebrows rising as she takes in my situation. "Wow, that's bold as shit."

Layla was cold back when she was fifteen. I'm sure twenty-year-old Layla is no different.

"So, what does this mean? Is there something wrong? Is Layla trying to hurt you?" Luxe asks, gripping the sides of the table and cocking her head to the side. She's getting heated, and a heated female Alpha is not something I wish for Layla to deal with, even if Layla hurt me.

"No, she's no trouble, I promise. She's a hurt twenty-year-old missing her brother. She's coming to visit me soon," I say, realizing that I have no idea when she'll be here.

"Is that safe?" Flora asks.

"Maybe we should be there too, in case?" Luxe asks,

worry shifting her fingers. Her claws are poking from her fingernails; she's probably trying to hold her wolf back from making an appearance. I didn't think she'd be this upset. I didn't want to... to make her upset. Maybe I shouldn't have told her that part about Layla? In her anger, will she realize being my friend comes with too much baggage?

"Luxe I'm sorry. I didn't want to make you upset," I sputter, trying to figure out how to resolve this. My problems don't need to be their problems. I should've kept this to myself. Now she'll notice I'm a burden. My breathing becomes more labored as the panic of losing a friend settles in my bones.

"No, Layla is going to be sorry. How dare she talk to you like that—"

"Pipe down a smidge Luxe, the girl is practically a kid. Is she a threat, Willow?"

"No. I promise," I say, hoping they take my word for it. Layla isn't me. She wouldn't hurt anyone, even someone like me.

"Is that all?" Flora asks. Her hand was probably covered in my sweat, yet she keeps it on my arm. Isn't she grossed out? She hasn't even moved her hand to wipe away all the sweat on it. She remains next to me.

Now that I think about it, she's always done that. She hired me, even when she didn't have any real positions open, and my resume wasn't ideal. When she had me organize the first lunch meeting, she asked me to join them. She visits, she calls, she's here.

This is what friends do, to keep my friends, I'll do that too. Though I can't help my eyes shooting to Luxe. She calmed down, her claws retracting into her fingers. Flora squeezes my hand, her eyebrows are raised in question.

I know she'll drop the conversation if that's what I wanted to do, and to be honest, I want to. I want to stop here. But I also find myself wanting to spill everything.

I want to tell them my heartbreak over losing Milo doesn't hurt anymore and how that scares the ever-living shit out of me since he was my mate.

I want to tell them that someone robbed me of a few bras and tea bags yesterday. Tell them how I've come to realize how much I've missed Layla all these years, and how the idea of her coming to visit *me* lights my skin with giddiness.

Regardless of my wants, I nod my head, telling her that is all I had to say. She stares at me for a minute before her eyes trail to the clock. I'm emotionally tapped out, and I hope she can tell. I'd hoped she'd take over from here, and the smiling Luxe across the table would understand that I wasn't as strong as she was. Luxe would have handled all this with assurance, with the grace that comes natural to an Alpha. But I wasn't an Alpha or a Luna. I need a moment to calm down.

"Enjoy your pizza slice, Luxe. We gotta get back to work," Flora says, getting up from her chair and collecting her trash.

"Damn, you girlies are leaving me already?" Luxe says with a smile that doesn't quite reach her eyes.

"Yeah, we have another design meeting to head to," Flora says, even though we have no meeting lined up right after this. It was open for me to revise Flora's to-do lists and for Flora to work on her designs. I appreciate what she is doing, though.

"Love you, girlies," Luxe mutters, pointedly staring at me while packing up her lunch too. She was only supposed to have a thirty-minute break since she was the only employee here today, so she has to go too.

"Love you too, darling," Flora says, blowing a kiss towards Luxe.

4

WILLOW

MOVING IN A SHIFTER TOWN ONLY TAKES ME A few days to do, and I'm grateful for it. Stalking house listings for the last few months helped me speed up the process. I didn't think I'd be moving this fast, but after the break-in a week ago and Layla coming to stay, I am more than motivated.

With an empty savings account and a mortgage, I am now the homeowner of a cute two-bedroom house on Lakewood Street. I have my car packed downstairs and a moving truck on the way for the bigger furniture. I find myself in my little kitchen, the last room to pack up. The more I stand here, the more I know it's time for me to move on. Besides the break-in, I'm ready to set deeper roots and live the life I am supposed to live. Happy and alone.

Shifters were never meant to live in apartments, since most have a no shifting policy. Our animals are usually too big to fit in an apartment. There are other features of shifters, such as claws, that always end up damaging walls or floors that keep renters from accepting our applications. I still somehow found myself with a hefty deposit to pay and keys to my apartment five years ago.

I was broke and moving fast. I needed something with little responsibility. This small apartment gave me the fresh start I needed. The fact that I'm moving on settles in my heart. I mean, I guess I could've stayed here; maybe the intruder was a couple of bored teens or something, and I'm blowing all of this out of proportion.

Still, the house I have now is worlds better than this, and I deserve that.

"Willow Buttercup?" a harsh, gravelly voice asks. I pause in my small apartment kitchen, where I'm packing away plates and cups.

I walk to the door, wishing I had a peephole or someway to see who is at my door. I'm not expecting any company, much less a man's company. I step away as quietly as possible. Maybe I can act as if I'm not home.

"We need to talk." This voice raises the hair on my skin. I have no idea who is out there.

The voice doesn't ring any bells in my mind, and the pounding on the door that follows makes my bear want to take over. She senses that whoever is standing on the other side of the door is a threat.

I let my claws shift through my fingernails; they'll have to be enough of a weapon. Where's Nola?

"Willow, open the door," he says again. He doesn't knock any louder or yell. He must not want my neighbors to hear the noise. Oh my goodness, is he going to hurt me?

I hurry away from the door. I can't let my bear out—I

can't deal with the aftermath of dead bodies, and a hole in the roof since my bear's head would probably go through it. Is the damage to the ceiling worth my life, though?

No, my bear is going to stay inside. I'll have to run this time. I grab Nola, her orange fur sticking up, and her own claws digging into my arm as I try not to scratch her with mine. Quietly stepping into the kitchen, I listen for the door, wondering how much time I have left and what is the best way to get out of here.

I hear heavy boots walking a few steps away. I think they're gone. The stranger's scent is getting less poignant as the footsteps get quieter. I think we're in the clear. With Nola still in my hands, I step up to the door with one hand. I don't sense anyone on the other side.

Every horror movie I've ever watched tells me I shouldn't open the door to check. The tension in my neck tells me not to—shoot, even Nola is actively trying to get out of my arms and away from the door. But I need to see with my own eyes that we are in the clear.

Maybe I am panicking for no reason. Maybe that was my landlord or something?

A sudden, yet particularly careful, pop has the door open, and a powerful force has the door whipping towards me faster than I can process. I want to shift, but with my concern for Nola and the wind being knocked out of me, all I can process is the harsh impact of me hitting the floor. Suddenly I can smell the intruder strongly, and I can barely see his physical form. He popped open my door far too easily—he must have done this before. Why does he know my name, and what could he possibly want from me?

Nola gets loose from my grasp. I snap back up, leaving barely any time for the intruder to get me while I'm on the ground. Yet I'm not nearly as fast as he is. Is he an assassin of some sort? Who would want to kill me?

Identifying the intruder is a whole other task as my human body recovers from my unexpected fall. He comes in as a blurred body, and I hear Nola's strained meow as I dash backwards to put space between me and the intruder. My bear might not give me a choice to handle this myself, and I'll need space to shift.

Dead bodies might be on the agenda today, I guess.

Except I'm not fast enough, and the man has a hand around my neck and is lifting me in the air.

"We could've done this peacefully, Willow, but you've forced my hand."

I gurgle, gasping for air as my claws dig into any skin that I can reach. I'm realizing you need to breathe to shift, and maybe this intruder knew that. My eyes instead flood with tears, and I can hardly see the man in front of me. Is this it?

No. Absolutely not. Layla is coming tomorrow, and I will not die on her before seeing her again. I can't leave her again.

I kick my legs out, and even with my height he dodges by swinging my body back and making his grip on my neck harder.

"I don't know what you did, but he's pissed." He cuts himself off and stares at my choking form. I think I see his brows furrow, and I think I see him shake his head, but the tears building in my eyes prevent me from seeing clearly.

"So, whatever you do—don't do anything stupid, and for the love of the Moon Goddess, lie low," he says, dropping me onto the floor.

As I sputter, trying to catch my breath, I move to stand. My bear is beyond mad. I rip off my shirt—my bear can have at him for all I care. Fur pricks through my skin, covering my body and my height extending about a foot before my vision finally dials in. I watch his blurry, but huge, form stride out of my apartment. He's out of here as quickly as he got inside, except this time, the door is wide open. It's probably broken and won't shut.

Now I'm officially not getting my deposit back.

Stopping mid-shift, I force my bear back down. I'll have to shift even sooner than I planned, since she's all riled up now. Shifters have to shift often to keep their animals happy; it prevents them from completely taking over and never giving us control back.

Nola skitters past me to the kitchen, and I walk over to take in the damage done to my door. I don't want to think about the damage done to me. My throat is killing me. I'll need to shift a couple of times to fully heal. The Moon Goddess made us so that we can heal from nearly anything if we have the conscious mind to shift and as long as we aren't decapitated. I'll have to wait until I get the movers to unload my stuff at the new place.

Shoot, how will I explain the bruising?

My stomach revolts with nausea, thinking of the attack. Now I must leave this apartment—I may have to leave this town. I shake my head. I can't run forever. I'll have to figure out how to handle this. I sigh, rolling my neck; my body aches everywhere. My bear is pounding in my head wanting to be let out. Can I even last much longer without a shift?

I bring my focus back to the broken door. I'll try to get my door to shut, then go find somewhere in the woods nearby to shift a couple of times before the movers get here.

Dragging my hand along the edges of the door, the horrible paint job chips at my fingertips. My eyes stay on the mat, remembering it was one of the first things I purchased before I could afford any proper furniture or decorative pieces.

The dirty brown mat is crooked, and a white piece of paper sticks out from underneath it. I squat down grabbing the paper and unfold it. When did this get here, and how did the intruder not move it with his speed or ruckus?

My eyes don't stray from the black letters as chills cover my skin, and my ears perk up. One sentence raises the hair on my arms and leaves me breathless. When did he have time to leave this?

Don't feed the monster - G.

When Milo first died, I searched like crazy for his murderer, his body, something—anything—to prove I wasn't crazy. I got notes with weird messages back then, too. Notes to stop searching, to leave it alone, to move on. This lasted a whole year before I had a big blowout with his family and my family, who staged an intervention of sorts. So, I listened to the notes: I stopped. I moved on.

But why a note? The intruder came inside to talk to me. Does he think that would've been a forgettable moment? Did he think I would've gotten the freaking message? What has changed since I moved here? Why is this happening again? The only real difference in my life is... Layla.

"Willow?" a shaky voice calls. Down the hall, I see Ms. Humming, and I let a small smile take over my face as my hand reaches my tender neck.

She's the only neighbor who stopped by to meet me when I first moved in. She brought store-bought chocolate chip cookies and came in for a cup of tea. We had monthly meetings with cookies and tea. I guess I could say Ms. Humming was a friend of mine, too.

I was wrong earlier. I've made three friends since running from—no—since moving here. Our monthly meetings were nice. I enjoy her company, but I can't burden her with my troubles. She lives a peaceful life from what I can tell, and now that Flora and Luxe know, there is no need to drag her into my messed-up life too. I'm going to miss those meetings, though. She is one of the few people I can sit in silence with.

"Hi." My voice sounds harsh, and I cough to try to cover it up, wrapping my other arm around my body.

"A young man left that for you," she says, walking closer, her cane in hand. She must be in her high hundreds. I've yet to meet a paranormal under three hundred who uses a cane. Shifters live for a long time, typically till we're eight hundred.

But age doesn't slow her down in the slightest. She loves the gossip that runs through these halls, and when we weren't sitting in a comfortable silence, she was retelling the stories she heard about our neighbors.

Wait, she saw my intruder. Did they speak before barging into my apartment?

"Did you see his face?" I ask as the blood drains from my face and dread fills in its place. I don't want to freak Ms. Humming out by telling her this person broke in and attacked me. He said not to do anything stupid, but what did that mean, and who did I anger to warrant this? I don't think there is a need to worry her—this seems incredibly personal.

"Yup, a Hispanic-looking man. About, erm, this tall, and he was handsome too. He had that nice soft black hair and tanned skinned, not like Italians, but darker. Oh, he was gorgeous. Definitely a bad boy, though. Covered in tattoos, even on his neck. Willow, dear, what a sight he was. You know him? He stood here for quite a while?" She gestures with wide eyes and a slick smile with one corner of her lips turned up. She's impressed by my intruder. The description is not helpful whatsoever, but it's more than what I had before.

I didn't want to scare the old woman—tell her I didn't know him, and that she should probably stay alert if she sees him again. That would probably land Ms. Humming in trouble. She isn't the type to back down.

"Yeah, he was a part of my life before I moved here, and, I guess, wanted to catch up. I can't remember his name, though. Did he tell you by chance?" I needed something, anything more than his initial is the letter G based on the note he left.

"Yes, he said his name was Ghost. The names these parents are giving their children these days blow my casket. Why would someone name their baby Ghost?" she says, turning down the outdoor hallway and back into her apartment.

I am left dumbstruck outside my apartment. Was Ghost the person behind the break-in too? It's a stretch, and maybe I'm paranoid, but could he be correlated to Milo's murder?

"Willow." Ms. Humming peeks her head out of her apartment, calling to me again.

I raise my eyebrow in question. I don't want my voice to giveaway that something is wrong. I can hardly move at this point. Thank the Moon Goddess I am moving today. I'll have to make sure that I don't directly lead Ghost to my new address. I have to go into hiding. I have to—

"If you know this Ghost fella, I wouldn't write him back. He's cute, but you're a good girl, Willow, and getting tied up in all that isn't worth it if he's not your mate. Don't let anyone get in the way of finding your mate darlin'—it's a lonely existence without one."

All I can offer is a nod and a weak smile. I listen for the click of her door lock after she closes her door. She must not have heard our commotion, and I'm glad she didn't. This is between me and Ghost, and maybe Layla.

I have something. I have a loose description of the man, his name, and his handwriting. Staring back into my apartment, the rug and carpet are dirty and scuffed up, but there's no evidence of a crime. Even the notes I got when I was in Kaler City were marked with an M, not a G. This could be something completely separate from Milo. What has Layla got herself into?

I think I should've told Luxe and Flora about the

break-in. They need to know. They're my friends. Friends want to know these kinds of things.

I don't want to be the friend who always keeps secrets or waits too long to say something. I let out a sharp laugh. I didn't want to be that friend, yet here I am, alone in front of my apartment after someone nearly choked me to death.

A human would call the police, but refraining from getting humans involved is one of the few laws the Council set for paranormals. Getting humans involved would get the Council involved, which isn't exactly the save one may think it to be. While the Council has a "let you figure it out among yourselves" mindset, they are quick to handle things, usually by death, once they are dragged into a problem. The Council comprises one of every species: shifter, vampire, fairy, and witch. They decide together what's fair, or whatever it is they do. I don't know. I've never been involved with them, and they sure don't advertise their services either.

The walk back into my room isn't nearly as bad as the walk to my nightstand, where my phone lies. I pick at my orange phone case, feeling the silicone peel as my face gets hot.

I have an itch for something I haven't done in years. Here I am like an addict, trying to think of a reason I need to make this call.

Standing over my bed, I dial a number I have memorized. I shouldn't make this call. This is stupid. I don't need it anymore. I let the phone ring before the voice I haven't craved to hear in a while finally fills the speaker.

"Hey, this is Milo. Leave a message at the tone."

This call didn't hit the same, but the small lingering

twinge of hurt will satisfy me. Maybe the hurt I feel is from loving him. Maybe the hurt is from not missing him anymore, I'm not sure. I need it to be the former. I need to know that I still love Milo. That I miss the man who was supposed to be my soul mate. This pang of hurt is the itch I've needed. Whether it's from missing him or the lack thereof, I need this hurt.

5

WILLOW

My video doorbell camera was the absolute best thing I could've ever bought. I get a live feed of my front door to my phone. I can decide right from my bed if I have enough social energy to answer whoever is at the door. The Mailman? Of course. Strangers though? Absolutely not.

It could prevent Ghost from breaking in again, too. At least I'd be able to see him coming next time.

Seeing Layla on the doorbell feed means I do indeed have to crawl out of bed and go answer the door. Sighing, I roll out of bed, pulling my yoga shorts that had ridden up back down to an appropriate length before making my way to the door.

"Please, take your time, Willow; it's only ninety degrees out here," I hear Layla say through the app on my phone. I stare at the woman on my screen as I move about my new house. Gosh, she is all grown up now. She straightened her black hair that reaches the bottom of her back now, and her face is covered in makeup in a way I wish I knew how to replicate. Layla is gorgeous, but she always has been. Good genes and all.

I make it to the door and open it wide, seeing my almost sister-in-law in person now. Her dark brown eyes peer into mine as she stands on my new welcome mat with three suitcases behind her and big fur boots covering her feet.

"It's about to be summer, you know," I say, finally stepping aside to let her in. I catch a strong whiff of Layla's scent as she walks by: sugar cookies. She even smells good. I took a sniff of my sweaty self, and while I don't smell bad, it isn't good either.

"The boots didn't fit in the suitcase," she grumbles, dragging in all three suitcases and twirling to face me. Layla is slightly shorter than me, standing at 5'5", but that doesn't stop the woman from pulling me into a soul-crushing hug. "Goddess, I missed you."

I hardly hear her, but I hug her just as hard. The twenty-year-old will probably never mutter the words again, and all I can do is soak in the moment. She was one of the closest people I had to family back then, and, by the Moon Goddess, I missed her, too.

"Now, show me my room, please." She breaks the hug and proceeds to gaze around my new house. I'm sure the boxes everywhere aren't impressive but—hold on. Why did she have *three* suitcases? How long was she planning on staying?

I lead her down the hallway to the second bedroom, where I've set up my old bed frame and dresser for her to use. Pulling a suitcase behind me, I show her the guest room.

"I checked this house out online, and it said there were two bedrooms," Layla mutters as she sits on the bed, pulling off her huge fur boots.

"Don't you find that creepy?" I ask. Something is off about her, and I'm not sure if it's because she's grown up or if something else is going on. Who would stay in someone's house after accusing them of being a killer?

Even if she is right about me being a—a killer. I didn't kill her brother. So why is she really here?

"That's not as creepy as the notes I've gotten." *Notes?* As in more than one? She opens her suitcases one by one on the bed and pulls out clothes and puts them in the closet as if her statement didn't make me freeze up. I swiftly turn to face Layla, shocked and confused.

"You got one too?" I ask, sitting in the rocking chair in the room's corner as I watch her unpack.

"Too? I don't mean letters in the mail, I mean notes left at my doorstep, in my window. Creepy stalkerish notes. Do you even know what I'm talking about?" I suddenly remember how annoying my almost sister-in-law can be.

"Yes, I got one yesterday!" I exclaim. Stomping towards my room, I grab the note from my nightstand, and I drop it on Layla's lap in the guest room, where she is already making herself comfortable. "Does this look like an admirer's handwriting?"

"How do you know it's not typed? Maybe they chose that weird ass font. This may not be the same thing as what I'm getting." She cocks her head to the side with an eyebrow raised, and my anger flares. I let out a long breath before answering her ridiculous question.

"There are marker strokes. There's no way this is typed."

"So, who is sending them?" she asks, pulling a stack of notes from her bag and laying them next to the one I got.

"How am I supposed to know?" I ask, amazed at how many notes she's gotten. All with similar messaging to my old notes. Mainly to stop searching, but what does that even mean?

"I was just asking," Layla says, holding her hands up in surrender. "So, do you know who killed Milo?"

"You know I don't know. Don't you think I would've reported them by now?" I'm already tired of this conversation. I need some tea. Walking away, I make my way to the kitchen and fill up the teapot with water before setting it on the stove.

"Yeah, I know," Layla admits, following me to the kitchen and plopping down in my new velvet dining chairs.

"So why did you accuse me of—" She cuts me off with a loud sigh, twirling her hair in her fingers as she watches me move around my kitchen preparing tea.

"I needed you to give me your new address."

"Why?" I ask in utter confusion.

Layla flips her hair over her shoulder, glancing around my kitchen.

"These chairs are cute," she says, wiggling side to side as if to snuggle herself in them. "I needed a place to go. Whoever sent those notes knows my address. I couldn't risk my family, and I need a fresh start, anyway. It was a win-win situation to find you. Plus, you're smart. We'll figure out who is sending these messages before one of us gets hurt."

I blush at the smart comment; it's not one you get often when you drop out of college, and everyone thinks you've gone crazy since your mate died.

Even so, whoever is sending these letters knows something. We need to figure out what's going on before it gets worse.

"If you're getting the notes too, this must be related to Milo," I conclude. But why? What were we doing that would provoke someone to warn us? I stopped digging into his murderer years ago; why threaten us now?

Has Layla gotten herself into something different, something bigger, than Milo's death? The teapot goes off, scaring me out of my running thoughts. Pouring the hot water into two mugs, I adjust a tea bag in each of them and sit down at the table. I stare mindlessly at the table as my head tries to connect dots that appear to be worlds apart. I have no clue why someone is bothering us five years after his death. Apparently, I made someone mad too, but I have no idea who, and it somehow bothers me more than the attack yesterday. What did Ghost mean? I made someone mad? All I do is go to work and go home. Who could have a problem with that?

"What do your notes say?" I ask, in case I missed something from them earlier.

"To stop. Stop digging. Leave it alone. Move on. The works," Layla says, dipping her tea bag twice before setting it off to the side in her teacup.

"Mine used to say things similar to that, but this one is

different. Who is yours signed by?" I wonder who else has received them? My notes from when I was in Kaler City were signed with an *M*, but the one I got yesterday was signed with a *G*.

"I've been searching for Milo," Layla admits with a sheepish blush on her normally deadpan face. A blush covers her face, and that alone is a signal to take it easier on her. No need to be as hard on her as her parents, who probably already dug into her for it. Why was she suddenly looking into his death? What did she know that I didn't?

"Someone must pay. He doesn't get to get off scotch free. Lives have been ruined since his disappearance." She doesn't look at me as she spots off her reasons.

"What do your parents think?" I ask, dipping my tea bag in my cup a few times.

"That I'm a heartbroken fool like you."

I scoff, but already knew that is how they thought of me. My almost in-laws and I got into many heated arguments surrounding Milo's death. We immediately grew apart. They think he got cold feet and ran away or something. They tried not to think about it much, obviously, because then why did he leave his family and school too? Why did any existence of him besides a darn coffee mug with his prints on it disappear? Because someone killed him and was trying to cover it up.

"They shut down when I bring it up. They're a dead-end when it comes to him." Layla sighs, taking a sip of her tea. My tea remains on the table; I thought tea would help, but I'm too distraught to think, let alone drink or do anything.

"So, what's the plan now?" I ask. She must have made

her way here with something concocting in that brain of hers.

"I move in here?" she asks almost nervously, gazing at me over her teacup.

"Move in here permanently?" I confirm, making sure I heard her right.

"Yeah, and we figure this out together."

"Layla, I can't support two people on my salary," I admit. Flora pays me well, but I'm only an assistant. With most of my income now going to this house, to feed and support her too is going to be tight.

"I'll... get a job." She raises a shoulder as if the suggestion is simple.

"What about school?" I ask.

"I'm not college material, Willow, and you know it." This time, Layla rolls her eyes. A sharp laugh escapes her lips.

"Okay, what about the notes?" I ask as more and more questions pop into my mind. Is Layla going to stay here for real?

"Gosh, Willow, do I have to come up with everything?" she says with wide eyes as she sets down her tea.

"I'm figuring out where you're at," I say, still partially in another place mentally.

"Ahead of you?"

"No, you're behind. The man behind the notes is a tall Hispanic man named Ghost," I say defensively.

"That's it?" She raises an eyebrow. Her attitude was raising the hairs on my skin.

"It's more than what you have." I couldn't help the retort as our conversation gets progressively more heated.

It's as if she is attacking me, and my shoulder blades tighten with tension. Her sharp gaze cuts through me. I'm older, I'm supposed to take charge, but I'm not that much older, and I'm—it's all too much. I'm not built to deal with these kinds of problems.

"So, Milo's killer is Hispanic. So, that gets us… nowhere." Layla nods her head, surveying my home; it was mostly empty at the moment since it's worlds bigger than my last apartment. "I knew I could only live with another bear shifter," Layla comments, leaning back into her chair.

"Why?" I ask. This girl could be incredibly random at times; it was hard to keep up.

"Because only a bear shifter would keep the house this cold."

"True," I mumble, letting the steam from my mug warm my face; gosh, it was too early for this conversation. Finally, taking a sip, I let the soothing hot liquid slide down my throat. For once, I'm not embraced by the comfort tea gives me; instead, I have the instinct to spit it out.

Sniffing the steam, it smells the same; I think? My skin lights up with heat regardless, the sweat dripping down the back of my neck intensifies, and sweat bubbles up at my forehead. My tongue is getting puffy, as if it's out of place.

Oh my goddess, did I purchase the wrong tea?

"Layla, does your tea taste funny?" My words are coming out all weird and wrong, but I try anyway.

"It's finally not that bland, harsh-ass black tea you used to drink. You exploring different flavors now?" she says with a weird stare at me, taking another sip of hers.

"I haven't. Someone must have done something to my

tea bags," I gurgle. When could that have happened? I just got here. I just got that box... oh my goddess, did Ghost find my new address? I can barely get the words out as my tongue is stiff. I grab her mug and mine to dump it down the sink. The effects of one sip are instant. My eyes puff up and water, and golly, when did it get hot? Is my AC still working? Am I truly having a reaction to something? What's wrong with me?

"Are you okay? You look like shit," Layla says. Grabbing my mug, she sniffs it before her eyes shoot up to me. She grabs an unused tea bag from the box I purchased a few days ago and rips it open, letting the contents spill on the counter.

"This isn't your normal, Willow. Did you get the wrong kind?" I can't keep my weakening body up anymore. I turn from the sink and in my attempt to reach a chair, I fall to the ground. The hard wood slams into my arms as I try to break the fall.

Shift. I need to shift to my bear. Activate the healing.

This is an allergic reaction. I used to recognize these symptoms faster, but I couldn't smell anything. Why was Layla able to smell it, but not me?

"Oh, my goddess. What am I supposed to do?" Layla shouts in a panic. "Call 911? Wait, no, that is for humans. The Council would kill me. Shift, Willow, shift! Oh my goddess, she can't hear me. Where's your phone?" Layla snatches my phone off the cream-colored table. All I can see is Layla's hair whirling back and forth as she panics. She reminds me of a dream, hazy and moving in slow motion. My eyes are closing as Layla moves the phone towards her ear, and that is the last thing I see before my body has had enough and calls it a day.

As embarrassing as it is, I, a full-blooded bear shifter, have an allergy to bananas. Shifter bodies could heal themselves from almost anything. As long as the bullet or object was removed or our heads weren't fully cut off, we could heal our bodies by continuously shifting between our animal form and human form. The act would activate the magic properties that allow us to turn and amplify the animal's ability to heal. Our healing ability doesn't activate without shifting, and that is hard to do unconsciously.

This is where witches and fairies came into play. As the doctors and healers of the paranormal world, it's a good idea to have one in your back pocket. The problem in my case, is that moving to Rainfall Avenue and going no contact with my family caused me to lose my family witch's number.

So, the fact that I'm still alive means Layla must have witch powers, or she called someone that I now owe a favor.

I'm in my room, that much I can tell. Turning my head, I can now see that Layla did, in fact, stick around, and that she is still here, rocking away in my rocking chair next to my bed. She lets out a sigh of relief as she makes eye contact with me, putting her phone down on the side table beside the chair. "Oh my goddess, Willow, that was some scary shit. I forgot shifters could have allergies."

"What happened?" I ask. My body is still heavy, but my eyes and tongue have gone back to normal.

"You don't have a witch on speed dial. Now you do, by the way. I called your emergency contact, Flora Enchanted.

I told her what happened, then she called someone named Dylan while rushing over here. Then Dylan called an Alpha named Jackson, and—"

"And now you're stuck with me, sweet pea."

The grocery store hero, also known as Eddie Enchanted, stands in my doorway, a smirk and those darn glasses decorating his face.

❧ *6* ☙

EDDIE

A CHANCE TO SEE WILLOW AGAIN IS SYNONYMOUS to a chance to laugh till your stomach hurts—something you wouldn't give up even if it meant the world would burn down to a crisp. I'll admit, seeing her doused in sweat because of witch magic and being deathly sick isn't the most ideal situation. But it brought me here, so who am I to be picky?

Sitting beside her bed, I decide then and there that she will have a hell of a hard time getting rid of me. As much as the fact that someone tried to hurt my Willow completely pisses me off, I now have the perfect excuse to be around her twenty-four seven.

"Sweet pea." I huff out a laugh, leaning back in my chair while resting my arm on her bed, my hand on her leg. A bedsheet separates my hand and her skin, and as much as I want to touch her skin, I think she would jump a mile if she noticed me touching her. For that reason alone, the bed sheet stays, for now. "If you wanted to see me that badly, you could've called. You know—"

"You're funny," she cuts me off, whipping her bedsheet off her sweat-covered body and glaring. My sweet pea is looking at me. Glaring, yes, but she's looking at me. A win if I've ever seen one. "Why are you here?"

"How could I not be here? You were poisoned." Snappy Willow is a new side I've yet to meet. I wonder what's putting her on edge.

"I know that, but what does that have to do with you?"

"Whose witch do you think came to save you?" I ask, a full-blown smirk covering my lips. She knows how the game works and yet is playing right into my hand.

"Oh," she mumbles after a breath. Her frizzy hair sticks up straight as she tilts her head. I can see the realization of her situation settle in her body as her eyes shoot up to mine. Finally, her full attention is on me.

"*Oh,* is right, Willow; the favor you owe belongs to me." It would technically be owed to my Pack, but Jackson, after far too much pleading and begging, let me take the lead on this one. Favors are an enormous deal among shifters, and owing one is akin to owing a debt to a shark, dangerous as hell.

"What do you want?"

"Ah, ah, ah. No, no, Willow. I'll save this favor for now and cash it in later," I say as her body tenses up. "More importantly, why is someone trying to kill you?"

"I... I don't know," Willow says, glancing at Layla, the friend I met about an hour ago, before settling her gaze on me. I didn't think she'd play me for stupid, but I'm not quite ready to push her yet. Not on this. I'm saving that for later.

"Then we can kick off this guarding gig by making room for one more in this little home on the prairie." The plan is to be glued to her hip, and I couldn't do that from a dozen blocks away. I'll push as hard as I can on this and find out who is behind this little incident later.

Little does she know, she isn't getting rid of me.

"No, absolutely not. There's no room for you here," Willow says. Her curls are wet with sweat and sticking to her forehead. She's absolutely tantalizing when she's a hot, sweaty mess, but I can't stand that she's uncomfortable. I reluctantly get up, losing my physical contact with her leg, and pull the rest of her bed sheet down.

"I could sleep in your room with you," I say. The most ideal solution, but with her constantly pushing me away, the most unlikely.

"As if," Willow replies with a sharp laugh.

"You could come live in the Pack house?" My Pack's house is a new build made with more than enough room to grow, and it wouldn't be the first night she stayed over. That night was a few months ago when Flora's coworkers tried to kidnap her. For what, I can't quite remember, but my sweet pea, Willow, stayed with Flora and Luxe at the Pack house. She abruptly left; for what, once again, I don't know, but I would safely assume it had something to do with whoever poisoned her.

"I have responsibilities here," she mutters, her eyes trailing everywhere but to me. This little move was her way of distancing our connection, but I'd get her eyes on me again.

"Like what, sweet pea?" Her fingers twist the blanket that sits beside her as she probably tries to come up with a reason why she can't come with me to the Pack house. The Pack house is where she would be safest, surrounded by eight other shifters and a teenage vampire.

"Like my cat, someone has to feed her and change her litter."

"Layla"—I look over at the woman on her phone—"Can do that while we go live in my house."

"Eddie."

"Willow."

Her deep brown eyes finally meet mine. I hold my breath to make the silence in the room louder so I'll be ready with any counter she may give me.

"Eddie, I don't need a bodyguard, and I can't leave Layla alone."

"I'll be a friend who never leaves your side." Did I fucking friend-zone myself? Damn, I'm off my rocker. I walk out of the room, hoping to collect the pieces of my mind that must have blown up at some point and find the thermostat. Finding it in the living room where my Pack sits, shivering, I adjust the temperature to sixty-two degrees.

"How is she?" Flora asks, getting up from Dylan's lap.

"She's good," I say, not wanting to tell them she's awake. I already had to share her attention with Layla, but I'd disappear if they all came to see her, too.

Those thoughts don't matter because Luxe, Flora, and

my Alpha, Jackson, stalk towards Willow's room while I trail behind them.

"Eddie, don't be overbearing. Girls don't like that," Ryder, one of the eldest of my Packmates says with a damning smile on his face.

"How the fuck would you know?" I say before entering Willow's overcrowded room. I can hear the rest of my Pack's laughter as I shut the bedroom door.

I sit, once again, in that uncomfortable-ass folding chair by Willow's bed. Once again, I rest my hand on her leg. She doesn't notice my hand, her attention being thrown to the Alphas who've stepped into the room, followed by Flora.

"Willow, what the hell happened? How did this happen? Why didn't you tell me someone is trying to hurt you?" Luxe, a female Alpha who prefers the female term for leader, Luna, storms in. Her blonde hair whipping everywhere as she steps in front of one of the many fans set up around this bedroom.

"I couldn't," Willow says as her face of annoyance melts to worry. "I was in the middle of an allergic reaction."

"An allergy to what?" I ask, surprised to hear she has an allergy. Most shifters don't have allergies since our bodies heal themselves when we shift, which begs to ask the question, "And why didn't you shift to heal yourself?"

"What part of having an allergic reaction are y'all not getting?" Willow says, waving her hands about as if this is something we all should know about. I sure as shit can't explain what happens when someone has an allergic reaction.

"Willow, we were worried about you," Flora says, sitting on the bed in front of my chair, blocking my view of Willow. My nerves itched to push her out of the way, which I'm sure would earn me a knife through the hand as her mate, Dylan, wouldn't appreciate my touching her. Spoken from experience.

"She passed out, guys," Layla says nonchalantly, as if everyone should know that happens. I could only glance back at Luxe, who is as confused as I am.

"Why are you wearing glasses?" Layla suddenly asks, pointing to her eyes as if she has glasses.

"Because I came from work. People take me more seriously." I answer with furrowed brows. Why did this matter?

"Even when shifters know you have twenty-twenty vision?" Willow asks, staring at my face. Fucking finally. I smirk, tilting my head slightly. I have her eyes on me again, and I'll always eat up every second I have of her full attention.

"Yeah, even shifters fall victim to perceptions." Not to mention, the glasses look good on me. Moon Goddess strike me down if looking good is a crime...

She doesn't strike me down.

"Willow, are you okay?" Jackson asks, stepping away from his position in the room's corner. He is more of a watcher than anything else. It makes him a strategic Alpha.

"Yes, thank you, Jackson, and everyone, for everything. I'm fine now, and you all should head home cause it's getting dark out," Willow says. She moves her eyes to the window and stares as the room settles. I lost her attention to the damn window?

"The witch said you'd be tired," Layla murmurs, moving to turn one of the fans towards Willow.

"So, what happened? For real this time," I ask again. As much as I could joke around, there is a serious problem here. Someone hurt Willow, and my bear, and I can hardly hold on anymore.

Willow huffs, staring at Luxe, who only raises an eyebrow. "I didn't want to worry you," she says, more to Luxe and Flora than to me. She moves her line of sight down to the damn blanket, instead of to me, the person who asked the damn question. "Someone broke into my apartment."

"What the hell do you mean, someone broke into your apartment?" I ask, leaning in closer to her. My eyes naturally search her body to make sure she is okay. I hope she knows that I'm sure as hell not leaving now.

"Explain, Willow. What's going on?" She explains how someone broke into her apartment twice, attacked her, left a creepy note, has left Layla notes too, and that someone laced the tea, which caused the allergic reaction.

These attacks are personal, and the only thing she isn't saying is *why* this was happening. I can tell Layla knows something too, by her tense body language. I want to hound them to tell me everything. I want to go kill the fucker who dared to hurt Willow, but Rome wasn't built in a day, and death would be too easy for the fucker. Tonight is not the night to try to do all that.

"What are you allergic to?" I ask. Luxe lies on the bed, getting comfortable next to Willow and Flora. I guess she is staying the night, too.

"Bananas," Willow quietly says. Her shoulders are

slumped, and I can tell she is drained, and yet I can't walk away.

"Anything else I should know about?" This line of questioning would only give me about thirty more seconds in Willow's presence. I know, yet I bask in these thirty seconds.

"No, that's everything." I know it's not, but for tonight, I'll let it slide, for real this time. I stand from my chair, walking around the room, sliding my fingers over the windowsill and double-checking the lock.

"I'm staying on the couch," I say, walking towards the door as Jackson rolls his eyes and leaves. He knows if this was his girl, he'd do much worse than I am. Willow is special; something in my soul is attached to her, and I can't shake it. So I'm not fighting it.

"No, you're not. Go home."

"You can't possibly believe that—" I say, and this time, she interrupts me.

"Eddie, I'm serious."

"It might be a good idea to let him stick around. It won't hurt—" Luxe agrees, maybe to stir the pot or because she genuinely wants me to stay, who knows.

"No, Luxe. He has to go. I can take care of myself."

Layla abruptly leaves mid-conversation, and now it's me, Luxe, and Flora, both of whom also refuse to leave. Not that Willow gives them any pushback. I guess it's no big deal for them, but me staying is an absolutely hard limit. I think the fuck not. I'm staying whether or not she gives me permission. There is no way I'll leave them alone. Not when someone is trying to hurt any of them—Layla, the newbie, included.

"Night, ladies," I say, moving to leave. Willow stays quiet and maybe she thinks she's won.

"Night," Luxe says, curling around Willow's body. These ladies are Pack. I mean, only Flora is, technically, but seeing them all together feels right. They are ours, and we need them. More than need, I want them. Willow, more than... more than anything. She's mine, and this, this is right.

I trail into the hallway and see Layla, who shyly opens her door.

"Do you want me to check your window too?" I ask as she gazes up at me. I have plenty of questions for her, too, how she is a part of this whole mess, and what she's doing here, now, of all times. But I'll mind my business for tonight. The important thing is to protect my Pack, and that's exactly what I'll do.

"Pretty please," she says, stepping to the side to let me in. I go to the window, locking it and checking that the lock is good before searching the room. Making sure no one is hiding under the bed or in the closet. I know no one is with my shifter hearing and smelling, and I'm sure she does too, but to be on the safe side, I check anyway. The lock is secure under my touch; this window is solid. We'll know if someone tries to get in here.

"You're good," I mumble, going to leave before she grabs my sleeve. When I turn to face at her, she glares, though. What an odd one.

"Are you staying?" she asks.

"You think you can keep me out?" I ask with a scoff.

"Good. Willow never knows how to accept help," she says, letting go of my sleeve and rounding her bed to get in.

I move to leave, but she isn't quite done. "Have fun on the couch."

"I will, little shit." I shut the door and pause at Willow's door. I'm sure she can hear me out here. She's probably waiting for me to leave before she'll go to sleep. She's probably waiting to hear the door shut and the car start. She probably won't rest until she does, and what she needs most is to sleep.

I don't want her to be tired.

I walk over to a window in the kitchen and slowly pry it open. Enough for me to slide back through. If a show is what she wants, then a show is what she will get. I walk through the front door loudly, letting the door close noisily. Getting into my car, I pull out of the driveway. The brisk air covers my arms. A quick shift to run through the trees would be killer right now, but I'm not leaving Willow alone.

I park my car about half a mile away before starting my trek back to her house. Hopefully, all of them will be dead asleep, and they won't hear me coming back in the house. Willow's house is surrounded by trees, a nice setup for a bear shifter. Being so damn big, it's harder to shift out in the open without being caught by other shifters or the humans who are immune to the presence of predators. The paranormal side of Rainfall Avenue leaves a lot of forest and greenery to help hide the shift, unlike the concrete jungle that the human side is turning into. Willow won't have to worry about being seen shifting with the forest that surrounds her place. It goes for a few miles out too.

This would be a great place. Too bad she won't be in it

for too much longer. If I had things my way, she'd be in the Pack house tonight. A man must have patience, I guess.

I sneak back through the window I pried open earlier, slowly shutting it. I quietly search the house, making sure the only living beings in this house are the same ones that were here when I left.

Ending up in Willow's kitchen, I can practically envision her hitting the ground in the throes of her allergic reaction. My skin bristles when I remember I wasn't here. It shouldn't. I hardly know this woman, yet my skin tightens when I'm around her, and she's on my mind fucking constantly. I can't fucking breathe without thinking if Willow is breathing, too.

I shouldn't have let her walk away. Not when I ran into her at the grocery store the other day, not when she was in my Pack house, not ever. Now I'm stuck playing catch-up, and she continues to look at me as if I'm a stranger, or worse, like she can't stand me.

She can look at me like that all she wants—it doesn't change anything.

I'm—she's—she's mine. She has to be.

Willow's kitchen is what you'd find in a classic farm style house. A huge farmhouse sink surrounded by light pink cabinets and tiny string lights. I run the sink as I pick up one of the little dirty plates; all these little dishes have tiny black angels and pink ribbons. I love a woman who does whatever the hell she wants, like using her china for everyday use. She's so damn cute.

After wiping down the counters, I finally break into her pantry. I can tell she recently moved in based on the lack of food and the amounts of takeout containers in her trash can. Plus, the boxes everywhere. The perfect place to get cracking on this cleanout is at the source of our current situation: the damn tea bags.

I take one and break it open on the counter. I get whiffs of bananas and tea leaves. It seems normal—did she pick up the wrong box? I tear another bag open and get the same results. They all have little bits of banana, but if she's allergic, why couldn't she smell them? If this is from the same stack from when she knocked over that display case, could all of them be ruined? My eyes trail over to the clock on her stove. It's midnight, and I'm losing time to clean out this kitchen.

I take the little ceramic box filled with the rest of the tea bags and dump it all into the trash. Turning to the fridge, I notice how its light contrasts against the little lights strung up around the room. Taking the first thing, a bottle of ketchup, I snap a picture with my phone before tossing it in the trash.

I pray she doesn't lose her shit when she wakes up to a new kitchen.

Taking the overfilled trash bag with me, I walk all the way to my car. Leaving the girls unattended again isn't ideal, but I'd locked up after stealing Willow's house key, of course.

I drive straight past the paranormal side grocery store where she got her original box of tea bags. The human grocery is only about fifteen minutes away. The employee on the intercom makes damn sure every shopper knows to get their asses out of here in twenty-nine minutes and twenty-five seconds the moment I walk into the store.

I check the photo I took of Willow's half-used ketchup

to match the brand of it to the ketchup in my hand. Taking those damn photos was the smartest thing I've ever fucking done.

After I'm done replacing everything she had, I go down the baking aisle. Does Willow eat pancakes? Or waffles? Who doesn't eat pancakes? I grab a box and some syrup, and what's pancakes without bacon, sausages, or eggs and toast? I should pick those up too.

"Five minutes before closing. Please make your final selections and make your way towards the front."

* * *

"RISE AND SHINE, HONEY PIES!" I sing as Willow, Flora, and Luxe enter the kitchen. The girls each have bonnets covering their heads and sleepy faces. Their sleep was either amazing or horrendous, but either way, I made a bomb ass breakfast. Therefore, Willow's anger that grows on her face as her eyes narrow should be canceled out.

"You stayed?" Willow growls, sitting at her small dining table. She quickly got back up to—I don't quite figure it out because she sits right back down. Her eyes shoot to me, following my movements as I place the plates and full mugs down on the table.

"Of course I did," I say. Worst-case scenario: someone tried to kill her last night—and she's asking why I'd stay. What kind of man would I be if I had left? Who the hell has she been hanging around?

Their mugs are filled with tea and Willow brings the mug up to Flora, who sniffs it wordlessly before taking a sip and then nodding towards Willow. I could've sniffed that for her. I fucking made that for her. Did she think I'd poison it?

Layla floats into the room soon after the girls sit, and I set a plate in front of her. Her hair is perfectly straight, and her face is covered in a white substance... in skincare? She is not shy at all while filling up her plate with four pancakes and drenching them in butter and syrup.

"I'm hungry," Layla shrugs as she stuffs her face. "You a chef?"

That is probably the closest I'll ever get to a *thank you* from her.

"No, ma'am. That would be my mom. She cooks at Eleanor's Diner and has taught me a thing or two." I say, sliding another pancake onto Willow's plate. I'm doing my damndest not to stare at her eating. I crave to though. Watching another eat, especially before you eat, is a practice only soul mates do, and on instinct, I swear, the pull is there. Does she experience this too?

"Your mom is the chef at Eleanor's Diner?" Willow asks, dropping her glare as her attention shifts to the pancakes in front of her. Her hands wrap around her mug as she slowly sips her tea. Her eyes move to watch me again, and I can hardly look away. Her gaze entraps me. I love her eyes searching my body.

"You've got some drool there, sweet pea," I say, pointing to the corner of my mouth. I laughed, and Willow snidely snickers.

"Why are you here?" she retorts, as if it's something I should be ashamed of. I smile. Ignoring the question. I move on to talking about my mom.

"She's been working there for twenty years now."

"And what do you do?" Layla asks.

"I save women from falling at grocery stores. Maybe you've heard about some of my work."

"Ha ha," Willow laughs dryly as she places a bite of syrup-covered pancake in her mouth.

"If you've heard about the tall, handsome man who has strong beefy arms saving a particular woman from hitting the ground in a graceful swoop, that was me," I say, earning a chuckle from the group.

Hearing the teapot go off, Willow makes a move towards it, but I'm faster.

"I didn't have pancake mix here last night..." Willow mumbles as she waits for me to pour more hot water into her cup. I smile down at her; she's got tired eyes and is gnawing on her lip.

"I bought you all new groceries this morning and threw away anything that was opened or unsealed," I mutter, leaning against the counter. I hadn't thought of a game plan to figure out what the hell is going on here, knowing someone is trying to hurt Willow. I'm not sure what the plan is with Flora and Luxe either and how long they plan on staying. "Any plans today, ladies?"

"I'm going to—" Willow says, but I suddenly have a better idea.

"Prep the house for staying with a big strong shifter to protect you? That sounds perfect, Willow. You can get ready first, then I can get ready at my house, and we go shopping for better locks and an actual security system." I say, interrupting the grumpy bear.

"I am going to work today," Willow says, furrowing her brows and cocking her head to the side.

"Flora gave you the day off," Luxe pipes in. While Willow is grumpy in the mornings, Luxe is more like a beam of sunshine that has finally pressed her on button. Flora only nods in agreement to Luxe's statement. She's become attached to her phone since she's sat down.

"In case you and Flora forgot, I have bills to pay."

"In case *you* forgot, Flora gives all employees thirty days of paid time off. You have twenty-nine after today," Luxe says, biting into her toast.

"What if I was going to use all thirty days for something else?" Willow questions, an irritated smirk covering her thick two-toned lips. I smile, a closed-tooth smile that lets her know I won this argument way before it even started.

"Then I guess you ask Flora for an extra day of PTO. Moving on. Chop, chop, ladies. Luxe, what time is your shift at work?" I say, clapping my hands and making a show of clearing the serving dishes. Luxe sighs, lazily gazing at the stove clock, pursing her lips.

"In an hour," Luxe says. She gets up to leave, but does her own surveillance of the house before she goes. Shifting into her wolf form, she does two laps around Willow's house, stopping and sniffing any scents she deems necessary before she takes off, presumably, to her own place.

I see Flora wink at Willow, which brings a blush across the woman's face. She leaves with a "Goodbye, darlings" as I'm sure her mate is here to take her to work. Willow finishes her meal, and before I can take her plate, she snatches the plate from the table.

"I am perfectly capable of cleaning my own dish, thank you."

"We're feisty in the mornings, aren't we?" I say, gently taking the plate from her hands and washing it before taking a seat at the table. I pull a pancake to my own plate; I'll wait for her to get ready before dragging her back to the Enchanted Pack house.

Willow dresses in wide-legged pants and a small tank top, her shoulder purse resting on the counter. Her beautiful auburn curls cover her shoulders. All this to say, she is gorgeous. Can I convince her to stop at my place for a change of clothes and a quick shower?

YES, I was indeed successful at convincing her to stop at the Enchanted Pack house. After a quick shower and a change of clothes, we were on our way to buy safety gear.

"Is this necessary?" she asks, lolling her head into her hand. She's leaned against the counter of the tech store in the home security department. I stand with her, paying for her alarm. I wanted her to pick it out, though—it was her house, after all. I have no idea why she's allowing me to drag her everywhere, but she has, and I'm not gonna waste it.

"What about this stick thing?" I ask her, turning around showing her the object. It's a white rod with a red bottom that props against the door, keeping it shut. I don't think it could keep a shifter out, but the banging noise of it hitting the ground would at least notify her of an intruder. I drop it on the floor to be sure that it would make a loud-ass noise, and based on the glare Willow is giving me right now, it's loud enough.

"Eddie, I'm about ready to leave you here."

"Except I have the car keys, sweet pea. Plus, you are way too nice to do that," I say. I am getting over the shopping too, but Willow's safety is more important than her irritation with me. We walk towards the cash registers; she's getting this stick and a couple of other little things to help protect herself when she can't shift into her bear. The person after her knows how to prevent a person from shifting and is obviously experienced in whatever the hell is going on here.

"You're lucky I didn't want to make a scene with all this noise you're making."

"As if you'd make a scene in there. Your cheeks are already blushing." Her hands fly to her cheeks, pressing them together. It makes her look borderline adorable.

"How would you know that?"

I stop and turn around to face her, letting her body crash into mine. Her chest against mine and her shoes bumping into my own makes my bear perk up with excitement. "Cause, Buttercup, I can taste the heat coming from them."

My fingers draw up to draw light circles on her cheeks where her blush tries to hide. Her breathing becomes as shallow as mine. My heart races, and I'm sure she can feel it with her hands pressed up against my chest.

"How do you know my last name?" she stammers, shocked. Her wild eyes search mine while I step away and move so her hand is interlocked with mine.

"I saw it on your ID," I lie. The witch had to know her full name yesterday, but I don't want to remind her of that whole ordeal yet. She is freely walking beside me, blissfully unaware and carefree, and I can't ruin that.

"You're fluffing annoying. You know that?" she says, glaring at me. She still hasn't taken her hand from my grip yet. Thank the Moon Goddess.

"Only for you, Buttercup. Let's go," I say, still not letting go of her hand. The only way she'll get her hand back now is if she realizes I have it and lets go herself.

❧ 7 ❧
WILLOW

My happiest place is the local bookstore. Standing in Written Memories, Rainfall Avenue's biggest bookstore, always makes me happy, yet this time I am racked with nerves.

Paperback books line the shelves as I walk straight to my favorite section with a pressing stare on my back. Eddie is following me. He said he wouldn't be my bodyguard, but it sure appears as if he is. Breathing down my neck and following my every move, how could I not be racked with nerves? I have a permanent blush flushing my face from the closeness of his presence, and there is no calming it down.

My flush only gets deeper as I walk into the romance section. The book covers suddenly seem more scandalous than usual and incredibly embarrassing as I now had company with me. My eyes constantly track between the covers with shirtless men and Eddie, as if he could follow my line of vision and is judging the crap out of me. I'm getting shy.

Why was I here again? Could the carpeting swallow me whole? Watching Eddie gaze over the covers, both innocent and not-so-innocent, my face is completely ablaze. I watch every tick of his arm and slight raise of his eyebrow as his eyes glide over the shelves that hold all my favorite books.

"These are some interesting covers, Willow," Eddie says, turning his attention back to me. His brown eyes melt into mine. I can hardly breathe as he stares down at me. He has his glasses on again: half-round rims with black hardware at the top. His braids stop at his eyebrows, and his teeth shine. Darn, even his teeth shine. His smell. Oh my Moon Goddess, his smell. I can't focus on much more beyond his smell. He smells euphoric. Vanilla and tobacco. Am I fawning over him right now? I can't. I can't be into him.

"I'm not in charge of the covers," I murmur as I scan over the covers. Sure, some of them were... interesting, but it's a huge part of the story. These books captivate me, whisk me away to dreamlands I can only find in these stories. If I wanted to be a bakery owner in a small town and fall in love, I could. If I wanted to fall in love with a mafia capo, I could. It is one dream world after the next. How dare I be ashamed of what I like? I love these covers, naked men and all.

"Which one do you want?" Eddie asks, looming over me with an intense amount of eye contact that warms my insides. Looming didn't happen often for me, seeing as I am 5'7", but Eddie is tall, and his wide, lean build swallows my own wide frame. I never thought I would enjoy being loomed over, but here I am with my heart fluttering and my forehead breaking out in a sweat. I had completely forgotten I dragged him in here for a specific book.

"Um, uh. This one." I try to play it off as if I hadn't been eyeing the book for weeks now and have the description on the back cover memorized. I am only now convinced that I deserve to walk out of Written Memories with this book in hand.

"I'll get it too," Eddie says, grabbing the copy in my hand and one more for himself.

"No." I honestly don't think I could get the word out any faster. Whipping my head towards him, my curls whip with me. Is he teasing me?

"No? Why not? You're getting it," Eddie asks with a too-big and too-goofy smile on his face.

"It's spicy. Look at the cover." I try to reason. Romance authors are clever and enjoy being funny with their discreet covers. I know better than to think of the words cute, soft, and fluffy when holding a cartoon cover in my hands. The book would have as much of a chance of being filthy, slutty, and a completely different type of good time as a book with naked people on it.

"It's cartoon characters," he says with a shrug. His eyes stalk over my face, stopping at my eyes, then my nose, my lips, and deviously slow back up to my eyes. This man is tempting me.

"It's not just cartoon characters; it's on a romance book cover." He has no idea what he is getting into and would think I am crazy once he figures it out.

"You're not explaining what's wrong with me reading the book?"

"Cartoons don't mean that there's not an intense level of spice in this book," I whisper, stepping closer to him, hoping he can hear me better. With this romance book grasped between his fingers, he is stepping into dangerous territory, and he doesn't even know it. He'll either be disgusted or fall so deeply into the hole there will be no light to be seen on the other side—a first-class ticket straight to hell.

"Spice is what exactly?" he asks, tilting his head closer to mine. Are the bookshelves closing in, or is it me? I can't pull my eyes away from his, and I'm sure he can see my bottom lip tremble. The smell of books can't calm me down when Eddie's body is all I can process. His forehead is nearly touching mine. Gosh, why is he asking me these questions while staring so intently at me? Is it bad I kinda want to reach my hands around his neck and bring his lips to mine? Yes, yes, it is bad. All I can smell is his scent surrounding me. It is too good—distracting.

"Spice is..." I mumble, scrunching my face, trying to think of a polite way to put it. "Tension, heat, sex."

"It's always the shy, quiet ones that are freaky, huh?" he jokes, and all I can do is break eye contact and swat his arm.

"Put your copy back," I say, trying to reach for the book in his hands.

"I think I'll give this spicy book a read, Miss Buttercup," he says, walking towards the cash registers.

"Eddie, wait," I say, pulling on his arm. "At least read the trigger warnings."

"These books come with warnings?" he sputters. We continue on our trail to impending doom that's waiting for us at the registers and beyond. My cheeks couldn't be any redder.

"Willow, I've read these kinds of books before; I'm only yanking your chain." He couldn't have mentioned this five minutes ago? I lift my head up as embarrassment slowly drains from my body and wonder replaces it.

"When?" I couldn't have asked in a tone any lower than I did, and I know I sound like a kid, but you don't meet many men who read romance.

"My mom had these all over the place; they were the only books she'd read." He's so nonchalant, confident, uncaring. It unsettles me, and I hate it. It appears easy for him to be the super cool jokester. It makes me wonder if it's a facade.

"She sounds amazing."

"She is."

Checking out isn't nearly as painful as I thought it was going to be, and walking side by side with Eddie is as easy as breathing. Except that every time I get a whiff of his scent, I lose my balance, and wow, why does he smell enticing?

Why am I not quite ready to go home? It was my unplanned day off, and here I am with someone besides myself, walking the streets of Rainfall Avenue without the need to rush home. It's a cool summer day, and while I am still covered in sweat, so is Eddie. I had forgotten how nice it is to hang out with people who have the same shifter animal as me. Not only is my bear swooning inside due to the handsome company we have, but I feel at peace. Sure, someone tried to kill me yesterday, but Eddie's here, and Layla, Flora, and Luxe. Never did I think I would have such a comforting group of people surrounding me, yet here I am.

"Watch out," Eddie orders. His arm shoots out in front of me as his head turns to the opposite side of the street.

"What?" What could he have possibly stopped me for? Was someone following us? Oh my, was I gonna die?

"You are about to step right into spilled ice cream," he says, wrapping the arm that stopped me around my shoulders, guiding me away from the direction of the car. "Speaking of ice cream, let's go get some."

The ice cream shop is small. It is designed as a carousel, and the center is where we order and get our ice cream. He got a s'mores-flavored bowl with gram crackers on top. I've never tried that flavor, never wanted to venture away from my cookie dough, but with Eddie here, the s'mores flavor is calling to me.

I watch as he sets our—I mean *my*—shopping bags down and sits at a small round table with a golden pole coming up from the middle of it. Even as I sit across from Eddie, a big, strong bear shifter, I can't help surveying my surroundings constantly now since his abrupt ice cream spillage warning.

"Willow."

"Yeah?"

"Eat your ice cream." I can't stop searching around, lifting my spoon without looking at it. What if Ghost is here? Following me here, right now? "I think it's time."

"Time for what?" I nearly shout, jumping at the

sudden sound. Everything is super loud, sensitive, and like there is a knife pointed at my back, even though I know there is no one behind me.

I wasn't jumpy at the supercenter when we picked up the protection supplies or at Written Memories when we were browsing books. But now that I'm sitting down, outside, out in the open, my nerves are shot. I'm not safe anywhere. I'm not safe here, I'm not safe in my old apartment, and I'm apparently not safe in my home. Where can I go? What can I do?

"To figure out what we are going to do about this."

"You mean what *I* am going to do," I sigh. "I have no idea." It's not every day I have to deal with someone trying to kill me. I've never thought someone would hate me enough to try to kill me. I'm a homebody, I rarely go out, and when I do, I'm nice and kind—at least I thought I was.

My breathing is getting heavy, and my vision is blurring. Shoot, I need to calm down now, right now.

Eddie shouts my name, and I can't help but study him. Really peer at him. His brown eyes dig into mine. His plush lips set in a straight line. His nose is wide and smooth. He has clear, flawless skin. He must shift often to have such beautiful skin; only shifting magic could make skin that soft. He has a white T-shirt on that wraps nicely over his shoulders, at the right amount of tightness: not too small but enough to show his muscles. When did he have time to work out—?

"Willow, I have an idea," he says, scooping some of his ice cream and reaching his spoon out to me. My gaze trails to the spoon and back up to him. I part my lips as he continues talking. Milo never shared, never wanted to, yet Eddie is without so much of a flinch. In fact, he offered it first. This is... this is nice. "We have to find out who is trying to hurt you and take care of them ourselves."

"I'm not a killer, Eddie," I say as he puts his spoon in my mouth. I drag his ice cream off the spoon with my lips, letting the flavor sit on my tongue. It is good, cold, yet warm, with the chocolate syrup and warmed crackers on top.

I say the words *I'm not a killer* almost instinctively. As if Eddie wasn't there the night I killed Cassandra. But he was. He was, and yet he sits here with me still.

"Doesn't mean I'm not." He bristles as he says it. Is he the same as me? Are we monsters? "Or Dylan, Jackson, Felix, hell, even Ryder, who is all about the law and doing right, might even get his hands dirty."

There was the difference.

He could never be a monster. He's never had to be. Neither did I. I didn't have to kill the woman who kidnapped my best friend, but I did. There is no we in this; it's only me. I am the monster. Maybe I deserve to be alone. Maybe the Moon Goddess is mad at me for the instinct she knows I have.

"I barely know them. I barely know you. They wouldn't—" I try to explain, but he's shaking his head before I can get the sentence out.

"They would. *I* will, Willow," he says, and it makes everything final. There is no room for debate or argument, barely room to think. I feed him my spoon of ice cream, and he takes it, biting the spoon for a millisecond before giving me a closed lip smile.

"So, we are going to kill Ghost?" I confirm.

"It's the only sensible thing to do, Buttercup," he says, giving me the last scoop of his ice cream. I try giving him my last scoop—it's only fair—but he shakes his head.

"Together?" I sure as hell didn't want to do this alone; protecting me and Layla is already a battle in itself since I'm the older one, and I can't run anymore. I bought that house. Own it. It's mine. I shouldn't be hightailing it away. I'll be running forever, and that's not fair to me, my cat, or my friends. I have people here worth fighting for.

"We do this together."

Together. What does together mean for us?

8

EDDIE

I'M NOT QUALIFIED FOR THIS. NOT IN THE slightest. I am an architect, not a bodyguard. Yet here I am, and here I will continue to be, right by Willow's side. I pull my car into Willow's driveway, glancing in the rearview mirror at the stuff I shoved in the back seat. I'm staying at Willow's place until further notice, and I only hope she'll be on the same page as me. She was silent when I was packing the stuff in the car, and silent on the ride here. She's stuck in her head. Maybe the realization of her situation is settling in.

"How long are you going to stay?" Her voice is too quiet. I wouldn't have heard her without my enhanced hearing. I turn to face her; her face is as alluring as it was when we were sitting at the ice cream parlor earlier. She draws me in, holds me in space and time, and all I can do is be consumed by her attention.

"As long as you let me, Buttercup." When her full attention is on me, my breathing becomes slightly faster and heavier, and my eyes are glued to her in the best way possible. I have to fight to keep my hands to myself on this side of the console.

"Okay," her little voice says before she rests her hand on the door handle. She's scared. Scared to move, scared to be out in the open, seen, followed. I wish I could eradicate these fears, wrap her up in bubble wrap, and carry her to the door myself; maybe she'd let me while she's in this state.

Willow Buttercup is a magnet, pulling me into her no matter how far away I am. The first time I met Willow was in that same grocery store where we bumped into each other a few days ago. She had toppled over me in the freezer aisle, and I caught her. I'd caught her scent before I saw her. Her warm buttercream, pancake-like scent had me following her around the store. She was so determined in following me that when I stopped abruptly, finally connecting the dots that the scent I was following was *behind* me, she fell straight into my arms. That moment, her in my arms, changed everything for me. Never in my twenty-nine years on this earth have I felt this way before.

Since then, she's been part of my every thought. The second time I met her made my thoughts of her stronger and more compelling. She came to stay with Flora at the Pack house for protection. She didn't stay long, disappearing to go, who knows where, but when she came back, Flora had been kidnapped, and her bear wasn't having it. Willow's bear took on a panther, one of the scariest mother fucking shifting animals in the United States, and she tore that bitch apart for hurting Flora.

I jump out of my car and speed around to open her

door. Willow wouldn't have to do this alone, not while I'm around. Her hand falls to her lap, but I grab it, guiding her to get out of the car. She stands still for a moment, gazing at the forest that surrounds her house before walking towards the door. I grab my bag and game console, following after her.

"Willow, you're back! Finally, I have some news," Layla says, bouncing on her heels and dragging Willow by her hand to the kitchen table. "I've already put on your tea. I need your full attention. I got a job!"

"Congrats! Where?" Willow asks. She's smiling now and gripping Layla's hand with more excitement than the lost girl in my car moments ago could have dreamed of mustering up.

I go to the living room during the rest of their conversation. My new bedroom for now. Setting my overnight bag in the corner, out of sight. I don't dare disrupt Willow's careful decorating of candle lighting, blankets galore, and sherpa seating. I set up my game console. Realistically, I won't have a ton of time play since we *are* searching for an attempted murderer.

"Moon and Stars Tattoo Parlor, isn't it great?" Layla says with a bright smile and a twinkle in her eye.

"Tattoos? Since when do you know how to do that?" Willow asks, now confused.

"No, I'll only work the front as a receptionist. All I'll do is make sure people come to their appointments, answer the phone, and take payments. I'll give them our paperwork, make sure they are comfortable, things like that."

"I'm happy for you. That was fast," Willow says. I

make my way back to them, getting three mugs out, pouring each of us a glass of boiling water and dropping a tea bag in each one. I wait for the tea to settle in before taking a sip from Willow's mug. We weren't having a repeat of yesterday.

I am as capable as Flora is. I can check her tea from now on.

My eyes find hers already staring at me. She slowly lifts it, taking the slowest sip, and I swear she puts her lips right where mine were. Are we kissing now? Is this woman flirting with me? I love it. The smile is impossible to stop, I don't bother even trying. I sit with my own mug.

I swing my hand under her chair and yank her closer to me, smiling down at her. Willow, my dear lovely Willow. The light is back in her eyes, and I fight the urge to kiss her plump lips. Man, oh man, am I a strong guy.

Or am I? Leaning towards her slightly, I watch her eyes drop to my lips and back to my eyes. Her skin glows with softness, and I yearn to trace it with my finger, down her cheek and neck. Her buttercream scent surrounds me, and I'm drawn in even more so. Wow, the way this woman stares at me.

"Willow, what are we going to do about... what was his name?" Layla asks suddenly, twisting her fingers. Her eyes shoot between me and Willow, and it reminds me that she's practically still a kid. It's like she's looking at her parents. Which we are not, but I find I don't dislike the idea. Still, Willow jumps away from me, turning her attention back to Layla as the light in her eyes dies out.

"Who are you talking about?" I ask, putting my mug down.

"Ghost," Willow murmurs over her teacup.

"What do what we have? Layla, what do your notes say? You've gotten more than Willow has. Maybe we can tell more from yours?" I ask, realizing I haven't heard her side of the story yet.

"They say to stop looking, but that's it. Nothing more has happened to me," she explains.

"Looking for what?" I ask, and by the silence that follows, maybe I shouldn't have asked, but I don't care because I ask again. "What have you guys been looking for?"

I could hear Willow's breath hitch as if she'd been punched in the stomach, yet she sits almost isolated at the table. Besides Layla, who is sitting across from her and no longer gripping her mug. Willow's staring into her mug like it will tell her all the answers she's desperate for.

"He's trying to help," Layla tries to convince her to spill whatever it is. A minute passes before Willow's eyes meet Layla's before a sad smile takes over her face.

"I'm not used to talking about it," Willow says, staring at Layla, who only stares back at her. Being an outsider never hurt as much as it does right now.

Willow should be finding comfort in me, not Layla. I want her to share everything, every little thing, about herself with me. Whatever she's got to tell me won't change the way I see her—nothing would. What is she scared to share? I release a shaky breath, staring at the side of Willow's head. She won't look at me. She's shutting me out. I—

"Do you still love him?" Layla asks, reaching her hand

to cup Willow's, running her thumb up and down the side of Willow's palm.

Him? Love him? Is there another man in the picture? Am I too late?

"I don't want to talk about that," Willow mutters, her eyes glancing at me before settling on Layla.

"We might be past that, Willow."

"I know." She sighs, and a tear trails down her face. The blush that adorns her face is long gone, and my heart is hanging on by a thread. There is a whole life of Willow's that I don't know about. Which I knew, but there are details that might break me, and I almost ask her to not tell me.

I turn in the velvet dining chair, my body completely faces her. Whatever she is afraid of or worried about sharing will be embraced by me. I will be the best listener she has ever talked to. I don't even prop my head up by leaning on my hand, wanting to show her that I'm paying attention.

"In high school, I found—"

"Fell in love," Layla interjects. Willow pauses, glancing over at her with scrunched eyebrows before continuing on.

"Fell in love with Milo Barrow, Layla's older brother. We were inseparable. We were soul mates, Eddie."

Soul mates. She had already found her mate. What—I mean, how—why am I so entranced with her if she's not my mate?

The thread my heart was hanging by snaps.

Something vile and burning spreads throughout my body, but I remain still. I don't blink; I don't breathe. She has a mate. She had a mate. Where is he? Why isn't he with her? I can hardly stay away from her. How could he?

I thought, I thought this is what mates would be like... the connection gets stronger than this?

"Milo and I were planning our mating ceremony about two years into college, and the night before our big day, he was murdered."

"How was he murdered?" I ask. I hate the way it came out, all dejected and shit. My heart has fucking dropped, and my soul nearly left my body when the word mate left her lips. Mate. She had already found her mate. She was going to mate her soul pair, and he died.

I've been flirting and imagining a future with a woman who lost her soul mate. Her one true love is dead, and here I am, following her around like a lost damn puppy, hoping maybe she'll see me differently.

"I don't know."

"You don't know?" Wait a minute, she doesn't know? Then how does she know he was murdered? How does she know that was her true mate?

"I woke up the morning of our mating ceremony to his side of the bed cold and his stuff completely cleared out. He disappeared off the face of the earth, and his murderer made sure there would be no evidence, no trace, nothing besides a used empty teacup sitting on the counter."

My eyes switch from Willow to Layla, then back to Willow. "Do you know how he was murdered, Layla?"

"I know it sounds crazy. Trust me, I know, but something is weird here. Things don't add up, and now that I've thought about it, him being murdered is a real and high probability. Milo was a family man, as most bear shifters are, and he wouldn't up and leave Willow. He wouldn't leave Mom and Dad either. Something is going on."

I don't know if I'm being crazy jealous over a woman I barely even know, but I don't know if I believe this man was murdered. Why would a murderer take all of Milo's stuff? Clean out his closet, drawers, and everything?

Even if I don't believe this story, there is no way I'm letting Willow see any sign that I don't. People must have brushed her off, and that must be why she's here and not wherever her hometown is. I have to be careful about this.

"Okay," I say, my gaze switching between the two women sitting beside me. "Was there a body?"

"Yes, but the body wasn't found until weeks later and was barely identifiable."

"Who identified it?"

"My parents did, and they did it by scent. It smelled exactly like Milo," Layla explains, rolling her shoulders. There's a possibility he wasn't murdered; scent could be easily masked. Milo's clothes and blood on the corpse would make the body smell like him. Maybe Milo's in trouble, or was kidnapped, and even then, how could I tell his... *soul mate*... who believes he's dead that he might not be?

Even then, how does this explain Ghost and all the coincidences that have happened since Layla began her search for Milo?

"So, we need to find out why Ghost is sending the notes and who it is that hired him to attack Willow. The only place to go from here is to examine the notes."

"Let me go get them." Willow jumps up and sprints

off to where she must keep her notes. I can hear her slippers shuffle on the floor as she goes. The steam from my tea is touching my face, as if in a calm spa, and I try to focus on keeping calm.

I've never been heartbroken before. Not if it feels like this. My chest aches as if a knife has been stabbed there, and it's stuck. It may be there the entire time I'm here, or forever even, but I can't leave.

They need me. I still need Willow. I can't walk away from her scent, from her smile, her presence. I'd rather wither away in pain and still be able to see her than walk away and heal my wound.

My wound will reopen every time I see her, and I'll have to accept it because there is no damn way I can leave now. It's probably a good thing her mate is dead 'cause he'd have to kill me to get her away from me.

"I should go get the notes I got, too," Layla says, disappearing into the hallway. I wait for them to come back, and Willow is the first one I hear, though her steps are slow, too slow, and calculated. She takes a couple of pauses before she makes it back to the kitchen.

"Willow?" I call out. She's right outside the kitchen, standing out of sight with labored breathing. Shit, she's hiding. I stand to meet her. She's got her curls in a loose bun on top of her head and has taken off her jewelry. A harsh blush covers her face and neck, and her bottom lip is at the mercy of teeth. She carries what could be a hundred notes, and all her cuteness falls to the shock that takes over my mind as I realize the amount of notes she has.

"When the fuck did you get all these? I thought it was only one." I take her pile from her arms and turn to spread them across her small round table. "How long has Ghost been after you?"

"These aren't from Ghost. These are from *M*. I've never had a physical encounter with *M*. The majority are from right after Milo's death. I spent months searching for anything that would prove he was killed, and these notes were my biggest piece of evidence. I showed them to his parents and mine, but—" She stops. Her eyes search up at me, waiting for some sort of sign that I probably don't believe her, but I do. I may not fully believe that Milo was killed, but something is wrong here. No one sends this many notes without hiding something fucking huge—something on the level of murder.

"What did they think?" I ask to urge her on. I need every detail, no matter how small or large, if we are going to figure out who is behind this.

"They think—they think I made these myself." She lets out a harsh breath as she sits back down at the table. I quickly follow suit, sitting right beside her. I grab a note; all of them are on note-card-sized sheets of white construction paper. Black lettering covers the center of each, with different messages ranging from "Stop Looking" to "He's Gone."

The lettering was made with a thick Sharpie, and the handwriting is messy. It sends a chill down my spine. Willow hardly touches the notes, seeming more content with watching me go through them. Layla comes back with her notes. She keeps them in her hands, separate from all of Willow's notes, but the paper, marker, and handwriting are the same between her and Willow's notes.

"When did the notes start back up, and how many have been sent recently?" I ask.

"Mine arrived about three to four days ago; I've only gotten one since Layla started looking again. When I first moved here, they stopped, but I had also stopped looking. I haven't dug into his death again either, but maybe since Layla has, Ghost wanted to make sure I didn't get involved too?"

"Layla, what did your parents think about you receiving the note?"

"That Willow was the one who sent it to me," Layla murmurs, carefully glancing at Willow, who remains quiet as if she suspected that's what her in-laws—nearly in-laws—would think. "Okay, what do we know?"

Layla is quick to change the topic, and I'm glad she's here. I inspect Willow's kitchen, grabbing her little notepad from the side of her fridge. "We know the murderer's handwriting, that they know where you both used to live and maybe even currently live. They also must know that Willow is allergic to bananas. How many people know about your allergy?"

"Two families: mine and the Barrows," Willow says.

"So, someone in our family is a killer?" Layla exclaims, her eyes going wide and her hand gripping Willow's forearm.

"Not necessarily. It could mean that someone in the families has a big mouth," Willow quickly supplies.

"Or that someone is working with the killer," Layla adds. When I give her a look, she says, "What? If we're not honest about all the possibilities, then we'll go around in circles."

"Okay, how could Ghost get the banana in the tea bag without Willow knowing or smelling it? Layla, could you smell it?"

"Not the banana smell, but I smelled that something was off—missing. It didn't smell like tea or anything; it smelled like nothing."

"They could have used scent blockers," I say. I could smell the banana, but if Layla and Willow didn't, then there was something else going on. Maybe knowing what I was looking for allowed the natural smells to come through, or the scent blockers wore off by the time I got to them.

"I thought scent blockers were a pill a paranormal could take, not—" Willow says, but Layla interjects. The cub must know more than I thought.

"It can be made into a perfume. Spray it on anything, and it'll take away the scent."

"So, they got the banana and scent blockers into her tea bag. How? They are sealed in plastic at the store; how did Ghost get the banana in there?"

"He had to have broken in and put it in after Willow had bought it; when did you get your latest box?"

"I—um, I might've used—oh my gosh. I found a couple of tea bags in one of my cabinets. Maybe those were the ones that were laced with bananas." The blush on her face is never going to go away at this rate, and while it's worrying that used tea bags she randomly found, I'm not upset with the blush on her cheeks; gosh, that blush is all mine. Not mine. I mean, not mine.

"Anyone could've made that mistake, right? I'm not even sure if the ones I found were the poisoned ones because I mixed them in with the others. How was I supposed to know that Ghost would try to kill me in that way? I thought he'd be a hands-on guy."

"It's okay, Buttercup. I checked a lot of those bags, and a lot of them were contaminated." Her ramblings are better than listening to music, but she's worked up in all the wrong ways, and I can't watch her get more upset. Layla even has the nerve to let out a small laugh, which she tries to cover with her hands over her lips.

"Oh my goddess, we would not survive on our own," Layla laughs, and Willow even lets out a strained giggle. I don't know if the haze of an attempted murder is clouding our judgment or what, but I find myself smiling, too.

"So, when Ghost attacked you in the apartment, he must have left the tea bags then? Maybe you carried them with you from the apartment when you moved, but where could Ghost get the scent blockers?" I wonder.

"A fairy, or a witch, but probably a fairy. They would know how to get a banana and scent blockers into a tea bag without the consumer knowing. Maybe an earth fairy would know," Layla says between her giggles of insanity.

"We need to find the closest fairy village," Willow says, leaning her head on her hand, mindlessly running her fingers over all the notes.

"Won't have to go far; there's one about forty-five minutes in the opposite direction of Kaler City, a little over an hour from here," Layla says, pointing as if that would tell us exactly where it was.

"How do you know so much?" Willow asks.

"I dated a fairy a couple of years ago. Didn't work out."

"Oh," Willow mumbles.

"Let's go this weekend then," I say, then peek over at Willow. "And don't even think of going without me."

"You'll have to go without me, though; I work this weekend." Layla rolls her eyes as if working is such a drag. She hasn't even had a first day yet, and she's already over it. What happened to the excitement from ten minutes ago?

"Should you be working, though, Layla? Ghost is still out there," Willow asks.

"Oh, I know he is, but he isn't going to stop me."

"He or this *M* person could have killed Milo, and he definitely attacked Willow. What makes you think he won't attack you?" I ask.

"He won't in a public place. Being alone here would give him an opportunity," she says, rolling her eyes as if *we* are the stupid ones tempting a murderer.

"Okay, as long as you'll be safe, Layla. I mean it. Call me if you suspect anything. If you think that you're in any kind of danger, call us. In fact, call me every hour—" Willow says, scooping the notes into her arms.

"I'll be working. I can't do that."

"Then text. I'm serious, Layla. I need to know if you're okay." Willow stares at the girl, and I swear for a moment, Layla is her cub. She's deadly serious, and I hope Laya doesn't fight her too much on this—I don't think Layla will win.

"Okay, I'll text."

"Good," Willow says, turning on her heel and walking out of the kitchen to put the notes back, I assume.

"Eddie," Layla whispers, waving her hand in front of my face. "Can I tell you something?"

"Yeah, anything." I'm still distracted by Willow's departure, but if she has something important to add that maybe Willow didn't, I need to know. If it'll help protect Willow, I'll take anything anyone would give me.

"No matter where her crazy-ass family is or whatever the hell my broken-ass family thinks, I am always on Willow's side, and if you hurt her I, Luxe, and Flora, we will beat your ass. So, act accordingly."

All I can do is smile. Fuck around and hurt *her*? I'm more worried about her hurting me. I can't tell this woman no, let alone hurt her. Nothing I could possibly do could hurt her more than finding out she can't be my mate hurt me.

But at the end of the day, Layla is Willow's family. Whether or not she mated to Layla's brother, knowing she has people who have her back is more important than being offended by a twenty-year-old cub's threat.

"Promise?" she asks.

"Oh, I absolutely promise."

9

EDDIE

"Eddie, go to work," Willow says through her video camera doorbell. Hearing her voice over the speaker makes the rock settled on my chest dig deeper into the spot where my heart is supposed to be. How can I miss someone who was never mine? Doesn't she know she's killing me?

I walked outside to get her mail and get some air and maybe even some space, and when I turned around, the damn door was locked.

Now I'm here knocking on the door and ringing the doorbell, knowing she's standing on the other side.

"Willow, let me in. I'm not staying for long." A partial truth. We are both going to work. We won't be staying here for much longer this morning.

"I don't need you to take me to work. I am perfectly capable of driving myself. I'll see you after," she says with a giggle.

She must know I can't leave her. Even if a *killer* wasn't after her, I couldn't leave her.

"Willow, I'll kick down this door." The door was fucking solid, but that's nothing a quick shift to my bear form won't handle.

"I got new locks, remember?" Hopefully, she doesn't remember that door stopper we got yesterday, too, 'cause that would be a bitch to kick down too.

"A lock and an alarm system aren't going to stop an intruder."

"Then why did you make me get them?" I could practically envision her furrowed brows and her frown. I really want to see them in person right about now.

"So, you would know when someone was trying to get in. Now let me in, Buttercup."

"My last name is not your weapon, Eddie Enchanted," she growls. Goddess, I love it when she says my name. Every time she does, it's the same as a lock clicking into place. Something secure and warm settles in my chest, and I want her to say it more. But she also needs to stop. *I* need to stop—banish this multiplying emotion before it becomes too much for me to bear.

"Willow, I gotta get going. Let me in, sweet pea," I say. I'm dressed in dress pants, and a button-up, ready for work, and she's supposed to be getting ready right now, not spending this time locking me out.

The first official day of Willow and I's partnership, and we've kicked off the day with her locking me out. I'm supposed to drop Buttercup off at work. It's Friday, and while we convinced her to take yesterday off, today was nonnegotiable. Still, I tried, even though I can't afford to miss another day of work either. As much as I want to spend all my minutes and seconds with Willow, I'm working on something big at work, and I need to see it through.

"Okay," her small voice comes through the speaker, and the door finally opens.

"Good morning, sweet pea. That was awfully quick," I say, breezing past her and into the kitchen where that damn teapot is going off. She was so intent on getting rid of me that she'd let her teapot make this horrifying sound for who knows how long it's been.

"I know you must have your own life, Eddie. I couldn't sleep if I was taking you away from that."

"Willow, not sleeping wouldn't be the answer. Where's Layla?" I haven't seen the cub yet today.

"Off to work already," she says, sliding her hair behind her ear. She has her curls out today and is dressed in a corporate-appropriate matching set.

"She left without a chaperone? I could've taken her, or better yet, one of the Pack members could've. It isn't safe—"

"Try telling that to her. She wouldn't listen to me. But I got her to call when she got to work and text on her breaks," Willow says, her brows rising with each win she got out of Layla. She has a face of triumph, and I can't help but smile at her wins, too.

"Are you ready to go?" She nods her head, and I pour some water into her to-go cup before leading us back to the door.

"Then let's go." This time, I let her out first. She isn't

going to lock me out twice in the same morning, that's for damn sure.

"Where do you work again?" she asks, sliding into the passenger seat of my car.

"Cloud Designs. Are you working at Dainty Rebel headquarters today?" I don't know where else she would go for work, but she and Flora travel often.

"Yes, sir."

Yes, sir. She could say that again. In fact, I think I'll have to insist she say that again, and again. *Yes, sir.* Goddess, she is doing things to me that aren't fair. Do I have the same impact on her as she has on me? Is it suddenly hot in this car? I refrain from meeting her eyes. I can't handle her gaze right now. I'm nearly breaking a sweat in this small car from her innocent words. *Moon Goddess, I need you to help me now more than ever.*

Letting the music drown out the silence, I drive Willow to work. As much as I want to get her talking, I can't. Not when I'll hang on to every word and fall deeper for this woman who's not my mate. She can't be feeling what I'm feeling, and that proves she's not my soul mate. The thought crushes me further into a state of depression. I can't stare at her. I can't touch her. I can't be with her.

I park the car with Willow directing me to which spot is hers. Sliding out of the car, I walk around and pull her door open, too. I grasp the doorjamb to make sure she doesn't hit her head as she gets out. Even if she does, she'd hit my hand, which means she'd be touching me. All in all it's a win-win situation. My hand might get hurt in the process, but I can't give up a chance to touch her. I should jerk my hand away to avoid these kinds of incidents, but it's another thing I just can't do.

"You're walking me in too? You don't have to," she says with a shy smile, fidgeting slightly as she gets out of the car.

"I want to," I say with a shrug; it wasn't rocket science. I want to, so I do. Similar to how I want to check the security measures taken at DR's headquarters, and here I am.

I take her hand and let her lead the way to her office. Her hand is soft in mine, the perfect size, and my chest puffs, knowing she's by my side. We get to the front door, and she gives me another quick glance of *okay, you can go now*, but I'm not satisfied yet. I can't let go of her quite yet.

Dylan, my Pack member and an ex-assassin turned bodyguard turned back to assassin, has hooked this place up, I'm sure. His mate, Flora, works here and had previous issues being stalked and kidnapped. I'm sure his crazy possessive-ass has security cameras covering every inch of this place.

I would be surprised if he's not here himself, since when he's not working on an assignment, he's up his mate's ass. I'm making sure the crazy fucker will protect Willow, too, since she helped save his mate and is also his mate's best friend. My skills don't compare to his in the whole bodyguard and killing people aspects of shifter life, so I'll trust his skills in the protecting Willow department. That's what being part of a Pack is great for. We're a team even when we're apart.

"Eddie, how far are you going to go? I'm not sure if they'll let you through security," Willow says, pulling on my arm to a stop. They damn sure shouldn't let me through, but just in case, I'll make sure everyone's doing their jobs.

"Let's go see." I drag her along to the front desk, where a young man sits, dressed similarly to me.

"Eddie, no. Go to work." Embarrassment of denial or rejection is nothing to me when it comes to Willow. I'll let them drag me out of this building, testing security to its limits before I leave Willow here without checking.

"Good morning, Willow; we missed you yesterday," the man, whose name tag reads *Jason*, says, a huge-ass smile appearing on his face. Was this part of his job, or did seeing Willow make him smile that damn big? Damn, someone call Batman and let him know a more effective signal would be this fucker's smile.

"I missed you too, Jason; everything went smoothly yesterday?" Willow asks, only a small smile gracing her face. Good. Jason doesn't deserve to see her real smile. Not the smile she gives me. I selfishly hold possession of that smile.

"Flora was only late for two meetings, and each time it was only by fifteen minutes," Jason says excitedly.

"What an improvement," Willow giggles, more to herself than to Jason, which is the only reason I don't take him outside.

"Who's this with you, Willow?" Jason asks, that big-ass smile blinding me still. This smile must be a part of who he is, then. Good.

"Eddie Enchanted, he's... with me," she says. At least she didn't say I was a *friend*. I think I would've died if she'd said I was her friend; I already friend-zoned myself earlier, and I don't need the confirmation on her end.

"Unfortunately, he's not on the list of approved guests. I can't let him in today, but, sir"—He turns back to me—"If you provide your ID, our security team will do a background check. They work fast. We could give you access as soon as tomorrow afternoon."

"Dylan likes to know everyone who comes in and out of this building. I don't know why he didn't include his Pack members on the approved guest list, though," Willow rambles. "I'm sorry, Eddie, and thank you, Jason." Her cute pouty lips are calling to all my innermost desires and the building flush on her cheeks and neck is too. I'm sure she wants me to turn around and leave, but I'm not quite done here yet.

"Jason, are you sure you can't let me in today? I'm part of Dylan's Pack, it should be okay," I say, leaning on the desk. If Jason had any sort of training, he would know that nothing I say should change the fact that I'm not allowed in. Maybe this is why Dylan kept his Pack members off the list—to test the security team here.

"I'm sorry, sir. Even if you are a member of his Pack, you are not on the list. The most I can do is if you got Dylan or Flora to call me directly, then I could let you in."

"Even if I threw in three crisp Benjamins?"

"Even then, sir. Security is one of our utmost values."

"Even if I jump this desk and—" Willow pulls my shirt sleeve, and I can hear the gasp she lets out, and it takes everything to hold back my smile.

"Even then, sir. I take my job seriously, and I will shift if I need to."

"I'm yanking your chain. I'm only checking the security here; I'll let Dylan know you've done a good job,

Jason," I say, finally breaking and letting my smile stretch across my face. I turn towards Willow. She'll be okay here. I can go to work knowing she's safe here.

"I'll pick you up at 5:30, Buttercup."

"I can catch a ride with Flora or call a taxi." Her brows furrow in concentration. She's riled up, talking fast, but I pull her into my chest, breathing in her scent one last time before I go.

"I'll see you at 5:30, Buttercup," I say again before turning around and heading towards my car. I have to get out of here before I decide to stay. Even if I can only be in the lobby.

I get into my car and sit for a minute. My hands play with the radio and the air before I finally drive away. How am I going to be close enough to protect her but far enough not to fall for her?

The last place I want to be at the moment is at work. Working for the man is hard. As much as I want to be able to do my own thing, it's a whole lot more work to go solo in this field. I don't know I'm ready yet. Being an architect on my own means not having a consistent paycheck and working long hours, which isn't the worst idea, but I worry about the Pack. The Pack is still new, and I need to be as committed to them as I am to the job. While I moved up in the ranks fast, I'm still young for an architectural engineer, and seniority is everything here.

"Eddie, my man, how's it going?" I hear his irritating voice before I see him. My shoulders tense up, and I try to smother my annoyance since he hasn't *really* said anything yet.

"Don't know, Chance. I just walked in." Chance is the

one man I cannot stand and will not pretend to. He is slightly shorter than me and has a lanky form compared to my more muscled build. He's an average guy with an average skill level. Chance is a shifter, a flamingo, if I had to guess based on those skinny-ass legs.

"You hear they scheduled a meeting about your little project?" Chance says.

"My little project?" That fucking ass.

"The heat house idea. They're actually giving it thought this year."

"Why wouldn't they?" I ask. They give everyone who isn't an intern a chance to present their ideas once every year. In fact, if you aren't coming up with something new, you get demoted. Every idea has to be pre-approved, and my heat house gets rejected every time. Except this time, I guess. Higher-ups are considering it for next year's list of projects.

Shifter women, or anyone who can reproduce, go through a cycle once a year where, for one week, their bodies crave... well, a baby. It's similar to a human period, except shifters are only fertile when they are in heat and their body's reaction. The desire for a baby completely takes over the shifter's mind. They are so focused on sex that basic necessities such as food and water are forgotten. Typically, a mate will see their partners through the heat, but a heat can occur even if the shifter doesn't have a mate, making the cycle extremely painful, which is where my idea of a heat house came from.

"Yeah, but a heat house? Is that necessary?"

"Guess you've never been around a woman in heat then," I say with an uncontrollable roll of my eyes. Obviously, the girls aren't flocking to Chance like he says they do.

"And you have?" I had, not that it's any of his fucking business. The pain and suffering of a heat without adequate comfort and supplies is a burning memory in my head. If I could create a place where shifters could be protected and helped during their heats, then I'd get it done. It's been my passion project for years now. I'm going to get it done with or without the company's help.

"Get back to work, Chance. I'm busy."

"You wound me, Eddie, really."

"Chance," I mumble viciously and that gets Chance dashing out of my office. Finally, some peace and fucking quiet. I glance over at my phone, seeing my mom's name come up. It's always been my mom and me. She's been my rock ever since my dad left, and I couldn't be more grateful for the work she put into raising me and keeping us afloat. Being a single mom has brought a lot of judgment and prejudice from other shifters.

Finding your soul mate is everyone's life goal in some shape or form and having kids with another shifter before meeting them puts a damper on the relationship. Which I don't quite understand because if Willow had kids, I don't think it'd matter to me. My feelings for Willow are strong, present in my every thought, that I would love any and every part of her, kids included.

I pick up the phone and my mother's soothing voice comes through the speaker. "Eddie, honey, I was hoping you had a quick minute. Are we still on for this weekend? I have Sunday off."

Oh shit. Oh shit. I forgot. How in the hell could I forget about our weekly lunch?

"What time do you get lunch today?"

"Today?" she asks, confused. We stay away from doing weekday lunches. She usually does the lunch rush at Eleanor's Diner, and I work through my lunches, but I need the weekend clear if I want to stick to Willow's hip. "What's changed?"

"Nothing. I've been wrapped up in this other—"

"Is it a girl? A mate, perhaps? Tell me, son, did you finally meet *the one*?" My mom continues to gush over the phone, "Yes, yes, yes, we must meet today. I have lunch at two today. Come by Eleanor's, and I'll make us something."

"She can't be my mate, mom."

"Can't isn't not, honey. Is it someone I know?" she asks. Joy radiates from her voice and stabs the arrow in my heart deeper. It hitches my breath, and I stare out the window, pretending to take in the fresh air.

"It's complicated."

"If it wasn't complicated, it wouldn't be real, honey. I'll see you soon. I can't wait to find who this lucky woman is, Eddie. I gotta go, but I love you."

We say our goodbyes, and my heartstrings are pulled taut. Hopefully, my mother doesn't get her hopes up because this isn't a complication that can be fought through.

10

WILLOW

THIS MORNING ISN'T LIKE THE MORNING HE MADE pancakes. I don't have to act surprised he is here or be mad about how he ignored my wishes for him to leave. Eddie is on the couch sleeping, I think, based on his breathing, and I'm in the kitchen, lost on how to act with Eddie in my space. This isn't our first morning together, but that doesn't change the nerves racking my body. It is usually only me and Nola, but now I have two roommates. One of which is a man whose smell calls to me more than it should and whose presence sets my skin on fire in all the best ways.

I haven't reacted to a smell like his before, if I'm being completely honest. There is a note to his smell that I can't quite understand, and it's that note that brings me closer to him. Milo smelled of a fresh summer day—the perfect pool day, followed by a family dinner out on the back porch. But Eddie—Eddie smells like heaven. Eddie smells like the world's loveliest cup of tea. The kind that brings a different kind of warmth than the sun would. His scent calms me from the inside out, and I can just *be* in his presence.

It's not something I've experienced before.

My slippers make scuffing sounds as I pace, and now that I think about it, Eddie needs slippers too. His days of walking around my house with shoes on need to come to an end today. Wait, maybe tomorrow. Does Eddie own slippers? Should I mop my dirty floors today, or should I wait? I'll wait till I can get Eddie some slippers. It'll be payback for all the things Eddie has bought me since he came storming into my life.

"Good morning, Buttercup." Oh my goodness, his voice. My eyes shoot up to his; he's leaning in the kitchen's archway. Crossing his ankles, he smiles at me. I notice his broad shoulders take up most of the space there, and he still has his head wrap on.

"Good morning, Enchanted," I say, my voice low. I continue pacing about in my kitchen, more slowly this time, as to give myself more time to stare at his drool-worthy form. Did he take that pose from one of my romance book covers, or is it natural to him? Either way, it's too attractive for his own good.

"Calling me my last name doesn't have the same ring to it, does it?" he asks, walking to the fridge and pulling out some eggs. Enough for him, me, and—"is Layla here?"

We rarely see Layla anymore now that she is working full time. At least she has an Enchanted Pack member taking her to and from work now. Now I know for sure she's making it to work safely. "She's at work," I say, taking a seat at the table, giving up on my fleeting dream of making him breakfast.

"Have either of you gotten notes since moving in to this house?" he asks while frying the eggs and putting bread in the toaster.

"No. No notes, no calls, no trace. Layla deleted all her social media for the time being. She uses a... what did she say? It's an account no one knows is her? I think?"

"What about you? Do you use social media?" he questions, still manning the stove, and, by the Moon Goddess, nothing is more attractive than a man who can cook. Even when I'm not supposed to be attracted to the man, the sight of him still makes my cheeks tingle.

"Absolutely not. I deleted mine a long time ago," I say with a scoff. "I didn't want anyone to follow me here." I didn't want any sort of connection from my old life following me into my new one. I was alone, and, at the time, I thought I should be.

"Follow you?"

"Yeah, I went no contact with everyone when I moved from Kaler City. I couldn't take the heat anymore."

"Even from your family?"

"I only started talking to them again a couple of months ago. My father fell sick, and now I'm the bad guy for running away. Even if I ran away before he was even remotely sick."

"Is he doing okay now?" Eddie asks slowly. He's eyeing me, maybe testing the waters with his questions, and normally I wouldn't say anything. I typically keep things to myself, but talking to him is... it's nice.

"Yeah, he's better. Though we've been talking, it's hard

to forget the way they treated me when everything went down with Milo. As if I wasn't their daughter anymore. I was a failure somehow," I say, twisting and untwisting the oat-colored place mats on the table. The tassels give me a chance to be distracted as my deepest secrets spill out of my mouth for a man who should be mine.

I'm rambling on now, but I notice he's still listening. His back is towards me, and I am grateful I don't have to see at his face for the possible judgment that could lie there. I clamp my lips closed finally, before I go in on my mom. That is not something I want to dive into today, not even with him.

He plates the eggs and toast before sitting down across from me. I smile in thanks before digging in. He waits a beat after I start eating. A habit I wish I hadn't noticed but did. A habit that is saved for mates, and I can't help how my mind goes to Milo. Watching a mate eat allows the watching mate to feel pride in how they can take care of their mate. It's an honor to take care of one's mate. I can't decipher if I can't remember Milo having this habit, or if I don't want to remember. As if doubting Milo was my mate would justify my feelings for Eddie. I could almost laugh at my cruelty. This isn't who I thought I would be.

"We going to the fairy village today?" Eddie asks, shoveling eggs into his mouth.

"Yeah, we should probably get that out of the way. Let's leave at one. I'll drive."

"Yeah, fucking right, I'll drive, Buttercup, but nice try." I smile as I eat the breakfast he cooked. I knew I wasn't driving. I haven't gotten behind the wheel since I woke up from my near-death experience, and there he suddenly was in my room. He's completely inserted himself into my life, and I can't say I'm even remotely mad about it.

"You wanna shower first?" he asks.

"Yeah, I'll be quick though," I say, popping up from my chair and heading towards the shower.

"Not too quick!" he hollers, smirking down at his food.

"Eddie Enchanted, are you saying I stink?" I pop my head into the archway of the kitchen.

"No, Buttercup. You smell like roses."

"I should smell like buttercream and honey!" I shout, walking back to the bathroom. I took a shower last night, so while I might not need one physically, I need one mentally. I've never been to a fairy village, and I'm nervous. I've never met a fairy, and now I'm going to a village filled with them. I can thank karma for that, I'm sure.

With Eddie doing the driving, this ride will give me the perfect time to overthink the situation in its entirety. Ghost wanted to hurt me, kill me, and now I'm being whisked away to a fairy village. Wow, what a life I get to live.

I cut off the shower and step out of the tub, watching the water drops trail down my skin as I brace myself for this visit. At least, in this, I'm not alone. Eddie is going to be with me. The thought makes a smile, and I lotion up and get dressed before seeing the wonderful man waiting for me by the front door.

"Ready, Buttercup?"

I nod and follow him out to the car. Maybe the Moon Goddess isn't that cruel after all. I mean, Eddie may not be my mate, but maybe that doesn't mean I can't experience love again? I don't know. I bite at my lips as he pulls out of the driveway. This isn't what I'm supposed to be focusing on right now. I need to focus on the fairies.

It isn't long before we arrive at Thunderwood Village, home to all the fairies in the state of Michigan. Eddie pops out of the car and rushes over to my door to help me out of the car. Not that I needed it, but it sure is nice to be cared for.

Visiting this village is similar to going downtown, a park-and-walk-everywhere situation. The concrete road stops at the village's entrance, and the rest of the way is made of curvy walkways and train tracks. Dense forestry blocks a lot of the entrance, and we walk for a while before we meet civilization. The fairies guard their towns and villages with the elements, which stops humans. Other paranormals aren't as quick to give up. With enhanced strength, we can get through as long as the fairies maintaining the barrier allow it. They know we are coming. They may not know why or what for, but they let us pass through, anyway.

The sidewalks are lined with little houses and shops. It's all homey and cute. Pulling out my phone, I find the closest herb shop to us, figuring we can start there.

Fairies mostly kept to themselves. It's obvious in the way they clear the pathway for us to walk through, some even crossing the street to avoid us. I've heard fairies hate other paranormals for destroying the earth. Which could I blame them? The damage to the ozone, deforestation, sure we partook in that, but did we deserve to be cast as outsiders for it? Well, maybe, yeah.

"Woods, Leaves, and Bees. The map says we're here," I mutter, laughing to myself at the name of the little shop. It appears exactly as I would imagine an herb shop to. The outside resembles a tree stump, and the inside is decorated as if an earth fairy threw up leaves and vines everywhere. Wood shelves line the walls, and little shelving units take up most of the space on the floor. Glass bottles are lined neatly in rows on every available surface. Eddie, with a hand on my lower back, leads me straight to the checkout desk.

"There are too many shifters in this part of town," the shopkeeper mutters to herself, laughing sarcastically. Her long blonde hair almost matches the color of her skin. Her cheeks are strained, and her forehead lines don't hide her displeasure at seeing us.

"That's what we came here to talk about," Eddie says, leaning against the counter. He keeps an arm around me, and I can't help but lean into him. It's instinctual at this point. Every day that we spend together makes it harder and harder to remind myself that he's not mine to keep. "What other shifters have you seen here?"

"I can't tell you that outright."

"Can I ask what he came in for, and you can nod yes or no?" I ask, hope building in my chest and my skin getting tighter. I'd hoped she'd freely tell us what we need to know, but I can tell that's not going to be the case.

"Since you asked so nicely. I could help a cute bear like you out." She gives me a partial smile and that little gesture gives me hope that she'll help us catch Ghost.

"How'd you know we were bears?" Eddie asks, pulling me back slightly. I send a glare to the side of his head, which he doesn't acknowledge. I can't have him getting overprotective now that she's willing to help. He pinches my side, and before I can say anything, the shopkeeper speaks.

"I'm a fairy. I can just tell." She shrugs, rolling her eyes and focusing back on me. "I have an inkling about something. I'm curious if that's what you came in for."

"Okay, has a shifter come in here asking for you to put banana into tea bags?" I ask.

"I can't tell you anything unless you give me something in exchange for what I know." I furrow my brows and glance at Eddie, who finally looks at me. A favor? She wants a favor? What could she possibly want from us? What does she know that would be worth a favor?

"Oh, well," I say, trying to weigh my odds. I already owe Eddie a favor, which I'm sure he hasn't forgotten. Can I risk adding another favor, to a stranger no less, to my pile? "It depends on the favor—"

"Is what you know worth a favor?" Eddie challenges.

"I guess you won't find out, huh?"

I gulp. I mean, what could she really tell us? I saw him when he attacked me in my apartment. Sure, his form was blurry, and I'm not sure I could point him out exactly in a lineup, but... is this all worth a favor?

"I'll give you one favor. Did a shifter come in here purchasing a tea bag, scent blockers, and bananas?" Eddie says without hesitation. My eyes go wide at his words. He doesn't need to carry the burden of this favor; this information is for me. This goes beyond masculine gentlemanliness. I can't let him do that.

The shopkeeper nods her head yes. She knows Ghost; maybe she could help us find him.

"Wait, Eddie, this'll be my favor," I say, then quickly turn towards the shopkeeper, "I'll take the favor—"

"I need a bear claw." The words float into my ear and spin around in my skull. A what? She needs a bear claw? For what?

"Absolutely not. What could you need with a bear claw?" I stutter as I grab Eddie's sleeve around his wrist to drag him backwards with me. His arm is no longer around me, and his stare is intense and completely on the shopkeeper.

"You can't say no to a favor. You know that," the shop-keeper says, raising one eyebrow in defiance. Of course, I knew that, but my claw? Is my claw worth this information?

"What's his appearance? What was his shifter animal?" Eddie asks, and my jaw is hitting the floor, I'm sure.

"Eddie, no. We can find a different way."

"What happened to yes or no questions?" she asks with a smirk and raised eyebrow.

"Answer the damn question for the damn favor."

"Okay, okay," she says, motioning her hands in a *calm down* gesture. She eyes him before turning to me and leaning her head on her hand, completely relaxed with a tense bear shifter right next to us. I wonder if she's stronger than she appears. My bear isn't happy to have either of our claws up for grabs, regardless of if it only takes a few shifts between forms to grow another claw. It's the principle. Bear claws are not necessarily special, and I have no idea why a fairy would want one. A witch, sure.

They need to make and brew all sorts of medicines and spells, but a fairy?

"He had dark brown hair and equally dark eyes, and tattoos covering nearly every available spot besides his face. He had a pretty light tan and his demeanor was scary as hell. He asked for a small amount of banana, not enough to kill someone who might be allergic, but enough to trigger a reaction."

I gulp, nerves racking my body, causing me to sweat profusely. My bear is trying to shift, my claws nearly poking out from my fingertips.

"Willow, if you need a minute, take one," Eddie says softly in my ear. He runs his hand up the back of my neck to lift my hair into a makeshift puff with his hand as the ponytail.

"Why do you need a bear claw?" I ask.

"Not that it's any of your business—a favor is a favor, darling—but it's not for me, it's for a friend. He's sick, and the witch needs a bear claw. It's simple really," she says with a shrug, but I can see the tensing of her shoulders. She's either lying or genuinely worried about her friend. Maybe she thought she'd never run into a bear, and he'd die, or maybe she has something more sinister going on.

Still, if it's true and her friend is dying... his death could be on my hands. I'm—I can't be responsible for another death. Killing Cassandra was enough for a lifetime. This could reverse my karma for killing her.

"What shifter animal was he?" I ask, leaning onto the counter. As if getting closer meant hearing the shopkeeper's answers more clearly.

"I'm not sure I can say, legally, maybe."

"Why?" I whisper out of desperation. If I am giving this woman one of my bear claws, it needs to be worth it.

"I gave you a favor, didn't I?" Eddie grumbles.

"Let nothing trace back to me. I can't have an angry wolf shifter coming back here. How do I know that you'll keep me out of this mess?"

"There won't be an angry wolf shifter coming here 'cause he'll be dead. There won't be anything to trace," Eddie says, his hand still holding up my hair. It's weird hearing him say those things while simultaneously being sweet, holding my hair up off my sweaty neck, not because I asked, but because he wanted to.

"Eddie…" I say. I know we agreed to kill Ghost when we got the ice cream on our first day together but… Killing Ghost? Is that our only option?

"No, he's not getting away with this shit. You don't attack what's mine and get away with it."

His? No, I can't be his. I'm Milo's, right? What happened? Eddie doesn't wait around as I ponder in shock, and he stalks out the shop's door.

"Where's my damn bear claw?" she yells after him, and I know he shouldn't have to pay for the information I needed. This was all for me.

I half shift into my bear, enough for my claws to grow out and my skin to tingle. I yank a claw out, blood splashing out onto the title floor as pain radiates from my finger. My finger burns as if I'm touching a hot kettle, but I can't let Eddie do it for me. This is my mess to clean up, not his. I see his head shoot up from my peripheral, but I slam my claw down on the counter and rush outside to him.

"Eddie, it's okay—" I say, though I don't know where I am going with this. He doesn't give me the chance to figure it out. Shaking his head.

"It's not. I overstepped. I'm sorry. I shouldn't have called you mine, and I shouldn't have let you give her your claw," he says shortly. Not making eye contact is his best resistance to me, and my worst weakness. He stares past me and storms back into the shop, but I grab his arm with the strength of my half-shifted form.

"Eddie, listen to me, darn it," I say, standing directly in front of him. There was no avoiding me now. I need him to see me. "I don't know exactly what is going on between us, but I think it's time we called the bluff."

"That's not fair," he says, running his hand over the back of his neck.

"Fair to who? 'Cause it's sure as heck not fair to you. I'm sorry, Eddie."

"Why the hell are you apologizing?" he says, and a stressed laugh escapes his laugh.

"I—I can't put words to it right now."

"What happened to calling the bluff?" he asks with raised brows.

"I don't want to say it. It makes me feel—" I cut myself off. It's stupid to ask him to be honest when I can't even do the same. I wipe the sweat off my forehead and onto my short white skirt. Why does this have to be so hard?

"Feel what?" he asks, leaning his head closer to mine. I'm in his space as much as he is in mine. I'm giving him everything and nothing all at the same time, and it makes me feel like garbage.

"Like a liar." The heavy words fall from my mouth. Each one lands like a strike of lightning on my heart.

"Willow, you are anything but a liar." Of course, he's making excuses for my actions. Of course, he would be understanding and perfect and everything that I'm not.

"If not a liar, then a traitor, Eddie. It makes me a traitor. How could I feel this with you when Milo was my mate?" I whisper-shout. More to myself than to him. He is silent. But I'm not focused on him anymore. Tears stream down my face as a frustrated scream bubbles in my throat.

"Just because things change doesn't make you a bad person, Buttercup. It means you're alive."

"Eddie?"

"Yes?"

"What if—" Are you supposed to be interested in other people when your mate dies? Am I only destined to have one mate? What if the Moon Goddess is giving me a second chance? Am I destined to be alone if I feel this strongly for Eddie? Would she grant me a second chance? Is this truly a second chance, or did I just... not love Milo as much as I thought I did? "What if we give this a chance?"

"A chance?"

"A walk in the park?" I ask with raised shoulders. I want so much with Eddie, and yet it isn't fair. It isn't fair, and I can help but ask him for everything, anyway.

"What does that mean, Buttercup?" he asks, and now he's got his hands holding my arms. I can't tell if it's to hold the distance between us or to close the gap. Either way, I need his hold to have the strength to hear his answer. His eyes peer into mine, and for once, I can breathe, even if he's on the brink of breaking my heart. Even if this is the last time I see Eddie Enchanted, he has the right to know how I feel, and I can't keep dragging him along. I can't keep hurting him.

"I want to go on a date," I voice.

"A date? What about—"

"This isn't about Milo; this is about you and me." As much as Milo has taken up space in my life, so has Eddie, and as selfish as it may be, if Eddie is willing to look past it, then I can too.

"Willow, you need to shift. Your finger is still bleeding." His demand throws me for a loop that makes my chest drop to my toes.

"You don't want to go on a date?" Did I completely misread the situation and embarrass myself? Are my feelings one-sided? Oh my, my face is aflame, and the sweat dripping down my back is more akin to a waterfall than raindrops.

"Willow, when did you last shift?"

"Uh, sometime last week. Why?" Shifters have to shift often, at minimum, once a week. We share our bodies with the animals inside, and if we don't give them enough breathing room, they can take control, and we won't know when or *if* they will give it back. It is important to make sure that doesn't happen, but living next to a human town makes it hard to shift. Paranormals only have a couple of rules, and one of them is to keep our beings a secret from humans; there are exceptions, such as when your mate is a human. Even then, they have to be interviewed by all members of the Council, which is made up of one of each kind of supernatural: a witch, a shifter, a vampire, and a fairy.

"It's been too long, and you need to heal, anyway."

"What?" I say exasperated.

"I wanna meet your bear."

"Eddie, you're not even going to address what I said?"

"A date is not enough for me, Willow. In no world, or planet, or fucking universe is a single date going to be enough. I could consume you whole, keep you locked in my arms for eternity, and it still wouldn't be enough. If you can only commit to a singular date, Willow, let's not start this race. Let's put this cigarette out before the addiction even sets in."

If I felt like garbage earlier, I feel like a monster now. Rolling my lips together, all I can think about is him. His breaths are harsh, and his tone is even harsher, as if insulted by my suggestion, and he's right. I know he's right. One date would be painful. A constant reminder of what could've been.

Maybe it's time to admit how I feel. How I feel about him, about Milo, but how can I get the words out if I'm not even sure? What if Milo was my mate? What if this isn't a second chance from the Moon Goddess? Maybe I'm an attention seeking whore, and Eddie deserves more than that.

He deserves someone who will love him wholeheartedly, undoubtedly, and I can't give that to him. Plus, what happens when he finds his mate? I mean—I've found mine, and now I'm destined to live the rest of my life alone, and here I go, falling into a web of destruction and heartbreak. He's right.

"Willow shift," he demands. He's not an Alpha, but his words' impact me all the same. I don't think, I don't move, I don't breathe. I shift. In the middle of a fairy village outside the first herb shop we found, I shift into my bear. The favor we owe is long gone from my brain as my claw grows. It'll grow back bit by bit as I shift back and forth. I remain on two legs as I grow into a big brown bear, my clothes ripping off my body.

Her claws are long, and her fur is dense. Deep brown fur covers almost every inch of my body, and my nose changes into a snout. I love my bear, protecting her as she does me. We're both big and happy, and I wouldn't have it any other way. Being big was good as a bear shifter. Bigger was truly better, and I embraced that in both my forms.

I shift freely, without concern for collectors, since Eddie is with me. Catching two shifters is nearly impossible for the BSM, and that's why moving in groups or Packs is safest: it's not only animal instinct but for protection too.

My bear is not like me. She's not shy, she isn't careful, and she does what she wants, when she wants. If she wants to rub her back on the tree that's part of the structure of the herb shop, then she will. If she wants the berries sitting on the market's table, she'll get them. She'll pay no mind to the farmer's terrified face or the profits he'll lose from her thievery.

"How much for the berries?" Eddie says, pulling out his wallet. Being "awake" while your shifter animal is in control isn't always the case with shifters; it depends on your relationship with your animal and what mood their in. If my bear wants to block me out, she can, just as I can block her out when I'm in control. Right now, I can hear, see and feel everything going on around us, but I don't have control of our body, she does.

She likes him. She's always has, but now I think she loves him. Her happiness spreads through me, and we smile. She is the distraction I need, and the chance to get away from my ultra embarrassing rejection. She smiles, as much as a bear can, scaring the farmer with her sharp teeth, I'm sure. She drops to all fours, as gently as a bear can, and nudges Eddie's hand. She tries to put her head under his hand, like a dog asking for a pet. I know she can interpret my confusion —we aren't dogs, we don't get pets. She doesn't care, urging Eddie to keep his hand on her. What a traitor.

Eddie pays the man for the berries and walks away. He doesn't even look in our direction. He walks away. We don't like that, not one bit, and so she follows. Growling and nipping the air behind him.

"Mad you aren't getting your way, Buttercup?" he says, popping a berry into his mouth, glancing back at us. "Want one?"

My bear nods, speeding up to walk beside him. She tries to nudge him to look at her again, but he ignores her. Getting pissed, she knocks him down, and he falls. No matter how strong a human body may be, it won't compare to a full-grown bear. He's laughing, the berries still in his hands as my bear licks them off his hand. He sits on the ground and watches us. He's smiling, and my selfish shame in asking him out dies a bit.

When my bear finishes eating, she licks his face before backing off and walking off.

"I'ma need Willow back, honey pie," Eddie says as we reach the car. Leaning against the car, he crosses his arms and stares at me. "You won't fit in my car."

My bear shakes her head no before making a move to walk away. She doesn't want to shift back, even if that meant our claw would grow more than the little stub that it is now. "Wait, what if I promise to shift next time, too?" Eddie shouts.

She stops in her tracks, her ears twitching as if she's listening. Her enjoyment of the idea spreads through our bodies, and she gives me control, shifting back into our human body. Our completely naked human body. But before I can even process the redness building in my cheeks, my head is covered in black. His T-shirt. My arms are lifted and guided through the arms of the shirt, and I only stare as Eddie dresses me.

"Buttercup?"

"Hmm?" I'm standing stock-still, only dressed in his T-shirt and with my curls a flying, frizzy mess.

"Let's go home." He opens the car door for me, then after I'm seated, he reaches over me to put my seatbelt on, even though I am more than capable. He softly smiles and gets into the driver's seat. I can't help the silence or the guilt still eating away at me. I turn to face him, knowing I have to let Eddie go.

"Thank you, Eddie, for helping me. For keeping me safe, for helping me find Ghost, for everything. You don't have to stick around. I won't hold it against you if you want out. I get it, but I can't ignore my feelings for you, and it makes everything weird, and I can't keep hurting you. You deserve much more than this." I mean it, down to my core.

Eddie has his own life to live. He has a job, a family, and a Pack. He doesn't need to be saving me from murderers, yet he is here anyway. I'm putting him at risk by him even being here.

Where do I draw the line? He doesn't look at me, doesn't slow down or pull over. He sighs and lays a hand on my thigh.

"For you, Buttercup? I'd tell the devil himself to fuck off."

THE REST OF SATURDAY WAS ROUGH. SUNDAY, I
spent the day avoiding Willow from the comfort of her
living room. She spent the days avoiding me from her
bedroom. Now it's Monday, and in light of having to go to
work, I break our avoidance feud and further piss Willow
off by forcing her to attend my dreadful workday.

I don't think I could have accomplished this before,
but with this newfound guilt she must have over our one
date conversation, she is persuadable. She sits on the small
velvet couch in my office with a gently used book in her
hands. Her laptop sits open on the small coffee table next
to her phone. She wears a lightweight long-sleeved blouse
with a barely long enough skirt and heels. She's laying back
on the couch and lets her short hair hang over the arm of
the couch to keep it off her neck.

"If I knew your office was this cold, I would've
brought a sweater." I could smell the sweat from the
underside of her exposed neck, but I let her complain.

She's tense. I can see it around her shoulders and the way she barely lets her body move, and yet that doesn't stop me from forcing her to be with me.

Even with proof she's hot, I toss the sweater I keep on the back of my chair to her. She isn't working a full day today since Flora took the day to travel with Dylan. So, after rescheduling all their meetings, Willow is free to be with me. I stand at my desk, typing away a script for my presentation on my heat house project that is coming up soon. It isn't in the books quite yet, but I want to be ready. I'm excited, to say the least. I've been perfecting this plan for the last five years, and I finally think it's ready.

When I say I'm creating a script, I mean I am *trying* to create a script. I really am trying, but watching Willow in my space is far too distracting. She's like a painting, one deserving to be stared at for hours. One I wish I could reach out and touch, but can't.

She admitted she had feelings for me, and I left her hanging. I left the fruit on the tree, and now I am contemplating her suggestion.

A date, one single date, is all she asked for, but I don't think I can give her that.

I'll need more. I'll end up taking more than she can give and as strongly as I feel for her, I'm waiting for my mate. I was waiting for my mate.

I dated around in high school. I'm not clueless by any means, but once I entered college, I wanted more than a temporary girlfriend I know I have no future with. I wanted, still want, to find my soul mate. The one person I'm destined by the Moon Goddess to be with.

I thought Willow could be my mate—my instinct for

her is unrelenting and incomparable to anything I've felt in my entire life, but she's already found her mate. I couldn't forget that. I also can't forget she is on the edge and battling her demons; so much as one wrong move, and she'd be running for the hills. Or caves, in a bear's case.

"Thanks," she mutters, wrapping the sweater around her legs, knowing damn well she is too hot to put the sweater on. I stare at her out of the corner of my eye, the blank document on my computer screen screaming for my attention. The door suddenly shoots open, causing Willow and I to jump out of our skins with the bonus of a growl coming from me at the loud-ass intruder.

"Can I help you?" I all but hiss out. Chance's goofy ass is the offender. He stares at Willow for a touch too long. She tries to keep her eyes trained on her book, but her eyes shoot between the two of us.

"Yeah, since when do we get to keep pretty women in our offices? Is this a new policy? Why haven't you introduced her to me, your best coworker?"

"I'd rather keep her free of your existence," I mutter as Willow jerks up into a more proper sitting position. She straightens out her skirt as I stand to intercept Chance as he tries to get closer to her.

"I'm Chance. Nice to meet you, beautiful." He reaches a hand out to Willow, and her polite ass shakes it. I, of course, must fucking move since it would be rude, but if I thought Willow would let me get away with it, I would kick Chance's ass out immediately.

"Willow," she introduces herself shortly, quickly returning her hand back to her book. She keeps her thumb on her page. One thing I'd learned about Willow is that she doesn't use bookmarks. She doesn't fold the tip of the paper either. She remembers what page she's on. What beautiful-ass psycho does that?

"Chance, what do you want?" I ask, standing close to Willow, her legs brush against mine. Her contact settles me but I'm growing irritated with Chance's presence, and it is past time for him to go.

"Just to say good morning, Eddie. Gosh, what a downer." Chance smiles too big, his teeth too perfectly white.

"Goodbye, Chance," I say, finally glaring at the man in a crisp white button-down and slacks. I huff out a breath as I watch the man wink Willow's way and finally walk his annoying ass out of my office.

"Hello, Mr. Grump, I don't think we've met yet. I thought Ryder held that title." Willow giggles, lying back down on the couch. My smile is unstoppable around her.

"Chance likes to give me a hard time for moving up in the ranks so fast." I don't enjoy that we are talking about Chance, but I do notice that she remembers meeting one of my Pack members. Ryder is the lawyer and handler of all law-related things in the Enchanted Pack. He is also the oldest member, hence all his degrees and roles. The forty-five-year-old appears thirty at most, thanks to the shifter's slow-aging gene. He also wears glasses for the aesthetic but is a huge, muscled man that no button-down shirt could hide. As a newer Pack, we have to stay strong. Since we've gotten challenges from other Packs questioning our strength and morals, we have to be for challenges. We haven't had a challenge in the last six months, and hopefully, it stays that way. A challenge results in fighting, both in human and shifter form, and the winner is determined on whether the Alphas have deemed it enough. It's stupid to be honest, but as a Pack, we stick together through the stupid shit.

"How did you move up in the ranks?" Willow asks, putting her book down and coming over to my desk.

"From being good at what I do. Thankfully, Cloud doesn't focus on seniority but on the work we present too. It's allowed me to shine in what I do," I explain. Cloud Designs isn't a horrible place to work; in fact, starting out, I loved it. I'm not sure working for someone else is in my future. Needing to get plans and goals approved by higher-ups is a pain in the ass. But finding funding outside of a Cloud could be a pain too.

"When was the last time you shifted?" Willow asks quietly. Her gaze is on the photos of my Pack barbeques and achievements I've hung all over my office. "When was the last time you spent time with the Pack?"

"Don't worry your pretty little head over it," I say, but I can tell she's realizing how me being with her all the time has taken me away from my Pack. Another little thing she'll feel guilty over. "We can visit them today."

"And we can shift?" she asks.

"Yes," I say, sending Jackson a text, checking if it's okay with him for Willow, a non-Pack member, to shift on his territory. Willow is a Pack friend, but we need my Alpha's permission for her to shift on Pack grounds. Shifters played by some weird but necessary rules. Alphas rule lands, and if someone trespasses on an Alpha's land, that Alpha could deal out any punishment, including killing them on the spot. Death is a line commonly crossed.

I don't think I could let Jackson kill Willow. My bear

and I couldn't stand aside, and that thought alone scares the shit out of me. Choosing her over my Alpha would be a clear-cut sign she is my mate, but in this case, I don't know if I can trust my shifter instincts.

"Okay." Willow nods her head. "So now that you've dragged me to your place of work. When can I drag you to mine?"

"You could drag me through hell, heaven, and earth, and I'd still want you after," I say. My eyes shoot up to Willow, who is covering her cheeks with a hand and staring out the window to avoid looking at me.

I'm such a jackass.

I can't stop fucking flirting with her. That is an instinct I can't stop. As much as I wanted to take her up on her deal, I don't know if I could handle the heartbreak that would follow. I'm already attached to her. What if this intense attraction gets stronger?

"You know I haven't met your bear yet?"

"Yours is such a sweetheart. When will I get to see her again?"

"My bear is a possessive diva. Are you ready to handle her? She might not be nice next time."

"I know what she did to Cassandra." I laugh, remembering the event as if it was yesterday and not months ago. Her bear ripped a panther shifter into literal pieces after kidnapping Flora. She could be dangerous; there was no question about that.

She refuses to meet my eyes as her smile slips. "Yeah, be careful. I may be a marshmallow, but she's no teddy bear."

"I'll keep that in mind," I say as her eyes drift away from the window and back to my eyes. I shut down my computer, leaving the blank doc unsaved and unfinished. "Let's go."

"Where? Don't you have to work?"

"I can work from anywhere. I wanna show you something," I say, packing my laptop away and grabbing my bag. There is no way I'm getting anything done with this absolute goddess in my presence, so there's no point in denying her wishes of shifting and seeing my Pack.

"Welcome back, Willow," Jackson says as we walk through the front door of my Pack house. This is my home. We built this home from the ground up and one day, it'll be filled with tons of Pack members from different backgrounds and ages.

Jackson is our Alpha, our leader. Being an Alpha is something a shifter is born as, you can't become an Alpha like you could a Beta. Betas are chosen by Alphas and work as the second in command. Jackson and his Beta, Dylan, started this Pack together and collected the rest of us as if collector cards. Most Packs keep to their own kinds—wolves with wolves, bears with bears—but we are different.

Most of the Enchanted Pack members are wolves, but I am a bear, Flora is a panther, Felix, another member, is a crow, and our newest addition is a vampire. Jackson gets heat for accepting a variety of people, but our animals or paranormal power is only a part of us, and he believes if we fit together, then he'll fight tooth and nail to keep us together.

"Willow Buttercup!" Flora Enchanted yells, running towards the woman in question. "Does your phone not work?"

"What? It works fine," Willow says, pulling her phone out of her purse to check as she returns the hug her friend is trapping her in.

"Oh, why haven't you called me back outside of work?" Flora asks, raising an eyebrow and pulling back from the hug slightly.

"Oh, I've been—" Willow tries to explain her way through the missed calls, but Flora holds up her hand.

"It's okay, but don't forget about me again. I missed you."

"I thought she saw you last Friday?" Felix asks, walking into the room and jumping on the couch. Felix is a tall, heavily tatted East Asian man who eats and breathes technology. He's helping us track down Ghost, but paper traces aren't nearly as easy to track down as digital ones.

"It's been too long!" Flora says, pulling her friend's hands away from me and up the stairs to her room, or the upstairs living room, if I had to guess.

"Long time no see, brother," Jackson says, waving me over to sit on the couch with the guys. I see my older game console hooked up to the tv.

"Who's been in my room?" I ask as I watch Jackson and Felix play a car racing game.

"River," Felix says. River is Ryder's younger blood brother, who wears locs and a sheepish smile. He is the second youngest member now that the vamp has joined us.

"Hmm," I say, pushing River's head to the side as he lets out a laugh and tries to dodge my attack. "So, we just walk into people's rooms now, huh?"

"How're things going with the Ghost situation?" Dylan asks from the armchair next to me. The whole Pack, minus our newest additions, Remi, a teenage vamp, and Flora, is here, littered around the overly large living room. We had a recent expansion added to expand the living room since we realized if we grew any more, it wouldn't be big enough, but now the room echoes.

"Nothing has happened yet—knock on wood. We visited the fairy that sold Ghost the banana tea, but she was so damn unhelpful and impossible. It was a dead-end," I grumble. Maybe I fucked that meeting up. I should go get the answers from the shopkeeper before Dylan, or even Felix, gets any ideas and gets themselves thrown into shifter jail. They are the most violent members and are quick to pull a knife or gun out. It's caused more problems than it's solved, but they're working on it, I think. Other Packs don't appreciate that very much and neither does our Alpha.

Then there's Leo—he's got to be the calmest member of the Pack. He's sitting on the loveseat with a journal in his lap. He's a songwriter, and music is constantly playing in his ear.

"Can I have the notes, including Layla's? I'll investigate this Ghost character. Finding him through public surveillance has been a bust," Felix asks, giving the game controller to River.

"Sure, but I'm not sure what else to do. What more

can I do?" I've never tried to find anyone, let alone a motherfucking killer.

"Just watch your backs for now, and I'll see what I can find," Felix says, pulling out his phone. He is a tech genius and the second scariest Pack member. While Dylan is an assassin who loves to kill a bit too much, Felix is a vengeful fucker who has the tools to find anything and everything he wants.

"I'd appreciate it. While I'd do anything for Willow, this is out of my expertise," I say with a tense laugh. I watch Felix pull out his laptop and start typing away and drift my eyes to Jackson and Dylan. One observes me with a smirk and the other with a raised eyebrow.

"Willow Buttercup, huh?" Jackson asks.

"Number one, she's right upstairs, and number two, she already had a mate," I say, as if that little fact would convince them we weren't a thing, when it hasn't even convinced me to stop pursuing her.

"Yet you're together?" Dylan asks.

"I'm not answering that."

"When did bears get so secretive?" Ryder asks, joining the conversation and folding his newspaper. Who the hell reads newspapers anymore?

"And when did Eddie get shy?" River asks, a stupid smile covering his face.

"Eddie!" a voice that was too close and too soft to be any of the guys shouts. I turn my head to see Remi. Remi is of South Asian descent, with long, thick, jet-black hair and wide, bright brown eyes. She has dark milky skin and a smile dimmed by experiencing the world's cruelty too early in her life. We adopted her as a Pack member after finding her locked in a basement by the same people who kidnapped Flora a few months back. As a Pack, we are trying to give her a normal high school senior year and give her as normal of a life as she can have living with shifters.

Vampires outlive shifters. Remi will outlive all of us. The chances of her parents still being alive is a high possibility, but trauma locked her memories away, and she can't remember much from before she was kidnapped. So, the Enchanted Pack will take care of her until we find her parents.

"Yes?" I respond to her sudden shout, furrowing my brows, wondering what she could possibly tease me with.

"Willow likes you. She likes you a lot. You should go for it," she whispers with wide eyes. As if her little comment changes everything. As if the fact that Willow likes me too changes everything. When it changes nothing. She's not willing to commit to me, and with Willow, I'll commit everything I have.

"And how do you know?"

"I can sense it, remember?" she says with a hopeful smile on her face. I guess she likes Willow as much as she likes Flora and Luxe and would probably kill to get the whole trio of girls in the Pack house with her. Still, I'd forgotten she could read emotions as a vampire and around seven grown men that is dangerous. There were no secrets with this one around.

"It's not that easy. She loves another person more."

"Not as much as she loves you." Way to get my hopes up, vamp. Doesn't she know she is setting me up for the worst heartbreak of my life?

"Don't you think this is something I should hear from

her?" I say, trying to get the little vamp to stop spilling Willow's secrets. Remi brings her hands up to her blushing cheeks and dashes off faster than my eyes can see.

"Eddie!" another soft feminine voice calls. This time, I jump to my feet to meet Willow at the archway of the back door.

"Let's go before the guys continue their interrogation," I say, guiding her through the sliding door with my hand on her back.

"Time for a shift?" she asks, removing her shirt. Shifters aren't scared of nudity, if only because their clothes would shred in the shifting process anyway. Even so, I catch a glimpse of her downcast eyes as her shirt reveals her face again.

"Past time, Buttercup," I say. "But should shift one at a time at first. No need for your diva to rip apart my bear or anything."

"Eddie, I was joking earlier. My bear won't attack unless provoked. What about your bear though? Should I be scared?"

"Let's find out," I say as I lead her to the tree-filled forest that makes up the Enchanted Pack land. We have acres of land for our growing Pack and plenty of room to shift into our animals freely. "You want me to go first?" I wasn't sure how her bear would react to mine. She liked the human side of me last Saturday, but she might not like bear me.

"Yes, please. Keep him in control at first, then set him free," Willow says, standing in her lace bra and skirt. Shifters have two bodies and two minds. One human, one animal. While the animal typically lies dormant while in human form, it is always there. Since the animal lets the human side control the human body, the human consciousness backs off when in animal form. It's only respectful, and sharing a body isn't an easy task.

But expectations exist. If an emotion is too strong or if the other consciousness thought it is important enough, the opposite conscious could take over.

I shift into my black bear. My claws shoot out of my fingertips and my skin sprouts more and more fur till my entire body is covered. My bear falls to walk on all fours towards Willow. Even on all fours, he is taller than her. My bear has control, despite Willow's wishes, but I keep a watchful eye on him instead of fading into the darkness.

I let my bear circle around her as she stands completely still. He sniffs her scent, getting closer to the enticing scent of warm pancakes—that's what she truly smells like—and he leans into her hand as she welcomes him with a few head rubs.

My bear likes Willow.

Sometimes affection from the human side can bleed into the animal's emotions, but it most commonly happened with mates. It's another clue to finding your mate, so my bear's likeness towards Willow should be expected, but my human mind knows better. The fact that my bear is so comfortable with Willow would tell me she is a possible mate in a normal circumstance, but this isn't a normal circumstance, is it?

I know I need to let go of the notion that Willow could be my mate. It'll only end in heartbreak. I know, but I can't quite let go, and it seems my bear can't either. He takes a deep breath, inhaling her scent before stepping away from Willow. He sits in front of her and waits. He knows it's her turn to shift.

She's almost shy now, taking off the rest of her clothes. She immediately shifts into her brown bear, who is slightly shorter than my bear. She falls to stand on four paws and does the sniff and circle routine to my bear form. Her bear struts with a sassy walk, her hips swaying similar to human Willow's hips do, only her bear is more intentional about it. She wears a smirk on her bear lips as she sniffs us. It is sudden, and it is sexy, when her bear pushes us to the ground by leaning her body against ours. She's establishing dominance, and, boy, does my bear love that game.

Rolling over, my bear gets back up, this time on two legs, and pushes Willow down on her back before climbing over her. I have to jump in to push my bear to climb fully over her—this is a game, not a mating attempt. My bear sniffs at her, signaling to her this is play, and she sniffs back. With a push, she gets back up, drifting off into the trees, knocking into bushes and snapping tree branches I will have to clean later. Watching them, I realize this is their time, and so I give my bear full control and fade into the darkness.

❧ 13 ❧

EDDIE

Sometime later, I gain control back over my bear. Shifting at the same place as my clothes, I quickly dress, waiting for Willow's bear to get back. I hear a louder than normal branch snap, and I whip around to see Willow's bear. Seeing her bear coming at me at such a fast pace should scare the hell out of me in human form, but I'm hyped with happiness from the shift. She could maul me and run me over, and I don't think I'd ever be mad. She runs, and in only a way a bear can, gently wraps me in her arms. I give the bear a couple of pats, letting her sniff my human form. Once she is done, she backs off with a lick to the side of my head. The force pushing me back. Willow's human body quickly takes the bear's place with a deep blush and a small smile.

"I'm sorry, I couldn't stop her. She can move as fast as her thoughts. If not faster." As much as I know my bear will take that lick personally, there is no need to apologize.

I'd love for her to lick me again, and I'm sure Willow already knows that.

"I'm glad she licked me instead of biting off my head. I must have passed her test."

"That you did." Willow giggles. She dresses in her blouse and skirt again. She walks up to me with her hands wrapped around herself, tucked under her breasts. "Thanks for shifting with me. She likes company, but now that I'm not around family anymore..." she drifts off with a shrug.

"Your company will always be welcomed here, Willow," I say, taking her hand from around her waist and intertwining our fingers. "I wanna show you something."

Her hand is soft in mine, and it's perfect, almost like her hand would lock into place in my hand—a spot carved by the Moon Goddess herself. Her light smile and wobbly walk in her heels over the grass make me fall for her all over again. "A personal project I've been working on is a community house for shifters who experience a heat to have space away from other shifters during their heat. My goal is to make it comfortable and livable. To test it out, Jackson and I have been working on building one here."

"Jackson? How does he help? I know you are an architect, but..."

"Jackson works in construction; he literally builds houses for a living. I design it, he puts it together. That's how we first met. We were on a project together—those new pup cafés all over Michigan? That was us," I explain. We met three years ago, and we clicked. We hung out for days, weeks, and then one day he introduced me to Dylan, and though I'm sure I annoyed the shit out of him, we clicked too. Soon after, he asked if I wanted to join his Pack, and I took a chance and said yes. I shared my dream of this house with them, and Jackson's been as dedicated to it as I have been. Jackson is always thinking of the future, and I wanted the dream I've had since I was a kid to come into fruition. We didn't have members who experience a heat in the Pack at the time, but we want to be ready for when new members joined: female, male, or anyone in between.

"Can I see it?"

Can I see it? Is what Willow asked, but all I can hear is, *Can I see the bare bones of the project you've been working on your entire life?* She wants to see it. She wants to dive into my heart and soul that is sitting about half a mile out from here in the middle of construction. I'm suddenly shy about it; I can feel the weight of the blush on my cheeks. It's like I am about to bare my heart to her more than I already have.

"Of course you can see it," I mutter, pulling her to walk closer to me. We started construction on this house after we "finished" the main house, before all the additions were considered. We walk in a somewhat comfortable silence—besides my panicking and wondering what condition we left the house in—as the house comes into view. Willow matches my steps and follows my pace, which is slow as shit.

"Are the heels I'm wearing construction site appropriate?" Willow asks, as we step up to the heat house. "I can hardly walk in this grass, let alone around construction."

"Come here," I say quickly, turning around and letting her hand go. I wrap an arm around the back of her legs and hoist her up over my shoulder. She squeals and shimmies on my shoulder, but I'm not letting her go. Just like her hand, her weight fits perfectly on my broad shoulders and, more importantly, in my arms.

"Eddie, you could've asked!" she yells, her hand giving a weak pound on my back.

"We'll get there faster this way." Plus, I love the way she feels in my arms way too much to put her down now. She is fluffy and warm and perfect, and, goddess, I'ma hate when I have to put her back down.

"Eddie, I would've fit better on your back, not your shoulder," she says. I sense her brain running on overdrive trying to come up with a reason why I picked her up this way, but the reason is simple: I want to. I want to slow my steps down so I can hold her longer, but I know her smart ass would notice and demand for me to put her down. "I see the house now. Put me down."

"If I have to," I say, slowly putting her down on the small front porch of the first heat house in existence.

"Most of the hardcore construction is done thanks to Jackson. He's wicked fast at building shit."

"But the design was all you?" she asks with her wide, wondering eyes. I smile and the nerves in my chest settle down.

"Yeah, it was all me." Pride spreads in place of the nerves, and I'm glad she's the first one to see this project of ours. "The floors are solid and finished. You should be fine in your heels."

"Oh," she says, walking around the empty space. Willow's big auburn hair contrasts against the white unfin-ished drywalls. She's a light in this dull room, and I can't help but stare at her as she walks through the halls between the rooms of the first floor. There is a living room, a small kitchen with enough space for precooked foods and snacks. Heats are only something I know from the perspective of a child, and my mom was always too weak to cook during hers. I had to make sure she ate, and even when I cooked food, she didn't want anything elaborate, mumbling it was too much for her sensitive senses. Not that I could make anything elaborate as a kid anyway, but anything more than a ham sandwich was too much for her.

"Not an open concept? I'm surprised. The main house is an open concept dream," Willow comments as we move room to room.

"The idea is to be able to fit multiple people here as they go through their heats. So, all the walls are needed and are extra insulated to keep the hormones and scents contained and away from the main house. There won't be any attracting or tempting anyone as long as it's two miles away. One less thing a person in heat has to worry about," I explain as a small smile touches my lips. I'm proud of how far the house is coming along. I hope it will be ready for when Dylan and Flora went into heat. A nice, safe space to go through their heat. Theirs shouldn't be painful like my mom's were, since Dylan would be there to help Flora through it.

Since this is for the Pack's use, I don't expect it to be used by multiple people at one time. Once we build these in the shifter communities, I want anyone to be able to use it regardless of if someone is already there.

"How do you know it needs to be two miles away?"

she asks, pure wonder in her eyes. No calculation, no doubt, just curiosity. I appreciate that more than she knows. It's funny, the one-time I don't feel like I have to dive into my life story, is the one time I want to.

"My mom went through heats growing up, as your mom probably did too. My mom had to go through them alone. I'd have to get away from all the suffocating scents and painful cries from the cramps the body caused in response to her not being able to mate during that time. One day, I'd had enough and ran. I didn't stop running until I couldn't smell her sour scent or hear her wails, and that was two miles away."

"Yeah, as kids, we could always tell when my mom's heat was coming. Her scent turned sour, and the smell would hurt our noses. Isn't it crazy how biology can make one scent smell different to two people? My dad never knew her scent turned sour; in fact, he would become overly possessive over her when her scent changed. All us kids could think was, *when was the last time she took a shower?*" As adults, a person's heat would smell enticing and addicting, but as kids, the smell was sour and nasty. Willow's memory sounds more peaceful, and as much as I know about her family, I still wish I had a family memory like that. Even if my dad is a piece of shit.

"Your dad wasn't around? Other family you could stay with?" Willow asks as she leans against the small kitchen counter. She is in my space now. Her scent consumes me, and I know I'll spill anything she asks me at this point. She is Willow Buttercup, the one woman who could probably ask me anything and get an answer. Even ones I hate talking about.

"He... he wasn't my mom's mate. They chose wrong, and it wasn't meant to be. He left, knowing he had left behind a child. He left."

"How did your mom handle that?" Willow's arms snake around my waist. She rests her check in my neck, cuddling up to me all cute as if I hadn't shared the not so glamorous parts of my life.

"The best she could. Worked two jobs around the clock. Put me in the best schools. Did what a parent does. She didn't find her passion till I was grown and moved out. She wasn't always a cook, but when she cooked at home, she made the best dishes."

"And now she's happy working at Eleanor's Diner, making delicious food for the paranormals of Rainfall Avenue. Being the sole reason I don't starve," Willow says with rosy cheeks, her warm breath hitting my neck, heating the rest of my body like liquid fire. Tucking her head firmly into my neck, I lay my head against hers.

"Exactly." We stand in comfortable silence. I wait, loving that I get the chance to feel her in my arms again. I thought I'd be smarter about finding a way to prolong this moment, but all I want to do is stand here. Maybe I can memorize this hug, and it'll be enough.

"I finished the book we bought from Written Memories," I say, resting my chin on the top of her head.

"Did you enjoy it?" she asks with a rushed exhale at the end. She tries to look up at me, but I keep my chin planted. I don't want to ruin this moment.

"It was okay." I sound breathless. I have to slow myself down, slow my words down, before everything spills out of me and leaves me wide open for an attack.

"Willow, what did Chole tell Harry to do when his family's inn was on the verge of being sold?"

"Don't let a good thing slip past him."

"And what did he say next?" I ask, egging her on.

"That Chole was completely, and utterly right."

"Right," I say, biting my lip. I finally let her go, not completely, but enough to see her eyes, her round nose, and plump lips.

"What did Harry do next?"

"He kissed her," Willow whispers, leaning her head to the side as I wrap my hands around her neck. I finally kiss her. I'd wanted to be gentle, I'd wanted to be smooth, but the moment my lips meet hers, any semblance of control slips from me. She kisses me back as furiously as I came on to her. Pressing her body flush against mine. I can't get enough. I walk our bodies into the counter behind her. Caging her in, and even then, it isn't enough. I need to be one with her. This woman is going to fucking ruin me, and I can't stop her from doing so anymore. My hand lands above her head, leaning my weight on the cabinets behind her. Her hands have a field day against my chest, the cotton of my shirt rubbing my skin as her hands move. It is like having the spark of an idea for the first time, thrilling and overwhelming, and I want the feel of her lips on mine every waking chance I'll ever get. She could consume me now, and it still wouldn't be enough. But eventually, we have to break away.

"I can't let this pass," I say, truly breathless and with my heart hanging on a thin string between us.

"I can't either," she mumbles. She had a mate, she'd found her one true love, and maybe one day I will too.

We'll have to live in the moment if this is going to work. I will cherish our time together as if it will last forever. She pulls my head back down for another kiss, this time a quick one. "We'll go slow."

"As slow as the both of us need," I confirm, pushing a stray curl away from her face. I can't help the smile on my face; I'm a schoolboy again with his first love, and I'll take this childish moment if it means being with Willow. She smiles up at me, and, my fucking goddess, it lights the best fire in my chest. I let a small laugh fall past my lips. I can't help but whisper her name repeatedly, pulling her hands into mine. It is time to get Buttercup back home for dinner.

"Willow Buttercup, is that you?" an excited voice shouts from the front entryway. My mother steps onto the rug at the front door. Wiping her feet and coming towards us. Willow slips out of my arms with a jump. Her lips form an embarrassed smile, and a red undertone flushes her cheeks. She turns around, close enough for me to grab her and press her back to my front, causing a gasp to slip past her lips. It's nothing too crazy or too close since my mother is here, but enough that she can't hide from this, from me.

On the surface, I know Willow can't be my mate. We're taught as kids that each shifter only has one mate, but as we grow up, we learn nothing is ever clear-cut and perfect.

The Moon Goddess never created a book of rules with unambiguous rules for paranormals to follow. We learn of her and the ways of our world by word of mouth, which has proven time and time again to not always be the most reliable. Multiple mates exist. A person can have two mates, three mates, even, like a man I met on a project down in Texas: he had two mates and they were all mated to each other. The belief is that each shifter has one mate, but I've seen with my own eyes that there are exceptions. Maybe Willow and I are an exception. Deep down, something tells me to hold on tight to her, and I can't ignore my instincts anymore. Even if Milo was her mate, that doesn't mean I'm not also her mate. There's a possibility, and I'll have to spend the time she'll allow us to be together, proving I could be her fated mate.

"Mom, what are you doing here?" I have to let Willow go, all the way this time, so I can give my mom a hug. I saw her yesterday for lunch. She pressed and pressed me for details about who had my attention. I hadn't told her who it was, and now she doesn't have to guess who.

"I can't check on my son's biggest project yet? It's coming along well! The walls are finally up," she says, twirling around to view the house again. Her blue sundress twirls around her, and I can't say I'm mad at her for being here. She's so happy now. My mom has gone through hell, and she's made it out the other side with a smile and all her hair; no thanks to me.

"You've already been here for your weekly visit," I say, raising an eyebrow.

"Okay, you've got me. I was dropping off some chili when I saw you and a woman walk off in this direction. I had to meet her. Only to realize it's Willow," she says with a sheepish smile and turns her attention back to Willow. "Darling, how are you doing?"

"I'm doing good, Ms. Harrow. How have you been?"

"Oh, just living life, dear. Why haven't I seen you and the girls at Eleanor's this month?"

"Oh, you know, life. Luxe is picking up extra shifts, and Flora is off with Dylan doing lord knows what."

"Distracting him from his missions, probably," Mom says with a chuckle. "Well, I'll expect to see you soon. Bring Eddie along with you."

"Mom," I say, trying to warn her off the trail she is riding down.

"No, Eddie. You haven't been on a date since... What was her name? Charlie?"

"Kacy," I mumble with an eye roll. That date was fucking terrible, but at least I remembered her name. Kacy had no warmth to her. No shine, no spark that called to me. Before Willow, I was searching for my mate—that instant attraction, the instinct that that person is the one, and when I didn't get that, I dipped.

"One date is all he ever gives these girls, but I got an inkling about you, Willow."

"Mom, Willow's already found her mate," I supply before Willow can even think to respond. I couldn't have my mom getting her hopes up. Not yet.

"Then why haven't I seen him? Willow's been coming to the diner for the last five years, and I've yet to see a man come with her?"

"He's... dead," Willow says with a small, sad smile. Her eyes near on a spot on the wall, her mind in another world. My hope in us working crashing as my mother's face drops. Fuck. Does she regret kissing me now that Milo has been brought up?

My mom's lips snap shut, and her eyes stay steady on

Willow's. She stares at her in silence, watching the blush draining from Willow's cheeks.

"Did you love him?" Mom asks, grabbing Willow's hand in hers.

"Of course," Willow answers.

"I'm sorry, dear. I'm sure he was a great man with a heart as big as yours," Mom says. "Where is your bite mark?"

"We didn't—he died the day before our mating ceremony."

"You know, a bite mark is a telltale sign," Mom says, stepping in closer to Willow. "People think that the bite mark only makes the mating permanent, and it does. But that's not all. It's security. If a bite mark doesn't take, meaning it heals, that means your person is not the one. It's what happened with his dad." She nods her head in my direction, but it's almost like I'm not here. "I bit him, and he bit me, but our marks healed the first time we shifted. It was horrifying, but I'm grateful the Moon Goddess gave us a way to be sure."

"Oh," is all Willow can probably muster. The skin around her eyes is tight, and her fingers squeeze mine. She's shaking slightly, and I want to tell mom to stop, but the words won't come out.

"I tell you this to say, honey, don't be afraid to try again. You never know for sure without a bite." I've never wanted to duct tape my mom's lips shut as much as I want to at this very moment.

"Isn't your painting club meeting tonight?" I ask my mom, trying to get the attention off Willow while moving, so she stands slightly behind me. My mom isn't a threat, but I think Willow probably needs a moment, and the lost gaze in her eyes confirms my thought.

"Yes, I need to head out now. I'm leaving. Willow, darling, please bring my son to Eleanor's soon. I rarely get to feed him anymore."

"Don't let her fool you. She drops off a meal for the Pack at least once a week," I say, watching Mom walk away after giving the both of us quick hugs. Damn, she is pushy sometimes. It was okay when she did it to me, or even other Pack members, but Willow's face makes me wish I stepped in sooner.

"I'm sorry, she can be so—"

"No, it's fine. She's lovely. I've never actually had a conversation with the wonderful Ms. Harrow before," she says. Her gaze rests somewhere off in the distance, but she curls her body around me still, and I can breathe freely again. She leans on me as if I'm a support beam. I sigh with relief; at least she's not mad at me or my mom. I'll be mad enough for the both of us. I'll be her support beam for as long as she lets me.

"Want to go home?" I ask, swaying us a bit. It's relaxing when it's only Willow and I. The world's at peace when I'm in Willow's presence.

"Are you staying over?"

"I can if you want me to," I say, knowing damn well I was staying whether or not she wanted me to.

"Yeah, let's go," she says, grabbing my hand and leading us out of the house.

❧ 14 ❧

WILLOW

WORK IS ONE OF MY SAFE PLACES. ONE PLACE where I can turn the side of my brain with my personal problems off, but Ms. Harrow's words swirl around in my brain on an endless loop.

You know, a bite mark is a telltale sign.

I'd understood what she'd said. What bothers me is that I *want to believe* what she'd said. Yet I know I shouldn't want to believe her.

I want to call her a liar. I can't deny she has personal experience in the whole mates situation, but to say that Milo might not have been my mate to me, out loud, was scary.

She took a dip into my deepest, most inner thoughts, then brazenly gave a voice to them. I loved Milo. I was obsessed with Milo. We had plans; we had an apartment together; we were going to have kids—gosh; I want kids. He died, he was murdered, and just because he was murdered doesn't mean that I get to stop loving him, right?

This was my first time meeting the woman, and she already is spewing ideas about how Milo wasn't my mate. Why is everyone so comfortable telling me he wasn't my mate when they didn't even know him? It was me who he came home to after work. Me, who he came crying to. Me, who he loved. How would they even know if he was my mate or not?

Staring at my notebook is not part of my job description, yet I continue to do when I'm supposed to be taking notes. We are working on getting a new summer collection out, featuring accessories such as jewelry and hats instead of shoes. Flora is bubbling with ideas this time around, and she's sketching better than she ever has before. This also means she's losing track of time and has had a streak of being constantly late on the days I'm not around.

The design team is going over how realistic Flora's designs are for shifters. Being a shifter, there is a level of unpredictability that has to be accounted for in the designs of our clothes and accessories. If we shift suddenly, will the necklace choke our animals? Will rings safely pop off or will it damage our paws or whatever body part it is on when we shift? We have to go over these things because Flora tends to forget.

My notebook remains blank, and the guilt of wasting everyone's time seeps in as we walk back to Flora's office after the meeting.

"What do you think about the mechanics of press-on nails?" Flora blurts out as she settles in at her desk. "I'm not ready to mention it to the team, not until I can build a strong case on why it's a good idea."

"What?" Thrown-off is a state I'm found in often in this office. Flora can be incredibly creative, and I have to be the one to tone her ideas down. Thankfully, Dylan, who apparently still her bodyguard, has joined our makeshift design-police squad.

"Like, do you think press-on nails for shifters is a good idea? We could make them either strong enough to stay on someone in animal form or have them easily pop off when shifting," Flora explains, sitting back at her desk. Dylan sits in one of her armchairs in front of her desk, and I'm in the other.

"Yeah," I say, still lost in my thoughts of Ms. Harrow's words. Milo was my mate. He loved me, and I loved him. Our love was strong enough to be mates. Our scents matched. But I can't help but wonder why I grew apart from him, even in death. Shouldn't I be... enraptured by him still? Shouldn't I still be in love with him even after he's dead? How can I possibly love another when I already had a mate? Could that even be possible? I can't dig myself out of the mental hole that's made everything about me.

"That sounds crazy as hell. Don't lie to her, Willow," Dylan says with a smirk on his face. He is only challenging Flora because he thinks she is hot when she argues, but I can't bite the bait today, or yesterday, or the day before. I let their bickering fall by the wayside in my mind as Milo and Eddie take up my every present moment.

"Willow, darling, what's going on?" Flora asks, still typing away on her computer.

"Nothing."

"Willow, come on, what's wrong? Is it Ghost?" she questions, pulling away from her computer and staring at me straight on. It's harder to hide things while looking right at her, so I pull up my blank notebook to cover my face.

"No." Though it should be. I need to focus on the killer after me, not on whether the Moon Goddess loves me enough to give me another mate, or whether my first mate was even my mate.

She raises her eyebrows like a mom would, and suddenly I'm guiltier than I thought possible. I'm supposed to be working on sharing things with my friends, yet here I am, continuing the cycle of hide and deflect.

"I met Eddie's mom on Monday." The words tumble out, and it's more of a relief than anything else.

"How'd that go?" Dylan asks.

"She's... wonderful."

"She is, she really is, but I also think *pushy* is the word you're looking for," Dylan says, leaning back in his chair. He barks out a laugh as if fond memories of Ms. Harrow are playing in his mind on a slideshow presentation.

"She is sweet and kind, and I've never seen her outside of the diner, but last night, she said some things that didn't sit right with me. She wasn't rude whatsoever, but I can't stop thinking about it."

"Don't hold back now," Flora says. My eyes drift from her to a painting behind her.

I'm embarrassed to admit the one truth I've only now discovered was obvious to everyone around me.

I'm hurt that regardless of if Milo was my mate or not, I might have a chance at love, and I almost wasted it.

"Milo might not have been my mate, and I won't ever know for sure because we didn't seal our bond with a bite." The words I've hidden from are spoken out loud. I breathe more freely as I set the notebook in my hands down, and I stare at Flora and Dylan. They are mates, true mates. They've shifted from animal to human, and their bites are still there.

Milo and I could've been true mates, but we'll—I'll never know.

Maybe I wasn't supposed to know.

Maybe I'm meant to focus on the present.

"Damn," Dylan comments, acting as if he's distracted on his phone, but I've known the man long enough to know he is fully aware and attentive to everything around him, even more so around Flora.

"I'm sorry, darling. That wasn't fair of her to say."

"It's not only that she said it." I can't believe that I'm even having this discussion out loud, but they are mated; they would know what it's like. They are so wrapped up in each other that they alternate going to work with each other because the thought of being away for a workday's time is "unnecessary". They would be the best people to share this situation I'm in. "It's that what she said might be true."

Flora looks at me. Really look at me. It almost makes me shrink back into my solitary bubble, but I remain put. I don't move, and I hardly breathe. I'm here.

"People have doubted our relationship, and every time, I was sure they were wrong," I say, flushing with frustration at the situation "But I'm not sure he was my soul-destined mate anymore." I hope I'm not damned to hell after admitting this out loud. We checked off the right boxes: we had the love, we loved each other's scents, I thought that was all. But finding your fated mate isn't about checking boxes or having the picture-perfect life. It's about undying love, and our love died.

"And that makes you guilty?" Flora asks, but it's more a statement than anything else. The guilt is eating me alive. I reach for anything to bring back the love I had for him. His sweater that's hung in my closet, and the voicemail recording is all I have left, and yet every time I tug on those memories, I get nothing. Absolutely nothing.

No more heartbreak, no more sadness—nothing. Sometimes, not even guilt. If I can get over Milo, was he ever my mate? There's a connection, a spark, that is supposed to live forever when you meet your mate, and I thought I had that with Milo.

But our spark died.

And he's dead.

And I'm not alone anymore.

"Sometimes," I mutter, trying to hold back my tears and giving Flora a small smile. I hate to admit it, but it feels so good to get that off my chest. She nods and smiles, too.

"So, this means you're giving Eddie a chance?"

"Fucking finally," Dylan mutters with a smile.

"I'm giving *me* a chance," I say, knowing that it's Eddie giving me the chance and the other way around. I have to let go of Milo, even if he was my mate, because Eddie deserves the light, and I want to be the one that gives that to him. "So, you want to invent press-on nails for shifters?"

WHAT'S YOUR FAVORITE BOOK ON THESE shelves?" Eddie asks, entering my room and browsing my wall of bookshelves. My reading nook is my most prized possession, next to my custom-made rocking chair. I'd heard that you only need a thousand books to consider it a library, and it had turned into a challenge for me. My own little library filled with all my favorite books; isn't that something? I'm only at two hundred right now, but I've got my entire shifter lifetime to collect and read.

"This is an interesting cover."

"You won't like that one," I say, taking the almost naked couple book cover from his hands and putting it back in its spot. This, to another romance reader, would be a good recommendation. This book would probably freak Eddie out. Serial killer romances were my ultimate fave, but not something he should jump into. Staring at Eddie, I decide he would probably want something more than a cute country romance. Maybe an action romance or a suspense romance. Fake dating maybe?

"How about this one?" he suggests, pulling another book from my shelf.

"Do you remember what I said about the cartoon covers?"

"Yeah, but this one is dressed as a hero." And the female main character was a villainess. This... this could be his entry way to the darker themed books.

"You should read that one. I loved it. It was... different," I say with a small giggle. Gosh, I hope I'm right, and he likes this one. He is going to have fun reading this rivals-to-lovers novel.

"Why are you smiling like that?"

"No reason," I say, barely holding back my grin. I move onto my bed, holding his gaze as I sit. Gosh, Eddie is attractive. He had his mini braids redone and is sitting in the rocking chair in the corner of my room. He sits with the book in his lap but is on his phone.

I cuddle with my fur blankets, grabbing my book from my nightstand. The freezing temperature the house is set at allows me to snuggle with my blankets.

Here we are, sitting in my room, reading. The thought brings a blush that I hope he won't notice. My goal is not to stare at him during this reading session, but that doesn't mean I can't glance. Glancing was okay. Glancing wasn't harmful. In fact, how could I not glance at his beautiful, smooth brown skin? And he has his glasses on. I've never met a shifter with glasses, but they made the man in my rocking chair so fluffing attractive. Would he wear them during sex? Would they slip off or be in the way?

"Willow," Eddie says, suddenly breaking me from my accidental staring session.

"Yes?"

"How's your book going?"

"Oh, good?" I say. It's hard to go wrong with a *Beauty and the Beast* retelling. The book probably is good, but I haven't read a single page since Eddie entered my room. I set my book aside as I crawl to the end of the bed. I've got something else more interesting to take up my time.

"Oh, really? What's it about?" He laughs, shaking his head. He definitely knows I was *glancing* at him for long periods of time. His deep rumble of a laugh warms me. My skin lights up as if a warm fire is caressing every inch of my exposed skin. Smiling down at myself, I find I don't want this to stop. Eddie is like finally coming home after a long day. Everything about him is perfectly right, even though it probably shouldn't be. He fits perfectly in the puzzle that is my life. How could I have missed this?

He stands, setting his book and phone on the side table, and prowls his way over to me. Is it prowling? I don't know, but it feels predator-like, and my smile almost hurts my face.

"If you keep staring at me I'ma have to do something about it," he says, leaning over me. His hands flank my sides, running ever so lightly up my bare arms. Is he teasing me right now?

"What are you going to do?" I ask in a voice I've never heard before. Gosh, even my voice is heady. He must think me desperate. I shouldn't have—

"What I've I been wanting to do since you stumbled over that display case?" And his lips meet mine for the second time in this lifetime. He leans forward, his arms coming in closer to hold himself up against the bed as my hands come up to cradle his face, bringing him impossibly closer. My core aches from holding myself up, but my need to be closer to Eddie trumps that pain in favor of the pleasure that I hope will come.

"Do it. Do whatever," I say, letting our bodies hit the bed. He follows mine like a magnet, and I can only thank the Moon Goddess for our attractions being aligned. I'm sure he's the positive to my negative, and I wouldn't change it for the world. He chuckles and moves his kisses from my lips to my cheek, my chin, my neck, and my chest.

"If only you knew, Buttercup," he mutters as he travels down to my breast, his wet kisses damping my thin T-shirt. My breathing only gets more laborious as he stops right above my nipple. The ghost of his lips hovering right above where I want him has my desire pooling in my panties and has me huffing harder than if I were running a marathon.

"I need to hear you say it." One hand explores the mounds of my curves, following down my body, soothing any worry I have about him wanting me. I'm safe with him, and it makes me want to do dangerous things. Like fall madly in love.

"Say what?" My voice is heavy and breathless. I arch my chest up only for him to deny me. A blush covers my face and neck, but by the way his brown eyes go molten, I think he likes my blush. His eyes are glowing, the dark brown in them shine, and I'm sure mine are too. Shifter's eyes glow when their emotions are heightened, and mine are all sorts of heightened.

"How much you want this, want me? I need to know that this isn't—"

"I want everything, Eddie. I want anything and everything you can give me, please."

"I don't think you'll need this," he says as he pulls my shirt up, the cotton causing light touches of friction up along my stomach and breasts, and, by Moon, can I please hold on? Next goes my bra, and he wastes no time continuing his trail of kisses. This time, his lips meeting my bare skin. He jumps back up to give my lips a quick kiss before pulling off his own shirt and giving me the view of a lifetime. Moon, this man is attractive.

He is smart, funny, and perfect in every other way too, but he also happens to be the perfect amount attractive.

I moan as he starts his trail all over again, and, my Moon, I ache for more. I stare as he stares at every bit of exposed skin. I watch his eyes roam my body and sparkle, and it satisfies a deep part of me that doubted if I was enticing enough for him. He slides down my body, dragging my silk skirt with him.

"Something else I wanted to do since you fell into my arms."

"What?" I stare at him, my chest heaving. My anticipation is making me lightheaded. It's a battle of slow and fast, and I can't get the words out to ask him to give me what I need.

But to see him almost worship me, as if it's fulfilling some sort of need of his, makes me feel all the more powerful.

Wanted.

Loved.

Darn, this is gonna hurt if we're not mates.

"I've wanted to taste you," he says, breathing right over my clothed cunt. Moon. This man pulls my two hundred and forty-five pound body to the edge of my bed without even the hint of a huff and kisses me right over my panties. My back arches as if to move away from the touch, and the shyness I knew would come has arrived. My checks are beet red, so red they hurt, and my fingers grip the bedsheets.

"If that's not what you want, speak now, Willow. 'Cause once I get a taste"—he kisses me—"I don't know if I'll be able to stop."

I force myself to breathe—three in, three out—to relax enough to enjoy this; as wet as I am, it's been a while since anyone has been down there. Now that it's Eddie, I'm conflicted between pleasure and self-preservation.

I want this so bad. I want him, but I don't want to end up hurting again. I don't think I'll survive if Eddie leaves me like Milo did.

"Please. Eddie, please." Another wave comes over me, and I know I'll pick Eddie every time. Even if he leaves me tomorrow, the heartbreak is worth these moments with him. Pleasure wins. Goodness, of course, pleasure is going to win. I can't even stop myself from choosing him, from choosing us. My back arches, and a cramp tickling my back, but I can't find a care as he slowly licks my center and hums. This man hums and smiles, almost as if he's in a world of his own as he finds his way deep in my cunt. I don't think I could've possibly moaned louder before, and I'm sweating profusely. Everywhere. Goddess.

His mouth is incredibly soft as his tongue wets and teases my clit. I refrain from running my hands through his hair and holding his head, but goddess, when he lets those braids down, I don't think anything could stop me.

He adds a finger, entering and curling it inside, and the atmosphere's pressure builds and builds inside me. I crave it, and we chase it together. It's deep and with every stroke of his tongue and his fingers, it comes closer to the surface. My body trembles as it finally comes to a head, and I break like a dam, but he doesn't stop.

He doesn't stop.

He keeps going, letting me ride out the wave completely, licking up every drop of come. Only once my body gets riled up again does he stop and look up at me. Only then do I see his come covered lips, and the grin of a man who knows he's made of gold.

"Eddie," I whisper, as that's all I can muster up.

Seeing him like this only gets me hotter, and I have half the urge to bite him. To mark this man as mine and to steal him all for myself.

I freeze for a moment. My body goes stiff, my jaw aches as my canines start to protrude from my mouth. Holy crap. I force my eyes to the ceiling, trying to regain control. That's never happened before.

I drop my gaze back to Eddie, to see if I've been busted. He's motionless for a second, blankly staring as his brows furrow.

"Has that happened before?"

"No," I say, my eyes following every flicker of movement from him. "I swear I didn't do it on purpose. I promise, I wasn't—I wouldn't—not right now."

"Maybe we moved too fast," he mutters.

"No," I say, but I'm not sure if I'm being selfish or not.

I'm more bear than human now, and I'm sure I'm only thinking with sex brain right now.

I watch him, waiting for a hint of hesitation, anger, or desire. I almost bit him. I almost tried to mate him. He should be beyond mad, and yet he's stock-still. He's here, but he's not, and I'm the world's biggest jerk.

"I'm sorry. I'm so sorry."

"It's okay," he says, and he smiles. At least he tries to. He turns around, heading for the bathroom, and he comes back with a rag and cleans me in silence.

But I know it's not okay. I know that my instinct to bite, to mate, him will throw us off course. It confuses me as much as it probably does him, and I have no idea what this means moving forward.

And even worse, this never happened with Milo.

"Did you put on the kettle?" Eddie asks as he comes back in, deliciously shirtless, and sets my mail on the table as he goes over to check what's in the fridge.

The light blue envelope instantly catches my eye. My constantly sweaty hands damage the paper as I pick up the envelope in my hands. I already know what's inside. My mother gave me a heads-up that it was coming.

I rip open the envelope to my sister's mating ceremony invitation. I pull out a photo of my sister and her soon-to-be mate smiling back at me with the date, time, and RSVP number. I'm going, of course. I've spoken to my sister and mother about attending; they brought it up on my visit when my father was sick, but I honestly thought my sister wouldn't invite me. Maybe she'd forget to send the invitation, or maybe it'd get lost in the mail. Not receiving the invitation was going to be my escape from going. I love my sister, and I wish I could support her and be happy for her as a normal sister would, but we weren't normal. Not when she was just as cold and callous over my reaction to Milo's death as everyone else was.

"What's that?" Eddie asks as he plops down in the kitchen chair next to me. He nods his head towards the white cardstock bending at the mercy of my fingertips.

"An invitation to my sister's mating ceremony." I watch as he sets a cut up apple and a tub of peanut butter in front of me. He has one, too, but doesn't start to eat. I don't either. Turning to face him, I force out a strangled breath. Am I actually going to ask him to come to my sister's wedding? I want to. I know in my gut that we aren't cool or good, or I don't know. I had the urge to mate him, and we haven't gone over it since it happened over an hour ago, and I'm terrified to bring it up.

And that's not the only problem in asking him to go with me. Would he care that everyone will know he's not my mate? I don't... wanna go without him. The pounding in my ears gets louder as each second ticks on. Word vomit builds in my chest and rushes up to my lips. "Want to be my plus one?"

Can he hear my heart beating violently, or is it only me?

"I get to meet the family?" He smiles, and this smile is much more what I'm used to than the smile he tried to give me earlier. This is the Eddie I'm used to.

"I mean, if you don't want to—" I try to give him a way out, maybe he's actually mad but hiding it from me. Why would he want to go on a date with such a hot mess? I'm so broken and selfish, I can't even understand why I even asked him to go with me.

"Of course I want to go." He cuts off my excuse and

holds eye contact. It's forceful yet comforting, and I can't help but stare. "I hope we're on the same page. It's not that I don't want you to mark me. I want that more than you know, but I don't think you're—we're—ready for that yet. I want to get to know you more before I know if we're true soul mates," he says. I know what he's really saying, though. If I bite him, and the bite doesn't take, then this stops. We're not ready for this to stop. I'm not.

Oh, Eddie. Why couldn't I have met you first?

"I mean, if you don't want to go, if it's too weird or uncomfor—"

"I wanna go," he says with a confidence that leaves no room for questioning or doubt on my end, and I think that's just what I need. He is so sure of everything and himself, and, goddess, do I wish I could have even a sliver of that security.

"Then let's go together," I confirm, my cheeks burning. I want to let Eddie in, and as awkward as this is now, hopefully, it'll be less and less so the more I practice letting people in.

"We'll go together, Buttercup."

"Would showing up as my date make you uncomfortable? What if people talk?" Namely, my family, or the Barrow family. I can take their words made of swords, but I couldn't stand Eddie taking their hits too.

"All the more reason to go." He shrugs, as if it's no big deal.

If he's sure, if he's confident, then I will be too. "I would be pleased if you could come with me."

"Willow Buttercup, are you asking me on a date?"

"Yes, I am, Eddie Enchanted. Do you accept it?"

"I have another hot date that night," he says, with a shrug. I let out a sharp laugh and lightly shove him.

"Who's this hot date?" I ask, the smile on my face not budging.

"A beautiful woman with orange hair and warm, deep brown skin," he says, laughing, twisting his fork in my apple slices and picking one up.

"Auburn hair," I correct slowly, watching as he brings the fork to my lips. This is what mates do: they watch each other eat and wait for the other to eat before they do. I see his actions, and I know what he's doing, but I can't find a single reason to stop him. I often forget about habits that mates are suppose to have. It's more than a sign of mates, it's an otherworldly experience when Eddie does them.

Milo... Milo didn't have these habits. He never waited, and even as the thought floats into my mind, I know it's unfair. Milo was a sweet guy in other ways. He might've never waited to eat with me, but he—he always made sure I was dressed well, even going as far to do my clothes shopping for me. He cared for me in different ways, and I have to remember that. He loved me, too.

"Who said I was talking about you?" Eddie jokes with one raised eyebrow and a laugh.

"Eddie!" I shout as a harsh flush fills my cheeks. He takes this time to slip his fork between my lips, which I bite down on as he slides his fork back.

"Of course, I'll come with you," he says, picking up another slice.

"Yay," I say so low I hope he doesn't hear, but I know he does. He feeds me another apple slice, and I blush profusely but don't have the courage to stop him. "You own a tux?" I ask.

"Do I own a tux? Yes, I'm an architect. I'm sure I have a tux in a closet somewhere." Eddie winks before guiding another apple slice in my mouth.

"Is Layla going?" he asks, finally eating his own apple.

"Absolutely not," Layla says, walking into the kitchen and digging through the fridge. She mostly stays in her room, similar to how a teenager would, but in her defense, she only just turned twenty. "I probably have work."

"It's Harper's mating ceremony. I thought you two got along?" I ask her. The three of us didn't hang out often, as Harper was always off doing who knows what with Mom, but I thought they got along.

"Not enough to sit through a mating ceremony," she says. "It's not as if you see an invitation for me lying around here."

"You can be my plus one?" I offer. I mean, I'm taking Eddie, but if Layla wants to visit back home, I can call Harper. She loved Layla before everything that went down.

"Sounds like you have a plus one already." She sighs before storming off to her room. Hearing her slam her door strikes lightning down my back. Oh my gosh, is she mad about Eddie and me? Am I betraying her?

"Let me go talk to her," I mutter, following behind my hurt, almost sister-in-law. I knock on her door, praying she'll let me in. Gosh, how could I be this insensitive?

"Come in," she says, and I walk in slowly. She's comfortable here, to say the least. She rearranged the room and bought a vanity. When she did this, I have no idea, and that might have been the problem.

"Layla, what's wrong?" I ask, crawling onto her bed where my cat Nola is stretched out, her orange fur a stark contrast to the white sheets I knew better than to buy. Layla sits at her white vanity, staring at me through the big round mirror with little light bulbs lighting her face. She's applying a face mask, and she has a creamy velvet robe over her pajamas. She puts her plastic applicator down on a small towel before turning to face me.

"Will you finally tell me?" she blurts out.

"Tell you what?" I ask, incredibly confused. What does she think I'm hiding from her? I think back to everything that's happened over the last few days that could've hurt her, and I can't think of anything, which makes me flustered. This doesn't feel good. My stomach is getting sick from the growing guilt, and I hate to have hurt her. My breathing is getting heavier, and I try to keep that little fact to myself. I don't need her worrying over my guilt when I'm the problem. I swallow down a gulp and try to even out my breath, trying to count straight. One, two, then three in and the same out.

"Is he your mate?" She doesn't miss a beat asking me this question. She doesn't blink or breathe, and I don't think I do either. My heady breaths come to a stop, and my lungs constrict as the question rambles around in my brain. Shock seems to work in calming me down.

She's direct, and I didn't need directness. I need patience. I need time. It's the question I could hardly confront myself, yet here Layla is directly asking me out loud. A question I can't answer.

"I don't know."

"So, you think Milo wasn't your mate?" She follows up before my lack of an answer can fully leave my mouth. I can't gauge if she's upset or hurt or angry even. Milo was her brother, my mate, and here I am falling in love with another man. How is this even possible?

"I don't know, Layla. Everything has been a mess, and I don't know what to think."

"Well, how do you feel?" she asks quietly. Her brown eyes pierce through me, and by the Moon Goddess's magic, I wish I had a clear-cut answer.

"I like Eddie a lot." There is only one thing I know, and it is that I'm falling for Eddie Enchanted.

"Do you like him more than my brother?" Layla asks in a low voice. I know the answer; hell, I knew since the first time Eddie Enchanted wrapped his arms around me in the grocery store. But how can I tell her I love another when I had a mate, her brother, of all people?

"Honestly?" I ask, twisting the bed cover between my fingers. Layla is grown, and if she doesn't already know, then she'll learn that the answers we desperately want are the ones that are the hardest to find and the hardest to admit.

"Honesty only."

"I could've been wrong," I answer slowly. "About Milo."

"Just promise me one thing," she says, turning back around to face her mirror. She picks up her applicator but doesn't move to continue applying her mask. She takes a deep breath and stares at me through the mirror instead of straight on.

"Anything."

"Don't forget about me. My brother might not have been your mate, but that doesn't mean you can kick me to the curb, Willow. I don't care what anyone says. You are my sister." Layla's eyes are watering, and I know mine are too. She's more afraid I'll leave her when she's been one of the few people I consider family. Everyone had let me go, but not her. She followed me when she could and chose me. How could I ever leave her?

"Never." I say, a smile coming back to my face as I get up to wrap Layla in a side hug. Nola comes to sit in Layla's lap, missing the attention, I guess. I hold on to Layla, my arms wrapped around her shoulders as we stare at each other through the mirror. "Nothing could stain our relationship, Layla. Nothing." Milo might not have been my mate, but Layla and I were always meant to collide. No one can tear her away from me, not if I can help it. And between me and my bear, it'd be a darn hard task.

"Have you gotten anything from Ghost lately?" I ask her while she is still wrapped in my arms, and I run a hand through her pin-straight black hair.

"I didn't want you to worry, but since we're being honest," she says, going back to applying her mask.

"What do you mean? Layla—" I cut myself off, worst-case scenarios running around in my brain ass if they're at a track meet. I knew there was no way Ghost was done. I'm not dead, and that if that is his end goal, which makes my skin crawl, but what's a girl to do?

"I'm not sure, but... I think I've seen him," Layla mutters and rolls her eyes.

"Has he hurt you? Why haven't you told anybody? Are you okay?" I rush through my questions. I drag myself off of Layla to see with my own eyes that she is okay, and she shrugs her shoulders and sighs.

"He hasn't touched me. I think he's been following me, though."

"You think? Layla, even if you think it is only your imagination, I need to know. I need to know if you're okay. I need you to be okay," I say. Was she not comfortable telling me this?

"I am, though. I am okay."

"How long?"

"Since I started my new job." My heart drops as I realize that's after he attacked me in my apartment, but before the tea poisoning.

"What does he look like?"

"The same as you described. He doesn't get close, but I can see him through the shop's window. He leans against his car—a black Audi, I think, and watches me."

"Is he there every day?" I ask.

"No."

"Does he scare you?" It doesn't quite make sense to me why she'd wait till now to tell me or anyone. Did the Enchanted Pack members never see him? Does he come after they drop her off and leave?

"You won't understand," she says, shaking her head.

"Try me."

"No, he doesn't scare me."

"Even knowing he strangled and poisoned me?" She sighs and looks away, almost guilty, and that's when I have my answer. "He's tried to kill me, Layla." I say, even though my point feels moot. I don't know why he hasn't tried to come after her, even though she's the one that started this whole thing up again. I'm glad he hasn't hurt her; I'd rather him come after me than her, but I can't figure out why. Is it because she's young? Even if she has this connection to him, this doesn't change what Eddie and I agreed on.

We have to kill Ghost. As much as I may not want to, I don't think we have another choice.

"Why did you stop contact with my family?" Layla asks, snapping me out of my thoughts. She has curious eyes and even more questions, reminding me she was left out of the loop all those years ago. I had been dealing with the idea that Milo was murdered longer than Layla had. She was fifteen when it first happened, and her parents told her it was a hiking accident. When she began to think it was a murder, I'm not sure, but it brought her here, so I'm selfishly happy. Happy enough, I should probably tell her the truth about what happened.

"It was in the small coffee shop on Third, where I ran into your parents for the last time," I say. I grab a wooden comb peeking from her top drawer and focus on combing her hair as I tell my story. "They ripped into my *silly* belief that Milo was killed in front of everyone at the shop. I was embarrassed. I guess they had hoped to shame me into letting it go, and it worked."

I was hurt. They didn't have to agree with me. I understood why they wouldn't, but to make fun of me for thinking their son was murdered was too much. "Your mom told me to stop being selfish, to let their son rest in peace, to stop making everything about me. They got people around them laughing at me and talking down at me as if I was a kid. I mean, I guess twenty is young for shifters but—"

Layla rests her hand against my forearm. She knows. If anyone knows what Mr. and Mrs. Barrow are like, it is her. Layla is young, but I'm sure her heart hangs heavy after having to live with them.

"I'll admit, I'm not proud of this whatsoever, but I need to share the whole story," I say with a dry laugh. Even though I'm not proud of how things went down, I wouldn't take it back or change it if I could reverse time. "I asked them how they could move on so easily after their son was murdered. How could they vacation and party till the sun rose again when their son, their pride and joy, was killed under their nose? Almost as if—"

"They were happy," Layla finishes for me.

"Not one of my brightest moments, but what do you expect from an emotional twenty-year-old who lost her mate?" I shrug, trying to suppress the heat of embarrassment in my cheeks. I could only move on after that. My parents were so mad I'd spoken to the Barrows that way. They told me to drop the whole "he was murdered" act if I wanted to stay under their roof. None of them respected me, and instead of trying to be there for me or help me get better, they turned their backs on me.

I deserve better than that, so I left the same day, slept in my car until I found a cheap apartment in Rainfall. I deleted all my social media, got a new phone number, and have never been happier, even with a killer hot on my trail. I couldn't have dreamed of a better turnout than the one I have.

"Why didn't you take me with you?" The hurt in her eyes kills me. How I wish I could've taken her. I knew she loved me, in her own special way, but I hadn't thought it was enough to want to leave with me.

"You weren't legal. Eighteen is the minimum for a shifter to be considered an adult, and even then, your parents could've got the Council involved and won. You're here now; that's all that matters."

"You would've taken me?"

"Of course." I was young and had no business taking a fifteen-year-old with me, but if I could have, and Layla had wanted to, I would've taken her.

"I love you, Willow," she murmurs, and I land a kiss on the top of her head.

"I love you too, Layla," I say, taking a step back and sitting back down on her bed. Layla is probably the closest thing I have to a "normal" family, and I need to cherish her more if I want her to stick around.

"Plans for the rest of today?" I ask her, attempting to create some sort of normalcy in our conversation.

"I've got some practice to do. But that's it."

"For what?" I ask, scanning Layla's vanity. There is some... skin? Or something that appears incredibly close to skin and a tattoo gun. "I thought you worked at the front desk?"

"I do, but Tracy, a tattoo artist at the shop, is teaching me to be an artist. She sees potential in me, or so she says," Layla explains with a shy smile. She opens a drawer and shows me some... skin... she's already practiced on. "She had me drawing lines and circles for forever, but I've gotten to practice on some faux skin."

"Wow," I say in surprise. She's settling in, and it makes the bubble of sadness in me pop. She's making a place for herself, here, with me.

"Tracy says I'll catch on quickly, but all I do is practice since Ghost is out there, and I sure as shit don't want him to know where we live. So, I stay home when I'm not at work to give him fewer opportunities to follow me and find you, practicing gives me something to do." She pulls out gear I can't name, but she's happy. She glows as she preps her supplies and turns on her machine.

I find my way back into the hall, closing her door behind me and leaning against it. I find Eddie standing in the kitchen staring at me. I tilt my head in question. He jumps slightly, as if jumping out of a daze, and smiles. I return a smaller smile, but a smile, nonetheless.

Milo is a memory. One that wants to be left alone. It's been easy to forget him, and that alone makes me ... a horrible person. It gets worse when Eddie is around. Eddie makes me forget everything that is wrong and feel everything that is right.

"Willow." His sing-song voice reaches my ears. I nod my head towards the living room, and we both make our way there. His eyes melt into mine as he walks into the living room. Sitting on the couch next to my feet, he trails a mindless hand up and down my shin as I reach for the book I left on the coffee table. It's comforting to hold in my hand even if I have no intention of reading it.

"Are you reading the new book?" I ask, a flush

covering my cheeks. I always resort to talking about a book, I can't help it. The silence is eating at me and I can't help but to fill it. "It's okay if you haven't. I was only wondering." I don't want to pressure him to read the book, but I'm excited now that I've gotten over the embarrassment. Milo never wanted to read books with me, not the kinds that I enjoyed anyway. Even when I offered to switch to the kinds of books we would read, he still declined—Oh gosh, that's not fair. I can't compare the two. I have got to stop. I shake my head as if it would erase the thought like an Etch a Sketch. I hear Eddie clear his throat, and I look at him again, my lips snapping shut.

"Yes, I'm on chapter two. They've met, and she hates him already. Are you sure this is a romance book?"

"You just wait. It's a toned-down version of enemies-to-lovers. More like rivals-to-lovers," I say, remembering how the story progresses.

"I'll keep that in mind, but I wanted to ask you something else."

"Yes, Eddie?"

"Go on another date with me?" His smile widens, and I'm confused. We already had a date planned, I thought, did he change his mind about the mating ceremony already? I mean, that's fine, but I didn't think he'd change his mind this fast.

"A date?" I ask.

"Yeah."

"Where?"

"Let's go right now," he says, pulling me up by my hands off the couch.

"What about Layla?" I ask. We can't leave her alone. Not when she thinks Ghost's been following her.

"You think I leave her here alone when you and I are away? No, one of the Pack members is always here," he says. He furrows his brows at me as if I should've known better, and maybe I should have, but who is here in my house when I'm not here?

"How? Where?"

"With... a key."

"Where did they get a key from? I only have two?"

"From... Layla. Did you not know this?"

"No, hold on. She asked you guys to stay here with her? Oh my gosh, how many favors has she racked up?"

"Willow, we don't charge favors from kids."

"She's twenty."

"Yeah, a kid. Now let's go. Leo's already on his way."

"Leo?" Oh my goodness, I can't remember who Leo is. My face sets aflame, and my stomach fills with the ickiest form of goo. Oh, man. I really can't remember.

"Yes—"

"Hi," a man who's way too tall with lightly tanned skin and wavy black hair says as he walks past us and straight into my house. Now that I see him, I remember meeting him back when I first met the Enchanted Pack, but names and faces get blurry after a while. Gosh, I am such a jerk for forgetting his name. Do I apologize? I should, I definitely should, but that would also let him know I forgot him, and I don't want him to be mad at me or let him think he's forgettable.

"Let's go, Buttercup." I turn to face Eddie, who's dragging me to the front door, then out to his car. I follow silently. Watching Eddie in the sunshine and the green trees covering parts of the sky and the gravel trail to our parked cars is a sight I would pay to see. This gorgeous man is taking me on a date. Is this our first date? I don't think the trip to the fairy village counts.

This is my first "first" date in eight years. I'm going on my second first date ever. Milo was my first love; I know that will never change. I couldn't change that even if I wanted to, but this warm bubbly instinct to follow Eddie anywhere on this planet beats any love I've had before. Eddie Enchanted is a gut feeling, an instinct that is unignorable. Is this what it truly like to find your mate?

HE TAKES me to the new puppy café in Rainfall Avenue, one with reservations that have to be made months in advance. My brows furrow as he pulls into the parking lot. The café is downtown, on the human side of town, in a line of other shops circling the park that centers the downtown area.

Rainfall Avenue has two distinct sides, one for paranormals and one for humans, and we typically stay on our sides out of fear mainly. We fear the humans finding out who we are and the Council finding out that the humans know. The humans' fear is more instinctual, they fear the sense of predators on this side. It's why we don't stick our hands into a lion's cage. Not everyone's instincts have the warning not to stick their hands where they shouldn't be, but most do.

The spring breeze is getting warmer, and more people

are to venture from their homes now that the winter months are officially gone; the grass is more lush, and the sun shines brighter.

As we walk down the sidewalk to the little café, humans part like the red sea. As if they know we are different but can't tell how and are too embarrassed to ask. It puts us on display, and it makes me flush, but Eddie drags me along. As much as I hate the attention, which is why I rarely go to the human side, seeing this pup café outweighs my discomfort.

"Are we window shopping? I don't mind window shopping, Flora and I do it all the time." I ask, walking up to the window of the shop and seeing all the adorable puppies walking around. I have no idea how it isn't a health code violation, but I sure as heck don't want to question it. I've been waiting to come here since the shop opened about a year ago.

"I helped design Pup in a Cup."

"Wow, really? What did you design here?" I ask, noticing I barely ask anything about him. I have been so wrapped up in my own mess, I haven't been able to get to know Eddie Enchanted. Can I be mates with someone I barely know?

Did I let someone I barely know eat me out...

I would do it again, in a heartbeat.

"For this project, I was on the inside. I worked with an interior designer, and together, we created what the inside of this building would look like: the walls, the flooring, the flow, the windows—the works. I make the plans that the construction crew follows."

"Ohh, interesting," I say, pulling his hands in mine and

walking towards the café door. We are seated quickly, and I can finally take in Eddie's work. "Now that we're inside, what did you design?"

"The cutesy interior wasn't me. But keeping the designer in line with the laws of having pets within a food service establishment was me. I designed that dog pen over there. The dogs can't roam freely where food is served, but they can roam freely in the pen. High net walls cage them in, but also cage people out."

"Did you make that wood trim around the net pink too?"

"No, I would've chosen green," he says with a deep chuckle.

"Green would've gone with the white metal swivel chairs and the dark gray tile flooring," I say, picking up my mug. Even though summer is nearing, hot tea is always my go-to. The steam warms my face as I stare at Eddie's side profile. His eyes gaze around the café with a small smile on his lips.

I love staring at him. His eyes light with a joy that I crave. I could bite him, he's so darn cute. I watch as he scans the room, seeing his work being brought to life instead of watching for potential dangers. I like this look on him.

As I watch him, a dark figure catches the corner of my eye. I turn my body, now acutely aware of Layla's confession to Ghost watching her. Has he been watching me, too? I haven't seen anyone, but I've been with Eddie since the tea incident. Has that scared him away?

No, it couldn't have because the Pack members drop Layla off, and I'm sure he's seen them with her. I jump slightly in my seat, the loud music and ambiance distracting most people as I turn to try to catch a full view. The dark figure is a tan White guy in a black hoodie with the hood up, and I can't help but laugh at myself a little.

Maybe I'm thinking too much into this?

"What did you want to be as a kid, Willow?" Eddie suddenly asks, turning to face me. I can see his twitching fingers reaching for mine over the table. I meet his grasping hand halfway. One thing about my man is that he loves to touch. There is an undercurrent of constant contact that must fill his subconscious, and he fulfills that desire with me. I find that I love that too. Being wanted in this way is so—it's a thrill I can't stop chasing.

"A mom," I answer. Even as a kid myself, I always wanted kids. Even with Milo and as young as we were, we were going to try for a cub. I never fell pregnant, which isn't overly surprising because we were never together during a heat. A heat is the optimal time to try for a cub since that's all my body would want during that time. Shifters are the most fertile and horny during a heat, and for most, it only takes place once a year.

"Wow, really?" He is surprised, and I am too. The distance between my family and I tends to make people think I don't want a family, and I'd normally let them think that. With Eddie, I want to be honest. I want him to know what I truly want, and kids are something that I want to be a part of my future. I thought I lost that dream when I lost Milo, but maybe I didn't.

Or maybe I did.

Who knows?

"I wanted to be a mom. I've never had a dream career. I had a dream family and having a child was the center of it."

"I want a family too," he says, not offering much more than that. I won't pry, but it brought an unwarranted blush to my face. If Milo was my mate, I couldn't have kids with Eddie, right? I couldn't hook him to me if I wasn't truly his mate. "Let's go see the dogs."

"Lets," I agree, following Eddie's lead to the small line in front of the gate leading to the wonderland that is Pup in a Cup. Even with Eddie by my side and knowing that the figure I saw wasn't Ghost, I can't help the drag of my eyes back to the front windows of the shop. I try not to let Eddie catch my worry. I know I need to tell him about what Layla told me, but this didn't feel like the moment.

Looking back at the pen, the turf is a dull green, and the left side is lined with little obstacles painted in dainty flowers. Little teacup-inspired bean bags and chairs decorate the pen, and it's filled with all sorts of adoptable puppies. I step inside the pen among other people, and one puppy comes dashing over, booping its little nose on the toe of my sneaker. It is a Cavalier King Charles Spaniel. Brown floppy ears and big bright eyes greet me as I bend over to run my hands over the top of the dog's head.

"Eddie, oh my gosh, she's so cute," I gush, my head whipping from the dog to Eddie and back to the dog. Maybe I can take this little one home. Nola likes Layla more than me anyway; maybe this dog would be more loyal to me.

"Are these puppies up for adoption?" I ask as the dog circles me and jumps up on my calf.

"Yeah, they are. It's why there are all sorts of dogs—it's

a chance for them to find homes. This place gives them more exposure," Eddie says, squatting next to me and petting the dog at my feet.

"Is it impulsive to adopt this one right here, right now?" I ask more to myself than to Eddie, though that doesn't stop him from answering.

"See how you feel in ten minutes. You might change your mind."

❧ 17 ☙

EDDIE

"Nola, come meet your new sister!" Willow shouts as I push open the front door to her house. She has her purse hanging off her shoulder and a small King Cavalier in her arms. I sigh as the dog licks Willow's hand.

We waited ten minutes, then another twenty minutes while she hummed back and forth over how she would make caring for a dog work with her current lifestyle. After about three reminders that Nola is an incredibly independent cat and that Layla might not be around to help forever, I gave up on persuading her not to get the dog.

Shifters aren't usually the type to get pets, since we turn into dangerous undomesticated animals, but Willow seems to be the exception to that trait.

"I still can't believe you up and got a dog at the drop of a hat—are you sure you can take care of a dog?" I ask, even though I already know the answer. Once Willow started following the little dog around the playpen at Pup in a Cup, I knew there was no going back.

"I wouldn't have gotten her if I wasn't sure," she says, giving the dog another smooch on the top of her head as she rushes into the house.

"Oh my goddess, Willow! She's adorable. Wow, what's her name? Can I have her?" Layla and Nola appear from around the corner. Layla has her arms out and Nola is tangling herself around Layla's ankles, tripping her along their way towards Willow and the new dog. Leo gets off the couch, raising his brows at the new dog.

"Just couldn't help yourself, huh?" Leo says, giving the dog a quick pet before grabbing his little black journal in one hand and his keys in another. Willow blushes at his comment, giving him a weak shrug as Layla crowds the dog and Willow.

"Thanks man, I appreciate it," I say, stopping him from slinking away.

"Wait, why don't you stay for dinner?" Willow asks, and she has this innocent face—where her eyes are wide with wonder, and her brows are raised a bit. A face that's hard to say no to.

I shut the door behind me and throw my keys in the bowl on the entryway table. I stare as the girls gush over the dog, and I feel that growing warmth in my chest. This new level of attachment settles under my skin. I'm so damn happy, yet I'm not sure this will last. The constant undercurrent of nerves fizzles under my skin, and it solidifies the fact that I need Willow Buttercup in any way I can have her.

"You can hold her. Her name is Sunny," Willow says, as Layla fawns over the dog. Willow's hands become free, and I shimmy my hand into hers and pull her to the living room. It's been quite the day, and I want to cuddle my grizzly bear; I hope she'll let me.

"What do we want for dinner?" I ask, ignoring Leo's attempts to decline Willow's invitation. This is one of those moments I'm glad she's hard to say no to. In fact, it makes me feel better about how I wish she bit me earlier. The moment was tense, and the only thing that ran through my mind was how much I wanted her to lose control. Her canines popping down instinctually made me hopeful that her body thinks we could be fated mates.

The dinner question gets Layla's attention, who instantly turns towards me with determination written in the set of her perfectly even eyebrows.

"Pizza. One whole box for each of us. A meat-lover for me, with everything. Gosh, a pizza sounds good right now," she says, plopping onto the couch. Willow puts Sunny on a leash we got on the way home and has her following Willow's every move. She watched videos about dogs and new homes or something the whole way home. I learned quickly when it comes to pets, there is no such thing as half-assing anything with Willow.

As I get settled on the couch opposite to Layla and Nola, my phone dings with a text from my Pack's group chat. Felix's name comes up with the message to visit the house for dinner and to bring some food. Which probably means he doesn't want to leave the house and wants one of us to feed his grown ass. "Can we move dinner to the Pack house?" I ask moving to put my shoes back on.

"We can't leave Sunny here on her first night," Willow mumbles, still correcting and praising the dog around the house.

"Take her with us."

"Two new locations is too much. Can't they come here?" That question makes me pause, my hands freezing over my second shoe while I balance on one leg. She wants my Pack here? She wants to host my brothers for dinner? Willingly?

"Let me see what I can do," I mumble. I stand back up straight, setting the shoe back and taking off the other. My phone light glares at me as I figure out how to ask my Pack to come here instead. I have a bubbly sensation in my chest —am I nervous? They've met each other before. Why am I nervous?

I type out the text, and as soon as I press send, Jackson, my Alpha, comes through with four words.

We're on our way.

They're coming. To Willow's house. To have dinner. "They're coming."

"Good. Good thing you stayed, Leo, or else you'd have to turn right back around. I'll set the table. Can you order, Eddie?" She's so natural, so calm. Does she know she's got a Pack of rowdy shifters plus a vamp coming over?

I order six boxes of pizza and pray it's enough.

Leo shrugs with a smile before disappearing to the kitchen, probably to help Willow set the table. He's the only gentleman of the Pack, except maybe Ryder.

It's a mere thirty minutes of Willow running around her house cleaning for some of the nastiest guests she'll ever have before my Pack is at the door with eight boxes of pizza. Holding the door open for them, they all pile in.

"Hi," I mutter while holding the door still as they take off their shoes. Most of them have been here before, watching over Layla on days she's not working, and I'm not here, but they've never been over on a visit like this.

"Cat got your tongue, Eddie? Or maybe a certain bear around here? Why has it taken long for you to invite us over?" River, the youngest member of my Pack and a wolf shifter, says as he comes in with a few pizza boxes in his hands. He laughs way too fucking loud as I furrow my eyebrows, questioning the two extra pizza boxes.

"Where did the extra boxes come from?"

"Remi wanted cheese pizza," Jackson clarifies as the vamp floats into Willow's house. She's made a total one-eighty since we first met her after finding her locked up in a fox shifter's cabin for two years—she'd never have asked for anything before.

"Willow, darling, where are you?" Flora yells as she pushes the guys aside and searches for her best friend.

"Please behave. She barely tolerates me," I say to the remaining members of my Pack. I want them to make a good impression. This is my family. I find I really want her to like them.

"I highly doubt that by the smell of this house. You do that with a kid in here?" Ryder says.

"Layla's twenty."

"Yeah, a kid."

"Shut up, and let's eat. Willow's probably waiting," I mumble, trying to stop the smirk clawing its way through my defenses.

"Y'all thought you were going to have dinner without me?" Luxe's voice rings through the house as she flies past me. I chuckle, wondering if it was Willow or Jackson who texted her. Or maybe she had some sort of Luna instinct that we were all gathering here. Who the hell knows with that one?

I walk into the kitchen, where the boxes are set, and see Jackson opening the top box of each stack to showcase which toppings were where.

"Posing for Instagram, Jackson?" I ask, tilting my head to the side with a smirk on my face.

"Ha ha, very fucking funny. Go get everyone, and let's eat."

"I think that's my line, Jackson, thank you," Willow says, setting plates beside the assortment of pizza boxes on the counter. "Everyone, grab a plate and file into the dining room."

"Yes, ma'am," River says, waiting for the women to grab a plate, thank fucking goddess. We only have two women in the Pack, Flora and Remi, so we have yet to discuss manners regarding the opposite sex, yet here they are, being the perfect gentlemen.

Once everyone has filled up their plates, Jackson moves to get his. As Alpha, he eats last, making sure there is enough food for his Pack and guests to eat. He always follows this rule, even when we are eating at other places such as Willow's house or Eleanor's Diner.

I grab a pizza slice and sit next to Willow. I cheer my pizza with hers, before waiting and watching her take a bite. Only then would I allow myself a bite.

I know that is a practice saved for mates, but I physically can't stop myself from waiting. A sick sensation stews up in my stomach until I finally see her take a bite of food first. She isn't my mate, most likely, but, goddess, do I wish things were different.

"Good?" I hear Willow whisper to Layla, who is flushed in the face and sitting beside her. The younger shifter nods her head, taking another slice of pizza.

"Don't be shy. Eat as much as you want in front of these rowdy men," Luxe says from her spot to the left of Jackson. "I sure do."

"We know that," I joke, earning me a glare from the Luna. As much as I love spending time with Willow, my home is here. This is my Pack, and I'm most comfortable in a space with them in it. I'd love to move Willow and Layla into the Pack house, but I know damn well she wouldn't go for it—she didn't go for it. I'll try again, but I know her stubborn ass would fight tooth and nail to stay in her home.

"Not to bring the mood down," Felix says after finishing his third slice of pizza.

"Please, Debbie Downer, continue on," Luxe mumbles around her pizza slice.

"Layla, is there any information you know about Ghost that the rest of us don't?" Felix asks, turning to face her at the opposite side of the table. It's questions like these that make me realize how separate my life with the Pack is from my life here with Willow and Layla. It's times like these when I have the urge to bring these two sides together even more, but I have to remember that it isn't up to only me. It's up to Willow and Layla and my Pack too.

"Why do you ask?" she mumbles, keeping her head down. Willow wraps an arm around the young shifter and answers more for her.

"He's been stalking her at work." Willow doesn't hesitate in telling Felix, which makes my chest light with warmth at how comfortable she is with my Pack. That warmth dies as soon as her words process in my head. He is stalking her?

"For how long?" I ask. Why has she waited till now to tell us?

"I don't know. I only noticed him recently," she says, staring into her pizza slice like it's her only lifeline.

"Has he talked to you? Hurt you?" Jackson asks. I can see his brows set in a hard line and his shoulders square up.

"No, none of that."

"Is there more to the story? This isn't making any sense," Felix asks. My Pack members sit at attention now, and the same panic on my face covers theirs. What the hell is going on?

"It's not really your business," Layla snips. She turns cold, and I am convinced there is absolutely more going on. Why is she so on edge, and what does she mean it's not our business? After everything we've done to help them so far?

"If you know something, share it. Who knows how long until Ghost attacks again," Luxe says. She's got her hands clasped in front of her as if this is a business meeting, and I don't know if that raises Layla's hackles or not, but we need answers.

"It's nothing, don't get all riled up—"

"It is our business, Layla. Anything that could save Willow's life or your life is. Ghost is trying to *kill* Willow. Do you understand how serious that is?" Jackson argues back.

"He won't hurt her—"

"How do you know that? Is that something you're

willing to risk? Is her life that meaningless to you?" Jackson snaps back as his Alpha presence takes over the air in the room. This energy helps Alphas control their Pack. It makes those affected want to submit, and with it spreading around the room, I can see all our gazes flicker down. A part of being an Alpha or Luna is the energy they give off, and while respectable Alpha's use their energy sparingly, it's in their nature to control any situation as they see fit. Their energy can slip from their control in emotional situations, such as this one.

He stands now with his fist against the table, and I can't help the anger that rises in my gut. Has Layla not been truthful this entire time? I knew her digging into Milo's death caused this whole shit show, but there appears to be more to the story that she's withheld from us.

"No, of course not," Layla yells, but she can't meet Jackson's eyes.

"Then what is it?" Jackson says, his voice never goes above yelling. He's never had to yell. He's an Alpha. If anyone can get the kid to say anything, it's him, and right now, I need her to spill absolutely everything.

"Milo isn't dead."

Willow's head shoots up, and her eyes jump to mine. It's the briefest second, but in that second, my heart drops to the floor. *Milo isn't dead.*

"He's not dead. I don't know where he is, but he's not dead."

"How do you know? There was a body—the blood, the smell. How do you know?" Willow's voice comes out as a pained whisper, and I can't help but stare as her eyes widen and brows furrow. I shouldn't be worried about what this means for me, yet I am.

"It was all fake, Willow. He—he didn't want to mate you, or go to school, or work. He got scared. He and my parents faked his death."

"So, why are you looking for him now, Layla? What's changed after five years?"

"Nothing's changed. He's the same piece of shit he's always been and I want retribution," she mutters as her eyes zero in on the dinner plate in front of her. "He doesn't get off scot-free."

"Retribution for what?" Jackson asks.

"For selling his only sister," she whispers. The room is so quiet you could hear a fly breathe. I can't believe what I heard. Selling. There's only one place to sell a person, a shifter, and that's—

"The Black Shifter Market." The words drop from Felix's mouth, and I can't breathe. I watch Layla's shoulders drop, and I can't breathe. Her hair moves, covering her face, and I hear the gut-wrenching sob from Willow that breaks a piece of each of our souls.

What kind of monster are we up against?

"Faking your death is expensive and he needed money fast and the quickest way is through the BSM. Now he's scared, and he knows the one person I care about is Willow and is using her to stop me from finding him," she explains.

"Why is he scared of you specifically, though?" Luxe pipes up with concern.

"Because I made a promise when he traded me. I promised him I'd kill him," she says, almost in a daze. She's somewhere far away from this dinner table. "He knows I got out. It takes a seriously mad motherfucker to get out and survive, and I did. I killed everyone. My buyers, the collectors, everyone involved, and now he's next. He knows I am coming to find him, or I was. Then Willow got involved, and I stopped. Her life isn't worth my retribution. Then this Ghost guy got involved, and I'm not that strong, not strong enough to beat him. He's been at this game a lot longer than I have."

"Finding Milo will stop Ghost," Felix murmurs, turning back to his pizza. His fingers tremble over the slice, but none of us says anything. What can we say? Sorry? Nothing we can say can save the pain in this girl. We'll have to show her, be by her side, and protect her ourselves from now on. Words mean nothing.

"He's hiding now. I don't know where, but I'd say he's probably closer than we think. He was never stupid. Selfish, controlling, manipulative, yeah, but never stupid."

I can only imagine what's going on in Willow's mind. She sits frozen with one hand covering her heart, and the other on Layla's forearm, griping far tighter than is probably necessary, but Layla doesn't stop her. I reach out my hand, giving her shoulder a squeeze to bring her back to us. No matter what Milo has done, Willow will always be Willow. She will always be the light.

"Layla," Willow stammers, bringing the girl into a hug. I can see Layla's face, which holds a grimace. She probably didn't want Willow to know. She clearly cares for Willow, and probably knew this would break her, but we needed to know. We need to know how to stop Milo. "I'm sorry."

"Don't even, Willow. I'm the one that's sorry."

"No one here needs to be sorry. Milo does, and Ghost too," Luxe says. Her concern turns to anger as she sits back in her chair, fuming.

"We'll get them," Jackson says.

"We know Ghost is watching Layla at work, so that's where we'll get him, then we'll get Milo. Layla, what days does he watch you?"

"He'll be there next Tuesday. He never shows up on the first or last days of the week," Layla says.

"We'll get him then," Jackson says, pushing his plate away from him.

"He's intense," Layla murmurs with a small laugh, as if to lighten the mood. Willow shortly laughs with her, bringing a smile to everyone's face.

"Eddie, when is the big day for your presentation at work? It's been assigned, right?" Felix asks after he gets back from grabbing his fourth slice. We're all shaky, and it's hard to focus, but I can appreciate the attempt at some sort of normalcy.

The nerves build rapidly, and my hands become clammy. I am nervous as shit. I've been working on the presentation at work and letting Willow distract me when I'm not in the office. "It's tomorrow."

I've been waiting for this opportunity all my life, and it's finally here. I'm ready, confident even, but I also might vomit at the mention of my big day. It feels final or complete already, but this is only the first step. My project is getting its first real chance, and I should be more excited. The heat house prototype in our backyard is coming along great. I had hoped that Flora or my mom could have tested it before my presentation, but mother nature didn't work on my time schedule. She purely did whatever the hell she wanted.

"You ready?" Jackson asks.

"As ready as I can be," I say before completely turning to Leo, who sits across from me. "How's that song coming along?" He was a producer and lyricist for tons of artists, and he loves the behind-the-scenes of making music.

"It's missing something. I haven't figured it out." Leo shrugs it off. His black hair is long in the front but swept to the side a bit, and he keeps light facial hair. He is a homebody with a lean figure. Lucky son of a bitch. He was more similar to me in the sense of our careers being some-what lax compared to the careers of Dylan, Felix, or even Jackson, who is the CEO of a construction company.

Relief showers over me as the conversation moves to Leo and his latest work. The tension in the room lessens but never disappears. Willow run her hand up and down my thigh, and I can breathe easier. I didn't want to speak too much or get my hopes up about my project. I want everything to go smoothly, and I want my project to receive the utmost support, and there I go getting my hopes up. Willow's eyes peer into the side of my head, and, just this once, I'm having a hard time meeting her eyes. I do though. Her warm brown eyes soak mine in, and it's in moments like this that I forget she's not mine. She smiles, and my heart does that fluttering thing, and it makes the world right.

Goddess, letting her go is going to be fucking painful.

18

WILLOW: PRESENTATION DAY

"Plans for the day—go," Eddie asks. He flips his last pancake as he points a finger gun towards me. I stare at the handsome shifter manning my stove. He is in sweats and a T-shirt, my honest-to-goddess favorite outfit of his. He's made himself at home in my house for the past what... few weeks? And our whole dynamic shift.

We wake up together, though he is still sleeping on the couch. He makes me breakfast, and I keep him company as he cooks. Then we get ready, and he drops me off at work like clockwork every day. I haven't driven since the day he got here, still, and I'm not mad at it.

I love that he is here in my home with me and Layla, but as much as he smiles and says he's okay, I know he misses his Pack. That kills me inside. I feel guilty, it's my fault, but I also know that even if I sent him away, he wouldn't go, and that settles my rapidly beating heart.

"Work, then I'm having lunch with the girls. Catch up with them and whatnot. You?" I ask. It's weird to not talk about attacking Ghost since Layla dropped that news on us last night. It's hard to process that Milo isn't dead. The man I thought was my fated mate isn't dead. Instead, he faked his death and is hiding somewhere, and now he's hired a hitman to keep Layla away from him by having the hitman attack me.

If I think about it too much, before we can do anything about it, I think I'll choke, I need to push it to the back of my mind.

We have to wait a whole four days before we get to the bottom of this and try to catch Ghost at Layla's job on Tuesday.

I'm trying to remain calm about last night's conversation. I'm pushing it to the back of my mind, but I know I'll break at some point. I sigh, and the tears trying to poke their way through my eyes, but I hold them back and smile up at Eddie. He's already staring at me with a small smile on his face.

"I have my presentation today," he says slowly. Almost as if it sounds unreal or too good to be true.

"How do you feel? Are you ready?" I smile, rising excitedly from my chair. I'll put everything to the side for now. Today's the day for Eddie's dream project to be presented to his company, and he's been oddly shy about it. I'm sure everyone else noticed at dinner last night too, and I didn't want to feed his nerves by asking why, but he brought the conversation up first.

"I'm as ready as I can be, Buttercup."

"Okay, okay. Are you excited? No, I know you are. What are you going to wear?" I'm rushing around the house now, grabbing at all sorts of outfits and accessories that he has all over the house.

"Willow, come eat," he says, setting down the pancakes next to the butter and syrup. "I'm wearing my normal attire."

"Nothing special? No, that won't do—let me find something!" I shout from my room as I dig through my drawers. I have a lucky pin somewhere, and he should at least have that. It's a stupid little pin from when I first moved to Rainfall Avenue. It was the first thing I bought after I got myself settled in. I love this stupid pin. I find it on one of my bookshelves and rush back to the kitchen, where he's serving pancakes onto three plates at the table.

"I found it. Here." I push the pin next to his plate and sit, watching his face for an expression. I slowly realize I'm being pushy and admittedly weird, and I want to take it back the more he stares at the cheap pin.

"A bear paw?"

"It's cute," I mutter.

"It's definitely cute and a little corny."

"You don't have to wear it," I say, reaching to grab the pin before Eddie snatches his palm closed with the pin tucked tightly in his hand.

"I love it, Buttercup. Thank you. I'll keep it with me," he says, sliding the pin into his pocket. A blush flushes my face as I think of him having the pin all day and probably thinking of me every time his hand runs over it. Maybe I shouldn't have given it to him. Maybe it'll be distracting.

"Keep it in your pocket," I mumble, stuffing a pancake in my mouth. Gosh, he makes the fluffiest pancakes.

"Willow!" Layla calls from the living room. She has the

day off and is taking full advantage of it, setting up camp in Eddie's "bedroom."

"Yes, Layla?" I yell from my seat in the kitchen, rolling my eyes jokingly. Layla is a wonderful housemate when the girl remembered she was twenty and not fifteen.

"Can you help me? The TV isn't turning on." Layla is laid out on the couch and doesn't look like she's moved since she plopped herself there this morning.

"Layla, you're twenty and can't change the remote batteries?"

"I forgot about that," she mumbles.

"Try the batteries then come talk to me," I say, trying to contain my laughs. Eddie sure doesn't, laughing his butt off as he goes towards the shower.

"Quit laughing, Eddie. You're the one who lost the remote last night!" Layla shouts back.

"You did what?" I ask, my head whipping towards him. One thing that made me mad was losing the remote. Layla got an earful from me the first week she was here after she lost the remote. Thankfully, it was only under the couch, but I hope she learned to search before asking me.

"I'm taking a shower. Can't answer any further questions!" he yells as he shuts the bathroom door.

Shaking my head with a small smile, I mutter to myself, as if annoyed. But to be honest, I love having both Eddie and Layla here, and even more, I love the life that it brings every day. Sunny, my newest addition, has become loud too, running around and squeaking her toys. I pause outside my bedroom door, my hand resting on the handle as a thought runs through my mind. It is the reminder that this is probably the closest I'll ever get to a full house.

* * *

THE RUBY-RED SEATS and shiny white tables bring back memories of my life before Eddie Enchanted. My life when I thought I was going to be forever single. Back when I was hanging out with Flora and Luxe almost every day. We haven't had lunch for who knows how long, and it's completely my fault.

"So, can we talk about what happened last night?" Luxe asks as she takes her seat at Eleanor's Diner. The Luna isn't happy, even through her smile, I can tell. The disappointment radiates off her as if it's magic, right into my pores. Flora isn't as headstrong, her face screwed with worry as she slides into the booth seat next to Luxe.

"I—" I say but cut myself off. Layla, my sweet, innocent Layla, went through so much and... I wasn't there. I left, and she was going through hell. My eyes trail out the window, trying to process everything that was said last night. I don't know what to think. "Can't say we've been through this before, darling," Flora says, rubbing a hand up and down my arm. It's nice to be around my friends again; they are warm and comforting. Goddess, I missed them. I see now that nothing would keep them away for too long. Not even a killer on the loose.

"Willow, spill. What are you thinking?" Luxe says. Her short blonde hair is pulled up in a claw clip, and she's dressed in a maxi skirt that drags slightly on the floor, and a white long-sleeve crop top covers her chest. I wish I could wear cute long-sleeve shirts in this summer heat, but I'd sweat right through them.

"I think I'm in love with Eddie," I blurt out. "No, I'm absolutely in love with him."

"But what about Milo? He's not dead," Luxe asks as her mood switches from angry to compassionate in the second it takes her to reach her hand over the table to take mine. Luxe is a Luna, after all. She's built to handle crazy situations. To adjust to change and to lead. She is strong and beautiful, and I love her.

"I don't know anymore. Regardless of if he was my mate or not, my mind pulls towards Eddie, and I can't stop this pull. Maybe I got it wrong, or the Moon Goddess is giving me a second chance," I say, unable to stop my rambling. With each admission, a weight is lifted from my chest, and I crave that lightness. I can't stop the rush I get as the load gets lighter and lighter.

"I can't believe I thought someone who could sell their sister to the BSM could be my mate? What does that say about me?"

"It says you're a loving person," Flora quickly supplies as a guilt eats away at my gut.

"I mean, I was going to mate that man! How did I not know that he could be so evil?"

"Do you believe your bites would've taken? Remember what Ms. Harrow said about bites healing when you're not mates?" Flora asks, trying to be encouraging.

"I don't know. I guess I'll never know," I mumble in a slight panic. At least they believe in my character. I just —wow, I can't believe I loved a person who could do that.

"We don't need men. We should be our own Pack. The

three of us," Luxe says, pouting her lips and grabbing our hands.

"I'm technically part of a Pack already, but Dylan will understand," Flora says, nodding her head in agreement.

"We already are a Pack," Luxe clarifies. "We have our Luna, me, our momma bear, Willow, and our business head, Flora. Layla could be a member too, and Remi. What more could we need?" Luxe laughs as she goes over our "roles." I watch them laugh, and I start to feel better about the Milo thing. Not about what he did to Layla—that will never be forgiven, and I could kill him myself for that. My bear paws at the surface every time I think about it, but I don't think that is my place anymore. Layla's been clear that's been her plan since she got out, and I don't want to take away any sort of peace she could gain from that. She deserves that much. "So, back to Layla and Ghost."

"My heart breaks for her. She's young. I have no idea how to help her," Luxe says, keeping a watchful eye on the window.

"What's wrong?" I ask as she turns to stare fully out the window. I turn to see, but she stops me with a hand on my cheek.

"Don't look now, but someone dressed in all black is headed inside."

"I wear all black outfits all the time. That doesn't make someone suspicious," Flora says, trying her damndest not to look. I want to look so badly—it's our weakness. I replace Luxe's hand with my own to block my view.

"Is he a tall man with tattoos covering every inch of his skin except his face?" I ask, suddenly doused in a cold wash of fear from head to toe. Oh, my goddess. Would Ghost try to kill me here? With my friends here? Oh my goodness, what if he hurts them too?

"Yes."

"It's Ghost," I say. My breathing becomes labored. Oh, my goddess. He's here. He's going to hurt me, hurt my friends, in our favorite diner.

"We don't know that for sure," Flora says.

"Ghost is here," I whisper, slowly pulling out my phone to secretly text Eddie. I pray he has his phone.

Oh shoot, he's at work. He has his presentation today! His phone should be off.

"Who should we call?" I ask worried my text ruined Eddie's presentation already.

"You think I can't handle this?" Luxe asks, slowly getting up from the booth. Her smile is sly and flirty.

Sly and flirty?

What in the world was this Luna thinking?

"Luxe, sit the fuck down," Flora says, grabbing her arm and slamming her back into the seat. "I texted Dylan. He'll be here soon," she murmurs.

"A killer, Luxe? Really?" I say, trying to act normal, and maybe, just maybe, Ghost is not here for me. Maybe he is just getting a bite to eat.

"Really! don't forget I've got an Alpha bark." It is a gift Alphas and Lunas have. A way to control even the rowdiest of shifters. Respectable leaders don't need to use their bark on their Packs, but it comes in handy once in a while.

"What if he's an Alpha?" I ask as I try not to duck my head or appear obvious. My auburn afro is hard to hide, and even harder to not... identify, but there might be a chance he doesn't recognize me.

"What is he doing here?" I mumble, picking up a menu to hide my face even though he must be sitting behind us since I can't see him.

"You would have a better idea than me," Luxe mutters back, following my lead and picking up a menu, too.

"Act normal ladies, this is a public place, there is only so much he can do," Flora says, biting her lip nervously as if that is completely normal behavior.

"You're right. Act cool," Luxe agrees, her leg shaking under the table. I can hear her shoe tap on the floor.

"Yeah, act cool with a killer sitting a few booths over," I whisper.

"Not helping, Willow," Luxe says as she stops her shaking and sits up straight now, flipping a strand of her hair over her shoulder.

"I'm just saying," I say, and I get a whip of cool confidence through my veins. This man tried to kill me twice. He gets to walk around, stalking Layla, and hurting me, and he gets to be what? Free?

I sit up, wanting to confront the monster behind us. How dare he come and threaten me and Layla? What kind of person is he for working with someone like Milo? And how dare he come into this diner thinking I won't attack? I should prove him wrong.

"I think he's staring right at us," Luxe says. She glares in his direction. "Is he fucking waving at us?"

She shakes in anger, and I see her claws scratching the diner table. They are going to kick us out at this rate, but I'm ready to show this guy he can't hurt us.

"Felix is walking through the door," Flora says, confusion wrapping its way around the whole table and stopping me mid-move. What the hell is Felix doing here? I've only met him a handful of times, but he's the Enchanted member covered in tattoos and is extremely tall. That tends to be hard to forget.

"Sit back down and play it cool. Pretend you know nothing," Felix says, guiding Luxe to sit back down as he slides in next to me.

"Why are you here?" Luxe asks.

"I've been going through security footage at the tattoo parlor, and guess who I fucking found? Ghost, leaning against a black Audi, and then staking out here, I see that fucker pull up," Felix says. He peaks over his shoulder in the direction Ghost is with a menu in his hands.

"Why didn't you come in and have lunch with us?" Flora asks, scrunching her eyebrows.

"Because Eddie said this was a 'girls only' lunch," Felix nonchalantly says.

"Okay, let's go get him," I mutter, and I move to get up, but Felix remains rooted to the seat. It's a booth, there's no way for me to get out besides climbing on the table, and I didn't want to draw more attention this way.

"Felix, move, please," I say, half standing.

"What the hell are you doing? This is our chance," Luxe says, giving the man her wide eyes and barely containing a snarl.

"Our chance to mess everything up. Think for a second, Luxe. Why would he be this damn obvious?" Felix says, refusing to move and staring at Flora to ensure the Luna stays in her seat.

"I can't find out if y'all go brawling and kill the man. We need him," Felix says, stealing the menu from Luxe's hands.

"So, what should we do?" Flora mumbles her question. My shoulders are tense, and I can hardly focus on the discussion. Ghost is here. He's in the diner. He's within my reach.

"You should stay here. I'll handle it," Felix says, his eyes trained everywhere and nowhere at the same time.

"Just 'cause you're a man, you think—" Luxe gets heated, but I can't contain my anger at Felix either.

"You are kidding me, right?" I say, my eyes glaring into Felix's. "He tried to kill me, and you want me to stay here? And do nothing?"

"Yes, I want you to stay right here," Felix says with a shrug, leaning back in the seat. The action only pisses me off. I make a move to stand again, but Felix blocks my way. Flora reaches a hand over to me, silently pleading for me to stay.

"What he means to say is that it's better if someone who is trained handles him," Flora says.

"I can shift, and my bear can deal with him," I try to reason, but it doesn't stick in anyone's brain but mine.

"And be banned from Eleanor's Diner for the rest of your shifter life? I think not," Luxe says. She's right, and I'm being emotional, but Ghost is *right there*. He's now sitting a few booths down, eating. Like he is a regular civilian enjoying lunch. That should be me or Layla. Not him, sitting there eating freely, without a care or having to watch over his shoulder. He doesn't deserve to sit there after trying to kill me.

My eyes switch from Flora to Luxe to Felix. Unease fills my chest and racks my mind. How can I eat? How can I sit here and pretend everything is normal when a killer that was after me is behind me?

My breathing becomes labored, and I try to calm down. My eyes find Flora's, who's offering a comforting smile, and it reminds me I'm not alone. I have them and Felix, and Ghost can't hurt us all publicly in a diner full of paranormals. Inside the diner is a neutral space; it's the rule of public business. No shifting and no fighting. Save all that for the parking lot and beyond. I know this, yet my skin itches. I see my bear's fur pop out on my arms through my skin, and I have to push her down. Inhaling, I wait four seconds, then exhale. They are right. I can't do this now.

"He's getting up," Luxe whispers. She doesn't even pretend that she isn't staring him down now. Her glare sharpens as the sound of his footfalls gets louder.

"Order me a cheeseburger to-go, please," Felix asks while slowly getting up from the booth.

"Can I fucking help you?" Felix snarls at Ghost as he stops at our table. My arms shake as I see the man of my torment.

"Yeah, you can." His dead voice registers like a fire alarm in my ears. It makes me jump out of my skin even though I was awaiting his response. He doesn't waste much more time pulling a white cloth from his pocket and tossing it onto our table.

A white flag. Surrender? Why?

I stare back at Ghost, who gives us a half shrug before turning to Felix.

"Not here," Felix says, looking the man up and down as if weighing if he could take him in a fight. I'm honestly not sure who would win. I think Felix was a cage fighter, and Ghost appears he's been in as many fights as Felix probably has.

"Okay, then," Ghost says. Felix nods his head. I can't see his face, but I'm sure it's as intimidating as looking at Ghost is.

Felix follows Ghost out of the diner. He's leaving. *Leaving.* The man who's haunted me for the last couple of weeks is now leaving the diner.

I turn my head to watch Felix go. I hadn't *really* seen Ghost's face till now. He is a handsome man, like Ms. Humming, my old neighbor, said, with deep brown eyes and dark brown floppy hair. He has thick waves at the ends of his hair and light facial hair above his lip. He has tattoos decorating his hands and is slightly shorter than Felix, but not by much.

They don't exchange many more words as Felix strides up to him, bringing his hand around Ghost's neck as Felix comes up from behind him. I watch as Felix shoves Ghost into his car.

"I guess he was planning on taking care of it," Luxe mutters. I hear a gasp somewhere in the diner and a hushing from someone else.

"Is someone going to do something?" I hear one woman ask, but this isn't the human side of Rainfall Avenue; this is the paranormal side, and if you aren't ready to fight, you mind your business.

A waitress comes up to our table, and my friends order food, including some for me and the cheeseburger for

Felix. I take a deep breath, my eyebrows scrunching. "Did he just solve all my problems with a neck snap?" I say so low I almost don't hear myself.

"Maybe not all of them, but a lot of them."

"We still have to find Milo," Luxe says, a grimace from her destroying the joy that was building up in my gut.

"Umm." I stop to take a deep breath as the waitress leaves to put in our order. "Should we go after them?"

"No, Dylan says to stay put until they can get chains around Ghost. Once they get him tied up, we'll go. Let's enjoy our lunch, darling," Flora says, sliding her phone back into her purse. As much as I want to fight that, Dylan has much more experience, being an assassin and all, than I do. So it feels stupid to fight his instructions.

"Okay, so, well... I'm visiting my family soon," I murmur as normalcy settles into my bones.

"Family? Why now?" Luxe asks, eating her fries then peeking into Felix's box once hers runs out.

"A wedding. My sister invited me to her mating ceremony at the last minute. Wasn't sure I'd be up for it." More like she thought I would cause a scene at her ceremony, but I don't want to talk badly about my sister.

"Are you?" Flora asks. I tilt my head in question, my loose bun of curls tilting with me. Am I ready? Yeah. Admittedly, the thought of her having a mate and having a ceremony doesn't bother me, but what if it's different when I get there? Will the bubbling bitterness of jealousy fill my every pore like every one of my family members thought it would when I see the ceremony?

"I'm 90 percent sure I'm ready. I won't know till I get there."

"Is Eddie going to be there?" Luxe asks, waggling her eyebrows.

I blush, but I can't help but answer, "He is."

"What are you wearing? I might have something for you," Flora asks, her interest spiking. I'm not a dressy woman, but if she can find a dress that my intense sweating won't destroy, then I will wear whatever she picks.

"Now would be a good time to have a designer as a best friend, now wouldn't it?" I ask, a smile cracking on my face.

"Willow!" My name is yelled as I hear sneakers hit the title floor. My head whips around to meet Eddie's eyes. He takes a deep breath, sliding into the booth next to me. His legs press against mine, and his hands turn my face towards him and away from my plate of a burger and fries. His brown eyes search every inch of my face, then my neck and body, before he pulls me into him. His warmth and mix of tobacco and vanilla scent fills my senses. "I was fucking scared, Willow. Goddess. Why was he here?" His heart beats out of his chest under my touch. I cuddle into him despite my friend's giggles. I let his body practically swallow me up, and I breathe in his smell, helping me calm down from the whole show.

"Felix was here," I mumble lamely.

"Thank goddess. Are you ladies alright?" he asks, still wrapped around me so tightly, I can't enjoy my fries.

"Yup. We're good." Luxe smiles. She laughs as Flora tries to stuff her mouth with a bite of burger, probably to stop herself from making an inappropriate comment.

❧ 19 ❧

EDDIE: PRESENTATION DAY

AFTER DROPPING WILLOW OFF AT WORK, THE unsettling feeling in my gut intensifies each minute I am away. I knew getting into work today would not be the same as any other day, yet my stomach turns with more acid than I thought it would.

Is it hotter in here than usual? I pull on the collar of my shirt as I head to my office first. My meeting is closer to lunchtime, and I'm hoping that knowing Willow will be safe with Flora, Luxe, and Felix today will settle this need to rush to her.

Even my bear is pacing inside me, and I can't tell if we are excited or about to shit ourselves. Staring at the light blue walls and ugly-ass brown carpeting of the office isn't helping my nerves, either. Neither is staring at the slides of my presentation. Today is finally the day. The day I get my chance to change the shifter community as I know it. It's so surreal, as if the world is going to come crumbling down at my feet.

My phone rings, and I see it's my mother. I let out a quick breath of relief as I answer the call.

"Mom." Her name comes out, and I can't help but smile. I walk over to the window and stare at the town down below me. She's the reason I've worked hard to get this project up and going, and I needed her voice as much as I needed Willow's. The sensation of the bear pin warms in my pocket, and I remember that regardless of what happens here today, I've got two strong women standing beside me.

"Hey, baby, I had to call you before your meeting. I just—" I hear her intake a sharp breath, and it settles the nerves in my stomach a bit.

"I'm glad you called."

"I needed to say how proud of you I am. Even if those dogs don't take on your project, you've made it far, and baby, I'm so sorry," she says over hiccups and little sobs.

"Why are you sorry? There's no need—"

"You shouldn't have had to deal with your mother during a heat. No kid should, and I am so damn happy that you're trying to change that."

"No, mother should have to go through what you did, Mom. It's not your fault."

"It is, but you're fixing it. You're fixing it, and I love you so much for not blaming me," she says, and I can practically see her in the window's glass. I kind of wish she was here. I wish she didn't have this guilt. I'll have to fix that too. I'm not sure how I'll fix it, but I will.

It's 11:25, and I need to walk in and set up my presentation, but my stomach is filled with lead and my limbs are heavy. I tell my mother I love her, and I thank her for everything before I end the call. I have to be the person we needed back then. Someone to care for the women and people in our community.

I'm fucking Eddie Enchanted, bear shifter and member of the Enchanted Pack, and there's no damn reason to be nervous.

Even if this goes to shit, I don't need this company to accomplish my dreams.

As much as want to say fuck it and do the damn thing by myself, having a company backing me would eliminate enough problems to make this worthwhile. At least, that's what I tell myself as I finally turn the door handle to the meeting room. The board is there and so are all the managers. They would either reject this project or put it in this year's schedule to bring to life.

I roll up the sleeves of my white, pressed button-down shirt. I watch the rings on my fingers as I queue up the slides when I remember how Willow loved my rings this morning when she kissed each one as good luck. Maybe I should wear them more often 'cause, damn, I am pretty. The decorative pin Willow gifted me this morning is burning in my pocket, bringing a smile to my face. The bear paw is corny, but I love it. It's Willow's favorite pin, and she gave it to me for the day.

11:55 a.m.—it's time. It's time to convince the board of Cloud Design that a heat house for the community is a worthwhile project that could put us on the map.

"Good afternoon, ladies and gentlemen." I have my laptop hooked up to a projector, my slides appearing on the screen. Taking a quick breath, I smile. Teeth and all, I am ready.

I speak with conviction and grace. I lay out all my points on neat slides and stand strong in front of the board members and managers that make up Cloud Design. Throwing in personal experiences and facts to help persuade my audience, I pray it's enough. I'm normally a super confident man, and it's something I pride myself on, but today isn't the same as any other day. Everything is going right, but my gut is saying something is going to go wrong, terribly wrong, and I hope what goes wrong is not this presentation.

"Thank you for this presentation, Mr. Enchanted, but this is similar to something we heard earlier," one manager, Lacy, says with a pen twirling in her hand. I can't stop the twitch of my eyebrow, but I recover quick enough, considering what they are implying.

My innocent, jittery nerves dissolve into budding anger. I move from the podium and lean on both my hands against the front of the table, where everyone is seated. They have to be mistaken, right? I let silence eat at everyone in the room as I stare at each of the members surrounding the table. What the hell did they mean by *similar*? What is my heat house similar to?

"The goal of these presentations is to show us something new. Something no one has ever seen before," another member rambles off, using their hands as if fireworks sprouted off from their fingertips. "We didn't get that today."

My stare becomes a hard glare as I wonder what the hell they are talking about. This is new—to them, at least. Heat houses do not exist in the United States, let alone in the modern world. Last I checked. I have been perfecting this idea since I was seven; how in the hell have they seen this before, and where? How dare they question my originality and credibility after I gave the best damn presentation of my life?

"This is something new, sir," I say. "Unless there is something I don't know about." I had thought it was obvious this idea is mine, hell. Why would I make up the horror stories of me seeing my own mom go through her own heats alone for so many years? No resources or guidance are provided for women who are mateless, and it's about time for the shifters of the world to step up. I've worked on these blueprints and designs for years. Have I missed seeing a heat house? I'd searched the internet for one for months to admit my mom into. Had I missed it? Could she have been receiving care this entire time, and I just... I failed to find one?

"Another one of your colleagues presented this idea last week. While it wasn't nearly as polished or thought through, we declined a weaker version of this heat house idea last week."

"From whom?" My voice is calm compared to the storm brewing inside. While I'd love to pop off at the mouth and tell these fuckers someone stole my idea, I can't. I have to remain professional; shifters are known for going ape shit, and I don't want to prove them right. Vampires, shifters, a witch, and a fairy decorate this board of directors. I can't make an ass of myself, even if someone obviously stole my idea. This is a business and a game all wrapped up into one, and I'm finding that out the hard way.

"I can't tell you that information. It would only cause conflict in the workplace and is not worth the hassle."

"You know they stole their idea from me. I've spoken about it to you and to my managers and instead of acknowledging that, you protect the person who stole it from me. Tell me, is my work here not respected? Am *I* not respected here?" My voice comes out low as all the dots are connecting. I'm not stupid and neither are they. They know this idea is mine. Nobody could come up with this in a week, let alone in a year. Not to this level of detail and attention. I'd been working my ass off on this project, and they have the balls to tell me I stole the idea from a coworker? You know what? As nice as it would have been, I don't need them. I can do this shit myself. I don't fucking need them.

"You know, forget I asked. Thank you for your time. Have a wonderful day," I say, closing my laptop. I go to walk out of the room, pissed as hell, but free nonetheless.

"Chance," a member whispers as I reach the door. I don't pause or stop at the information being given. I really don't give a fuck. He and all these fuckers can continue in this rat race, but I'm out.

I continue down the hall as the member is berated for giving up information I didn't need. I had a clue, an inkling it was his untalented ass. He is one of the very few coworkers who knew. I storm to my office, close the door, and take a seat at my desk. Fuck. I want to quit. Can I? No, I am way too hyped. I can't make any decisions while heightened on emotion. My bear tries to take over, but I can't deal with that fallout right now. I'll deal with Chance later, too.

Right now, I need Willow. Picking up my phone, I stare at my background, a picture of Willow reading a book from her bed. I love this picture. I remembered taking the photo the night I borrowed a book from her for my next read and ate her out. Damn, what a day. She was so happy to give me another book to read she couldn't hold back her little laughs and that fucking smile. Goddess, that smile could save planets from self-destruction. I had to capture the moment; her moment of faking reading and shining like the beautiful woman she is. Looking past her image on my phone, I see a text had come through about thirty minutes ago.

I think Ghost is here.

Seeing the words Ghost and here in the same sentence makes my heart drop through my stomach and to the damn floor.

Shit, shit, shit. Willow is in trouble.

"Eddie, let me see him," are the first words out of Willow's mouth when Felix and Dylan get back from dropping Ghost off at wherever the hell Dylan's creepy-ass hideout is. Dylan had a house built long ago to stay at after he finished his assassin-ly duties, afraid that work would follow him home.

The uneasiness in my gut has settled now that Willow is with me, and as much as I wish for this shit show of a day to be over, it's probably long from over.

Willow's pawing my arm, which in any other case I would enjoy, but the request attached to the pawing is making it hard to enjoy. I gaze into her wide eyes and grimace. It isn't my place to tell her what to do, but I can't help but try to stop her from being in the same room as Ghost. I don't think any of us know what we're walking into. Based on the story I heard, it seems like he was surrendering, but that wouldn't make sense either.

Why? Why is he surrendering?

"Dylan and Felix are trained in this sort of thing, Buttercup. They are going to get way more information from him than we are. Let the professionals do their thing," I say as I lead us to the living room so we can sit and discuss what to do next as a Pack. I can't shake the instinct that this isn't over. I'm tired, and, fuck, I can't catch a break today.

I've had a shit day, no doubt, but at least I can sit with Willow, her head tucked into my neck. Even if we are arguing, or even if I practically quit my job today, Willow being where home is will never not make any day a good day.

I lean my head against hers as she continues to try to convince me with all the logical reasons she should be there for the questioning. I get it to an extent, but I want her wrapped in bubble wrap in my Pack house, preferably naked in my room for when I get back.

She's rambling, and I think she's as tired of this day as I am, and she finally huffs and digs deeper into our embrace. It's peaceful for all of two seconds before Felix walks through the door to update us. Dylan isn't with him; he must have stayed back to watch the fucker. Who would've guessed a major part of our problem would walk through the door of the only shifter diner in Rainfall Ave?

"Willow, this isn't a puppy. This is a killer," I say, my

hand running up and down her side, soothing myself more than her probably. I don't understand why we're arguing about this. Ghost will continue his stay at Rainfall Avenue in Dylan's basement in a location only Dylan, and now Felix, knows how to get to. There's no way Ghost is escaping our clutches. So, in my mind, there is no reason not to relax for a second.

"Eddie, he's my killer—"

"No, Willow, absolutely not," I say, landing a kiss on the top of her head. She's not going, not right now, not until Dylan and Felix do a round of questioning first. I've decided, and now I'm done.

"Willow, let us handle this," Felix says, but it's more of a command, and I can't argue with it right now. I understand her frustration, but this has to go beyond emotions. Ghost is dangerous. I could've lost her today. On top of missing her text for help, her following text message of a simple *nvm*, left me drained and tired. If it'll make her feel better, I'll stay here too. Fuck it. "Willow, let's stay here."

"Eddie, let me talk to him. See what he knows."

"Dylan and Felix will handle that. Let's just—"

"Just what? Go back to life as normal?" Okay, she's right, and maybe I'm being a selfish prick, wanting to keep her to myself when her world is crumbling around her. But I'm not changing my mind.

Why wouldn't she want to be wrapped up in my bubble? She has reliable shifters to depend on. Why does she have to do everything herself?

"Let me have a go at him. Let us wear him down, and then *maybe* I'll come to get you," Felix says. He makes no promises, and Willow obviously picks up on that.

"Felix," Willow pleads with him too. She pulls away from me, as much as I'll let her, because there's no way in hell I'm losing contact with her. I keep her hand in mine, but I let her turn to face Felix to get the pressure of being the bad guy off my shoulders. She's facing away from me, but I bet her eyes are all wide and cute as she slightly pouts her lips, trying to convince him to take her with them. Damn, she is adorable, but in all honesty, I want to keep that look for myself, not for Felix to see. Pulling her arm, I yank her body back, which instantly curls into mine, and I wrap my arms around her. She's mine.

"No," Felix says, running a hand through his long hair and furrowing his brows. Her fingers shake as she stares at me with tears welling in her eyes, and her cheeks are a shade of red that crushes my defense down. Fuck. I hate seeing Willow upset. I sigh, knowing she'll go without us, and she'll probably succeed at doing so, and the decision I thought I made was never really made by me, but by her. She's going, and I'd rather she goes with me than without.

"I selfishly need you right now. Let Dylan do the grunt work, and in a few hours, Felix will take us to question him, okay?"

"That's all I was asking," she says with a tiny smile growing on her face. The tears don't go away but they don't fall. On some level, that's a win for me.

"What? Eddie?" Felix asks, furrowed brows and a *what the hell* look on his face, but he doesn't get it, and probably won't until he finds his mate.

"It's okay, Felix. Call Dylan and let him know." It's settled. I get up and take Willow's hand, not checking to see if she will follow behind me as I lead her to my room.

There, Willow slips off her shoes, and I plop onto my bed. My room consists of graphic prints all over the walls, a desk for work, and a game center with a missing game console that is currently at Willow's.

She comes over and gently sits next to me. Her weight presses down on the bed, making me hyperaware of where she is and how easily I could reach out my hand to yank her to me. Her foot taps on the ground. She's working up to ask me something, and while I would try to alleviate those nerves, today I'll wait for her to work up the nerve to ask. I grab her arm and guide her to lie with me 'cause one thing I'm serious as hell about is taking a damn nap.

"What's wrong, Eddie?"

"Nothing, just a long day," I mumble, snuggling closer to her. We haven't necessarily laid in a bed together, and now that we have, I know the best kind of sleep I'll ever get from this day on will only be next to her.

"Don't think I'm forgetting about Ghost, 'cause I'm not, but how... how did your meeting go?" The million-dollar question I don't want to answer. I'm confused about where I stand on the situation. I'm almost happy to be free of the chains of working for *The Man*, but I'm also upset that my company didn't care my idea was stolen.

"I'd rather talk about Ghost."

"That bad?" Hearing the sadness in her voice cracks through me like lightning. As much as I want to bounce up and at least pretend everything is going to be okay, I can't. Not around Willow. I can't pretend around her, no matter how badly I want to.

"Yeah, that bad, Buttercup," I mumble, moving so that

I can hold her in my arms. She is warm and soft. Her smooth legs rub against mine and her sleeve-covered arms wrapping around my waist. This is what I need, and for now, something I'd selfishly take. She smells better than buttercream and warm pancakes. She smells like home. As much as this house and my Pack are my home, Willow is growing to be too. If I could set up a meeting with the Moon Goddess to ask to why this woman wasn't my mate, I would.

"My pin didn't give you any good luck, huh?" The paw pin was still in my pocket. I hadn't changed from my work clothes and wasn't planning to leave Willow's embrace to do so.

"It did, just not in the way we imagined it would," I say as her fingernails lightly trace random patterns on my forearm. I surrender the stress of everything to the promises of a nap, leaning back against the headboard and pillows.

"Have you figured out what this means for you yet?" she asks, her warm pancake smell wafting through the air around me. Inhaling her scent as much as I can without her catching me, I nestle my nose in her hair. I'm becoming enraptured with her, and there is no stopping the heartbreak that will follow. I have no idea what my failed proposal will mean for me career wise. I'm too tired to care.

"Nope," I say, closing my eyes. "Chance stole my idea and presented it last week, and even still, I think they would've rejected my proposal." It's a reality I didn't want to believe but knew was more than likely to be true.

"Chance? Was he reprimanded?" she questions, fire snapping from her tone. Her brows angrily furrowed, and her lips turned downward.

"Probably not. I didn't stick around to find out. I rushed out."

"I'm sorry about that. I forgot about your meeting. I didn't ruin anything, did I?"

"You couldn't ruin a damn thing if you tried." She'd always make things better. She shines and grinds for others as if her life depends on it. Her light can't damage anything besides my heart, and even then, I'd happily let her destroy my pumping organ if only it meant I'd get to keep her longer.

"What are we going to do next?"

"Lie with me, Willow," I say, lying back and finally giving into the urge to drag her body close. "Let's lie here till we can't anymore."

"Sounds fine to me," Willow mumbles, cuddling into my arms even more. I drag my thin navy-blue blanket over us and take a well-deserved and much-needed nap.

It's only for a few hours before Felix's impatient ass storms into my room with the green light from Dylan to head on up.

Felix is pissed he had to wait around with us as Dylan did the initial questioning. I'd take a grumpy Felix anytime if it means I can nap with Willow right beside me. Damn, I loved that. I can almost ignore the fact that we are meeting with Willow's almost killer with how damn happy I am. We arrive at Dylan's secluded cabin in the woods, and Felix takes us to the basement. The fact that Dylan has this whole torture basement is chilling, but what's even more frightening is that it's being used.

"Okay, ladies and gentlemen, meet James Herandez," Dylan says, waving his hands towards the man as an introduction.

"Is that all you got?" Felix asks, as he rounds the man in the chair, circling him as if he's bait. I'm not sure when Felix's aggressive side came to be or what pulled it out, but I'm worried about him.

"No, he isn't hiding anything—hasn't told a lie, hasn't refused an answer, and hasn't pissed himself," Dylan says with a shrug. Willow remains quiet by my side as we stare at the lanky man with a black bag over his head. He has tattoos lining his arms down to his fingertips, similar to Felix. James is tanned and muscled like the rest of us.

"Why the bag if he's giving information freely?" Willow mumbles, pointing to the bag on James's head. She doesn't step forward or get closer, and I'm grateful as my anger builds at the realization of just who this is. I guess I couldn't forget after all. This fucker tried to kill Willow. My Willow. My Buttercup. Mine.

I tighten my grip on her hip, holding her firmly to me. I don't trust James, and I sure as shit didn't care if he was giving information freely. He's a killer we don't know, and I only trust the killers on my side, and James has proven he isn't one of them.

Felix rips the bag off James's head. Long black hair falls around his face and his brown eyes widen at the sight of Willow. He tilts his head as if in thought.

"What's there to think about?" I snidely ask. No way was this piece of shit looking at Willow in surprise. He obviously didn't do his homework if he didn't know the Enchanted Pack had ties to this woman. My woman.

"I'm glad to see you're still here." James's voice is a harsh growl. Like he's spent years yelling and now can only whisper. It hurts my fucking ears. "He was pretty pissed when I left."

"Why? Why the stop at my apartment? Why try to kill me?" Willow's voice comes out strained and hurt, and all I can do is press her closer to me. I can't take away the hurt in her voice, in her eyes, and it pains me more than I'm sure it should.

"It's simple, really. I was paid," James says with a shrug. A damn shrug.

"By whom?" I ask, but he doesn't look at me. His eyes are trained on Willow, and I lead Willow to stand more behind me than by my side. This man is led by greed, by money, and a fucker like that is dangerous.

"I don't know."

"And this is where the questioning truly begins," Felix says, gripping a dagger tightly in his palm. I finally look at my Packmate, really look at him, and it's only now I notice his eyes are different. Changed, and I can't remember when the change occurred. Holy fuck, how long have I been wrapped up in Willow? Am I a horrible Pack brother to not have noticed this change?

"He doesn't know, and you know this, Felix." Dylan doesn't move from his stance next to us.

"I know." Felix shrugs with a half-lit smile. "I'm just ruffling feathers."

"How do you know he doesn't know who's paying him?" Willow asks. Her fingers curl tightly around my right bicep, and I swear this is the best feeling in the world. In a room filled with way more qualified protectors, she chooses me. She holds my arm, she trusts me to protect her, and, Moon Goddess, please tell me why you've hurt me this way by not making this woman unquestioningly mine?

"I've dug into his phone while sleeping beauty and her prince charming took their darling little nap. The name, number, and bank routing information all track to a Doug Small. A.k.a, a man who doesn't exist. But we now know that Doug Small is Milo."

"So, the real question is, why did you stop trying to kill her? After the tea incident, nothing enticed you to keep trying to hurt her, even with the pay raises Milo offered. For a simple man who will do anything for money, why stop?"

"I found something more interesting."

"Another job?" Felix asks.

"Not that it's any of your fucking business, but no."

"Then what?" Dylan pipes in, his brows furrowing in question, and I'm beyond confused about the motives of the stranger sitting before us.

James remains silent and still. The man doesn't have a fearful bone in his body, not even when Felix steps into his view and makes a move to let the weapon fly in James's direction. Willow tenses and goes to make a move towards James as if she'd stop Felix, but it wasn't necessary.

I don't have to tighten my hold, and Felix doesn't let the dagger fly because Dylan's words make us all pause.

"A girl."

James's body goes stock-still, and his eyes shoot to

glare at the assassin. Maybe one man to another, Dylan knew. Dylan could've only been guessing, but James's body language that's been nonchalant this entire time, suddenly bursts to life.

"It's always a fucking girl. Who?" Felix asks.

James keeps his lips sealed, but a damn smile is tugging at the corner of his lips, and all I fucking know is it better not be my Willow.

"You can stay here till you feel like sharing with the class," Felix says, walking towards the door and leaving. I guess he's done with this snooze fest.

"Why did you stop at my apartment that day?"

"I wasn't paid to kill you, Willow. I was paid to scare you. It was an odd request, but cash is cash. I kill for no real rhyme or reason, but when you get tasked with killing someone as innocent as you, Willow, it makes you more concerned about who ordered the hit than the target. What did you, Willow, do that someone would kill you for it?" He leans forward, as much as he can, with his wrists bound to the chair. He's curious, and maybe we can use this to our advantage.

"I have to know. Why did you break into my apartment?" Willow asks again, and I honestly forgot about that. This started before she moved into her house, but what would Ghost have to do in her apartment?

"I told you?"

"No, before then. Someone broke in while I was at work and stole some undergarments and went through all my stuff. It was the tip that someone was after me," Willow explains.

"No, hun. That wasn't me."

"Who then?" I ask. If that wasn't Ghost then it had to be Milo, right?

"What about the notes?" Willow asks.

"The notes? The one I left at your doorstep when you moved from your apartment, that was me."

"Okay, and the tea poisoning?"

"That was me. It's hard to hold back in a physical altercation, but when he told me you were allergic to bananas, I had the bags made and placed them in your apartment," James says. He flips his long hair out of his face, and I'm half tempted to leave him here, but he isn't as heartless as he may think. While I don't care to show this rock of a being that he has a heart, I do see someone with nothing to lose has the same goal as we do.

Eradicate the fucker who dared to hurt Willow Buttercup.

"I—it's not—"

"Think harder, why, Willow?" James says, and I growl at the man.

"Watch who the hell you're talking to."

"Do you want to find this deadbeat or not?"

"Arguing isn't going to get us anywhere."

"It's not me he's really after, it's Layla," Willow blurts, and I pull her tighter against me. No way is James running this damn interrogation.

"The other girl was on my list too, and I can tell she scares him. He wouldn't give me any info on her," James says, leaning back into his chair.

"Layla? You never went after her," Willow mutters, crossing her arms. She rests a hand on her check and leans into my side.

"Layla," he mumbles, more to himself than anyone.

"Okay, so we have to work together. Can you tell us exactly when Milo hired you and how?" Dylan asks, pulling out a clean folding chair for her to sit.

And here we are. Me, Willow, Dylan, and her almost killer, trying to piece together the puzzle of her mate's "death." What a great fucking life.

20

WILLOW

WE GET ALMOST NOTHING FROM CAPTURING Ghost. As much as I would love to have solved everything by capturing Ghost. I have to accept the fact that he's not the problem.

Milo is, and goddess knows if we will ever find him. To go on with life as normal is like walking on hot coals without flinching. It's hard.

Now I have this mating ceremony to worry about too. I'm supposed to be happy, pretend that everything is okay, and that Milo hasn't lost his mind and is probably better off dead.

I didn't think there would ever be a day where I would think that.

But I also didn't think Milo was capable of doing the things he did.

The cherry on this cake, Eddie and I are invited to a family dinner the day before the ceremony, so now we have to leave for Kaler City early. My family wants to see me before the ceremony, at least that's what they said, but I know they want us to hash our emotions out before the ceremony.

I knew this, yet I couldn't say no to the invitation. I didn't want Eddie to think I didn't want my family to meet him or think he is my dirty little secret, and for him alone, I accepted this invitation.

"Willow." His voice is low and sing-songy. Wrapped in his arms, Eddie shifts closer to me as he wakes up. He tucks his nose into my neck, his smooth skin brushing against mine. Sliding one of his legs between mine, he lands a gentle kiss on my neck. Smiling, I keep my eyes closed as he moves his leg between mine, creating a delicious friction that lights my skin up almost immediately. I haven't dared initiate anything beyond a kiss or a cuddle since I almost mated him, and it feels as if I've been starved of his touch for centuries.

I let out a desperate whimper as the pressure in my core builds and move forward. Just enough to get heated, just enough for me to rock on his leg more forcefully.

"I feel your want, Buttercup, but let me hear it," he rasps as his kisses get wetter and sloppier. His hands trail around my stomach but freeze suddenly as I've yet to respond. I turn my head to face his, his brown eyes wide awake now.

My hips jolt, trying to find the dwindling pleasure again, but he rests his hand on my hip and demands again, "Willow, let me hear it."

"Yes, Eddie. Moon Goddess, yes," I murmur, kissing his lips. His front is still pressed to my back and my neck is strained beyond measure, but I don't care. I need more.

Satisfied with my answer, he moves his fingertips to pinch my hot, swollen nipple crying for attention, and he doesn't hesitate to give it.

I arch my hips back, and my toe draws a line up his calf as I position myself to get more motion. Biting my lip, I try to keep my moans, surely loud and unpleasant, to myself, but Eddie has different plans in mind.

His hand then slips from my breast down my stomach and to my clit, where his fingers get more than a little slick before he slides two digits into me. I arch even further and gasp as my head is thrown back into his shoulder. My hands instinctively reach behind me, finding his cock over his boxers. Slipping my hand into his waistband, I finally get to feel him in his entirety. It won't be all about me this time, though that was admittedly nice.

My hand finds his cock, heady and warm. As my grasp on him causes his fingers inside me to go from smooth and languid to jerky and the change has me clenching his fingers in my core tighter. I hear him mutter a curse as his hips lightly move against my hand. I smile, loving that I'm the one causing him to lose control as I swipe the pre-cum off the head of his cock and use it to add some lubrication between him and my hand. I slide my hand slowly and unsure at first, up and down as much as I can from this position.

We're so close I can hardly comprehend where he begins and I end, but it doesn't matter. He's completely ensnared into my being that anything without him is unreal or minute. I get a rush of the sense of home every time my soul picks up on him being near, and I can't help but fall into him. Any guilt I have over the possibility of falling for a man who could potentially be someone else's mate is set aside every time his arms wrap around me.

Please, Moon Goddess, please make this man my mate. Please, I swear I'll do anything, be anything, to make Eddie Enchanted undeniably mine.

He yanks my shorts down, bringing my hips up to get them over and out of the way. He moves fast to get rid of his clothes, and just as fast, he's right back where he was behind me and swings my leg over his forearm. Wind harshly caresses my lips as the coldness bites at my exposed skin.

"Please, Eddie," I beg as he fists his cock and lines up at my entrance. I'm practically clenching, ready for him to take me fully. I grab at the bedsheet for purchase and to gain some sort of control as he slides the tip in. Slowly, so slowly, he stretches me. His eyes trained on me, watching my face for what exactly, I'm not sure.

"I've got you, baby," Eddie says as he slides in inch by frickin' inch before he's all the way inside me. We both groan once he's bottomed out and then slowly starts to slide back out, painstakingly, inch by inch once more. I huff, and he only smiles before going in again, faster and harder this time and the next. I writhe under him as he hoists me open wider, with the leg hooked on his forearm. I didn't think I was flexible before, but with Eddie, he can get me to open up in ways I never have before.

Just as my orgasm is about to peak, he abruptly stops moving. I whimper loudly as I try to move with his cock stock-still inside me.

"Eddie?" I nearly sob. The only thing I can focus on is

how I'm frustrated in a way I can't quite understand, but it's in a way only he can dispel.

"You're so beautiful, Willow," he says, and my body hums. Literally hums as he moves again. This time there's a level of desperation that entices me to ensure I orgasm. A hunger to finish drives my hips to meet him at every thrust, and yet something clicks when I meet his eyes and see his open mouth smile.

"I need you longer than one orgasm, Willow. I need you for as long as I can possibly have you."

Oh.

Ohh fiddletarts.

This man is edging me. And by the Moon Goddess herself, I swear I want to kill him and love him at the same time.

"Eddie," I growl yet slow my rock to meet his new pace. The pressure builds again, and this time, it isn't shocking when he stops right before I come, though it resonates all the same. My moans fall from me on a shutter. I'm no longer concerned with how I look or how I sound, just the feeling of us connected and the pleasure stewing in my core.

He holds my orgasm in his control, denying me once more before we finally come together. He releases his hold, and I come harder than I ever have before. It's like running a marathon once we're done. Our bodies become slack as he slides out of me. I lay my head on his chest, breathing harder than I ever have before. His hand lightly traces circles on my back before he kisses the top of my head.

"I need to clean you up, Buttercup," he says, not making a move yet, but I see his stomach tense and know it's coming. As sticky as I am, I need it, but I don't want to move. With a sigh and a more than pleased smile, I roll off him, and he moves to clean me off and once again I let him. I hum and this time I am more content than anything. Eddie Enchanted, taking care of me through and through, and I find that I am, in fact, the luckiest girl ever, despite everything. Because being in his arms beats being haunted by a killer or being cast out by my family. With him, none of that matters. It's only me and him, and I love that.

As he crawls back into bed, I snuggle in next to him and doze off, exhausted.

An hour later, I hear Eddie call my name a couple of times as he moves his legs to overpower mine, caging me in. I try to curl the thin blanket over my head, but he grips the blanket to stop me from doing so. The thing about Eddie is that he is a morning person. He can wake up, jump out of bed and go on about his day. Me, not so much. Getting out of bed is one of the hardest things I do. Every. Single. Day. I moan in frustration and keep my eyes shut, trying to fall back asleep and quiet my racing thoughts.

"Willow, I want to go," Eddie groans, curling impossibly harder into my back.

"Go alone," I mumble, tired and almost falling back asleep.

"I don't want to go to Lovely Memories by myself," he whispers in my ear, and my eyes shoot open. "There's a book I think we should read together, for real this time," he says as he slowly drags my body to face him.

"The bookstore?" I sleepily ask, slowly opening my eyes to see a wide-eyed Eddie with one of my bonnets on his head. When did he put that on? That wasn't on before...

"Yes, Buttercup, the bookstore. Let's go."

"Are you trying to make up for arguing with me about seeing Ghost—I mean James?" Gosh, it's almost as if that was centuries ago, but it was just yesterday.

We let Ghost free from his bindings, but he isn't allowed at the Pack house or my house or anywhere else without Dylan or Felix present. While James didn't react to these rules, he doesn't seem to be the type to follow rules. I guess we'll see how that plays out.

I was given the duty to live my life as I normally would. As if there wasn't a person out there who wants me dead. Regardless, I more than welcomed the idea of living as if everything was absolutely perfect. It's about time I caught a break.

"I can't make up for something I don't feel bad about."

"Eddie, you're not helping your get out of bed argument," I mutter.

"Let's go buy books," he says, and I contemplate. I'm tired. Tired of life at this point, but books? Should I go buy books on his dollar? It would be a hell of an apology. But did I want to get out of bed?

"I guess," I say playfully, rolling my eyes. "Let's go buy books."

"Great! I picked your outfit out already," he says, crawling out of my bed and heading towards my closet. Picked out my outfit? How long has he been up?

Rolling over, I set my feet on the ground, taking off my bonnet. I gaze towards the end of the bed, seeing the so-called outfit Eddie is laying out for me. He picked a maxi length black dress and one of my little shoulder bags to match. For browsing the shelves of a bookstore, you couldn't go wrong with a long and flowy dress, but I'd switch out the shoulder bag for a crossbody instead. My hands need to be free.

My eyes trail up to his face. His adorably concentrated face, and I didn't have the heart to tell him the shoulder bag isn't ideal. His braids have grown slightly and trail in front of his eyes as his head swishes around, looking back and forth between the accessories I own.

Sighing, I get out of bed with a smile I couldn't get rid of even if I tried. Once Eddie is done fiddling with my outfit for the day, he goes off to, I hope, the kitchen to whip up some tea and pancakes.

Goodness, I love tea and pancakes, and I love when he makes them for me even more. How did I get so fluffing lucky? My face is refreshed now that I've washed it, and it's time for the most dreaded, but most rewarding, part of my morning routine: my hair. My curls never, and I really mean never, do what I want them to do. I can only hope that we are on the same page, and today I'm guessing that we're on the half up, half down page. Wrangling my curls for about twenty minutes is all the energy I have for today for my hair. Thankfully, it comes out decent and I make my way to the star of this morning: breakfast.

"One of these days, I'm going to wake up early enough to make you breakfast instead," I say as Eddie is setting down plates and mugs when I enter the kitchen.

"How about lunch instead?" He smirks, as if he knows

I'm probably never going to wake up early enough to make my man breakfast.

"I can do lunch," I agree, sitting in my seat. I look over at Eddie, slightly surprised to see he has black cargo pants on, matching my black dress. Is he matching my dress? Black is a common color, right? Maybe a coincidence.

"Eddie, are we matching?" I ask. My eyes are glued to him. Even if we aren't matching, cargo pants are as attractive as dress pants, and now I'm thinking this man could pull off anything, and that in itself is really unfair.

"Would you look at that," he says. He slides into his chair and eats. "We're both wearing black." Hmm, maybe it was a coincidence.

We eat in a comfortable silence, and I'm glad. I love this time with Eddie. I don't have to keep up conversation, or host, or entertain with him. I can just be, and I haven't had this kind of peace in forever. With everything about the ceremony and the James situation swirling in my mind, I don't have enough room to put on my mask of normalcy.

"Let's get going," Eddie says. He takes our plates, and we argue over who is going to clean them. He wins, but I refill our to-go cups, his with water and mine with tea, of course.

* * *

"So, what book did you want?" I ask, pressing on to the romance section of the bookstore. It's my favorite and, honestly, the only section I bother with. That I, until today. My eyes glaze over new and familiar covers as Eddie grabs my arm and steers me towards a section I typically don't even process exists: the self-help section. "Eddie," I mumble, my bear growling with me.

Those books were, I'm not sure how to describe them exactly, smart? I could admit that, but where was the excitement? Where is the thrill? The love and angst? I roll my head to the side, bringing Eddie into view, who acts as if he is about to burst with laughter.

"It's Rich D—"

"Do you want me to read one of these?" I interrupt as my shoulders slump. I only then realize I might be dumping on a genre that he might enjoy, and the guilt of being a hater is filling my stomach with rocks. I stand up straight, trying to fix my face into a cheerful smile. "I mean, do you like this genre? What's your favorite—"

"I'm messin' with you. There is not a single book on your shelf that isn't a romance, and believe me, I checked everywhere. But I do have a book recommendation I think you might like." He guides me back to the romance section, searching through the alphabetized books. I'd probably already read it, but for him, I'd read it again.

He lands on a book with a couple holding a basketball in their hands. "I think we'd both love this," he says, pulling two copies off the shelf. "It's about a woman who falls for a ballplayer who turns out to be an ass, and then she falls for another ball player while trying to get away from the original one. It's got love, thrill, and sports. A little something for both of us. People rave about it online."

"You did research for our next book?" I ask.

"Yeah, your recommendations are great, but I wanted something that would be new to both of us."

"Eddie," I say on a ghost of a whisper, smiling so hard my cheeks hurt. Eddie is thoughtful. He is kind, funny, and cuddly. He's everything. I stare at him as he holds two books in his hands. His eyes meet mine, and his face flushes. Actually flushes. His shoulders become hunched slightly, and he quickly looks away, as if embarrassed.

"If you don't think you'll like it—"

"I'll love it. I just, I don't know, that is incredibly sweet." I cut him off before he can downplay the kind act he'd done for me. I grab his shoulder to raise myself to press a kiss to his cheek, catching the corner of his lip. It isn't nearly enough to express my happiness, but for now it will have to do. "Thank you, Mr. Enchanted."

"You're welcome, Buttercup." I can hardly hold his gaze. Intense instinct and hard-to-get-rid-of thoughts cloud my mind as I turn to gaze at the other books. Is this what being with your mate is supposed to be like?

"How do you spend your free time?" I whisper, standing so close the only thing that separates us are the two books in Eddie's hands. "We are always wrapped up in me, and what I do. But what makes you happy, Eddie?"

"Willow, it's not like that." He shakes his head no, but he knows I'm right.

"But it is, even if you don't mind it. You're as much a person as me. What do you like to do?"

He takes a deep breath, his eyes straying away from mine. He ticks his head and shrugs a shoulder, as if there was an expansive list of things that makes him happy. "Hang out with you."

I glare, waiting for him to give me a genuine answer. "Eddie."

"I play video games. I hang out with my Pack, I work," he says, a sad smile playing on his face. "That's it."

"What games do you play?"

"Shooter games, sport games. It's fun, but"—he shrugs dejectedly—"It's never enough for people asking."

"It's more than enough for me," I say, already thinking of things we could do together. I could learn to play a game; shooters may even be fun. He already has the game station set up at my house. I just have to figure out which kind it is. "Have you heard of a game called Cooked and Booked?"

One of his eyebrows shoots up as he thinks about the question. "No, you play it?"

"No, but I saw an ad for it, and I thought it could be fun. It's a cooking game. Let's get it."

His smile is soft now, and his eyes are glued to mine. I take his arm and lead him to the checkout line. "You know there's this cute panda character in the game, and I call dibs on it."

"You can have whatever you want, Willow."

To think I was sleeping on video games my entire life is a crime all in itself. I figured out that Eddie has multiple game consoles, and the one game I wanted to play was, of course, on a different one. So, once we got home, we picked a game he called "easy," but this game was honestly hard as a ceramic teapot. As much as I wanted to continue to try to get one win, the pre-ceremony family dinner is coming up, and we have to leave soon if we are going to make it on time.

As much as I want to "forget" the dinner and show up at the ceremony tomorrow all innocently, Eddie's excited to meet my deranged family. There's a twinkle in his eye, and maybe he doesn't realize I left Kaler City because of *both* Milo's parents and my parents. My parents were even more ruthless than the Barrows. Maybe that was because I sullied the family name by being left by my potential mate; even if it was by death, it was still an embarrassment. I guess it wasn't really by death, though, was it?

That disappointment is always an undercurrent in every glance and conversation we have together. I'm the disappointment in my family, and now that my sister, Harper, is getting mated, that pressure has intensified.

"Oh shit, it's already time to go. Are you ready, Willow?" Eddie asks as he turns off his game console. I sigh and lean back dramatically on my couch. I stare up at him as he starts to collect our bags and head towards the door. I should tell him the poop storm he is rushing into, but I also can't help but hope maybe my family will be on their best behavior. Maybe they'll even be happy that I'm moving on.

Big. Fat. Chance.

21

WILLOW

A HALF-HOUR LATER, EDDIE PARKS THE CAR IN the driveway of my childhood home. The home that wrapped its arms around me and squeezed till I nearly suffocated. My hackles are up; my bear is already pacing inside me, and I hate feeling this way. I have an itch to protect myself. This is my family. These people are supposed to choose me, and I them, over anything, over everything, yet it isn't, and probably will never be, the case. They choose reputation, and I choose myself.

"Eddie, don't talk too much," I say out of pure nervousness. I can hardly breathe as we sit in the car staring at the house. "Just smile and wave, nothing more, nothing less."

"Willow, I'm not going to spend the whole weekend with my lips sealed," he says with a laugh. Gosh, how I wish I could have even a sliver of his easygoing nature. *Share some of that energy, you selfish, unsuspecting black bear.*

"I might," I mutter, looking away from the house and back at him. "Eddie, it might save your life." And mine. It would definitely save mine.

"Let's go. I've got to meet the people who raised such a wonderful, beautiful woman and forced her to fight this world on her own," Eddie says, popping out of the car and opening my car door. I'm sick with nerves. I think I might throw up. I could cry and puke all at the same time as Eddie and I walk up the perfectly maintained pathway to the front door.

Landing a knock on the door, I take a step back and wait. Eddie is by my side. His tall stature shadows mine, and I'm grateful for it. I stare up at Eddie, who stands tall and strong next to me. He's smiling, as he always does. This would probably be the best part of tonight. It sure is the easiest. I hope he won't lose that smile of his tonight. I think this all would hurt worse if he lost that twinkle of joy in his eye.

"Willow, baby, come in." My mother answers the freshly painted white door. Her honey-slick voice coats Eddie's first impression, I'm sure. He gives me a quick look with a raised brow. *You wait, big guy. Just wait, Eddie Enchanted, you'll see.* A fake smile takes over my face as my mom dives forward for a hug. "I didn't think you'd show."

"I called yesterday to remind you I was coming," I say shortly as the dramatics begin to unravel from her too-tight top bun.

"Yes, but who knew if our little runaway was going to show her darling face again?" Her voice is sweet to the ears but sharp to the heart.

"I was here last month and a couple of months before

that," I remind her as our little group ventures to the dining room table where everyone is already sitting.

"So, this is the plus one? Eddie Enchanted, was it? It is nice to meet you, young man," my father says, standing from the table to shake Eddie's hand. "Dinner is at 5:30, so we started eating, but you can still make yourself a plate."

Dinner is at 5:30 p.m. every day on the dot, and as I check the time on my phone, it is 5:45. We are late. Traffic was terrible on our way here, hence our lateness, though my family wouldn't care. All that mattered was that we were late.

As we walk into the room, grimaces are worn on everyone's faces. *Way to go, Willow. Of course, this visit is going to start off on a bad note.*

"I apologize for my lateness," I mutter. The family here includes my parents, my sister, and her soon-to-be mate. Eddie and I load up our plates and sit at the table covered with a white tablecloth, surrounded by plastic-wrapped chairs.

Eddie is taking my advice and remaining quiet, and while I gave him the advice, it brings a whole new wash of discomfort. The stiffness in his posture tells me he is uncomfortable, and I bet it's because I told him to be quiet. Oh, why did I say that? I hate I did that. I should've kept my mouth closed.

I went and made the one person I care the most about at this table uncomfortable, and for what? So I could please people who would never be pleased with me? Gosh, this dinner is going terribly in the three minutes I've been here. I want to drag Eddie away and apologize, but I think he'd be more upset if I did. I don't know. Maybe he wouldn't? I don't know how much more tension I can take.

This dinner is the opposite of what it would be like if we had dinner in my own home. My velvet chairs are soft and cushy, and my table is a gorgeous wood, and most of all, it's comfortable. I've always had the desire to be loud when it comes to home decor. I once thought it was my version of a rebellious streak or a phase I was going through with all my newfound freedom. Except I never grew out of the phase, and now it is identified as a part of my personality.

"What a beautiful home you have, Mr. and Mrs. Buttercup," Eddie comments, gesturing his hands at my parent's home. It's beautiful in a way I could now identify as different and not bland or bad. It's an accurate representation of my parents who live their lives to be prim, proper, and orderly.

"Why, thank you, young man," my mother says. My mother wears pearls that would adjust to her bear shifter size. She is the type of woman who wears a tweed suit every day, not only for church on Sundays. A prim and proper woman, and I loved that about her as a kid, and maybe I still do love that about her. The more I think about it, it's not the persona she puts on that irks me anymore. It's the constant disappointment that I can't bear.

"See, happiness is out there for you. What a nice man you've brought home," my father quips with an easygoing smile on his face.

"Thank you, Dad. Eddie is quite wonderful," I say, offering Eddie a small smile hoping he will relax again.

"But is it appropriate for you to be dating again? Your

mate died, and now you're, what? Whoring yourself out?" My mother's words flare into a flame of rage in my stomach, and I can't help the tightness appearing in my smile. Eddie raises his brows as he drops his fork from his fingers and onto his plate with a crash. The crash that gets this party started. He turns his head to my mom, maybe to say something, maybe to stare in shock, but I quickly shake my head no. There's no reason to put him in the hot seat.

"I think the kids call it 'casual' nowadays, Mom," Harper says, raising her fork to her lips.

"Causal? This man probably has a mate out there that wouldn't appreciate him here with another woman."

"Eddie," I correct, my voice low, staring at Eddie's hand resting on my lap under the table. I know what she is doing and won't let it continue. Eddie has a name. He is more than a fling or an undeserving boyfriend who won't last.

"Excuse me?" my mother scoffs, openly glaring at me. My mother's eyes narrow and slice into my soul. As a kid, that would follow me into the pits of self-loathing and despair, but now, the cuts don't slice as deep. I straighten my posture and move my gaze towards the quiet crowd as if I am unbothered. If they want a show, I guess I will give it to them.

"His name is Eddie Enchanted."

"I know." *Then act like it.*

"Harper, congratulations on the engagement and the upcoming mating ceremony." Eddie slides into the conversation, giving my thigh a squeeze. I appreciate what he is doing, but my bear is riled up at the disrespect from our mother. One thing I can't quite get a handle on is my bear.

Even as a cub, disrespect bothered her to the core so much, everyone was surprised I didn't present as an Alpha.

"Thank you, Eddie. This is Jason. He's a shy one, but he's my one and only." Harper laughs as Jason gives her a quick kiss on her cheek. I see the shows of affection in slow motion as if it was a movie, the kind of love she's found. I am thrilled for my sister. The love glistens off her skin, and her face, gosh, her face glows with joy. Love looks happy on Harper, but it makes me wonder if love ever looked that good on me? My eyes are stuck on Eddie, who sits directly under one light from the chandelier. His brown skin is smooth and moisturized. It appears darn near edible. Being in his presence and having his touch isn't enough. I want to be fully consumed by him. I want every look and every emotion to be mine. His smile goes from cheek to cheek, and he appears happy now while engaged in conversation with my sister.

With my focus almost completely on him, the dinner flies by. We eat, and Eddie holds a polite conversation with everyone and keeps his left hand on my thigh the entire time. I wonder if he sees why I left. It feels dramatic to have left town and dropped contact, but I couldn't do this anymore. The constant insults, reprimands, and nasty comments—I couldn't do it.

It all is so normal when I'm in this house, surrounded by the wallpaper of my childhood. For a while I didn't know families didn't speak to each other in this way. It's only my mother and her circle here in Kaler City. It's generational too. Her mother spoke like this to her, and my mother repeated the cycle with me. My mother knows nothing different, or maybe she chooses not to know anything different.

I don't know why she chose to hate me. I don't know why she chose to repeat this cycle of hate. We are supposed to be a family, not whatever this is.

Even with her harsh words today, it doesn't feel that bad right now. It's not that bad when he's here. When I have him, nobody else matters.

The smiles disappear as my mom and I enter the kitchen with dirty dishes. My mom sets the pile of dishes in her hands into the sink and backs away to lean against the island.

"Willow," my mother's voice hisses out in a whisper. I stare as she crosses her arms over her chest. I wash the dishes from dinner as my mother begins her rant of the hour.

She's standing behind me, breathing down my neck. It's a tactic she's used my whole life, and yet it still makes me feel inferior. Heat radiates off her and comes to suffocate me as she takes a deep breath before opening her argument. "Don't you ever disrespect me ever—"

"Or you'll do what, Mother? Why is it okay to be rude to my guest, but, goddess forbid, I forget one of your guests' names at any of the events you dragged me to? Please."

"Milo's death isn't an excuse—"

"No, Mother. It's not about Milo or his death. It's about me growing up. I'm well past the age of taking disrespect," I say, keeping my back turned. I hate not facing her, but it's the only way I can talk back to her.

Our hushed tones don't keep the tense air from

moving through the rest of the house. I quickly finish the dishes, trying to end the fight before it gets worse. I dry my hands and move to walk out of the kitchen as if nothing happened. But I stop and stare back at my mother. Her brows furrow, and it's almost as if she's stuck in the moment. Her brows unfurl and she forcefully exhales.

She looks tired. Not as in sleepy, but tired as in she's lived a long life of regrets. She leans against the counter again and twiddles a kitchen towel. "I'm—I know," she mutters and throws her head back, exhaling with a sharp laugh. She's laughing at herself? Or at me? I hear her exhale again, as if she's taking calming breaths, when she suddenly swivels around away from me and into my father's arms. My mother's shocked gasp knocks me back into reality.

"Dear, please come with me," my father says with his hand wrapped around her arm. He is a changed man ever since he got sick. He is now a man who walks with a cane at an age way too young for a shifter. He got sick with what a witch thinks is similar to meningitis. My mother had to call a witch to come heal him, and even then, they called me to come home in case it was time to say goodbye. I'd never seen a shifter, let alone my dad, so sick before.

He shifted back and forth from his human skin to his bear many times, trying to activate his body's healing, but it didn't work. The family witch couldn't figure it out as it's never happened before. It left us stumped and confused and praying to the Moon Goddess more times than, at least, I ever had. This is my dad. Even with everything, this man is still my dad.

Magic isn't always reliable, and he can still get sick. He

gently grabs my mother's hand as if they were dancing in the kitchen, like they used to when we were kids. Bringing her hands up to kiss the backs, he leads her out of the kitchen. Instantly calming me down. He is the calm to my mother's storm. He is her rock, and he had been dying.

As much as I want to be mad at my mom, and him even, for the way they spoke to me now and growing up, I can't. Not forever.

I finally look around the room, my checks ablaze with heat. The tile floor is chipping at its corners, and the walls have grease stains. My family is falling down a deep rabbit hole none of us know how to crawl out of.

Eddie steps into the kitchen, leaning in the archway in front of me where I stand frozen. He brings his long arms out and scoops me into a warm bear hug, wrapping his arms around my back and letting me tuck my head into his neck. Gosh. I knew bringing him here would be hard. It's hard to let others see your crumbling walls and rocky foundations, and he got a front and center view of my entire family's crusted walls.

"I'm sorr—" He cuts me off with a hum and a squeeze. Lightly shaking his head no against mine.

He's my rock. He's my rock, and he's here. I have to remember that.

"You had to ruin the dinner right before my mating ceremony, didn't you?" Harper whispers, walking around us. Harper's anger is much like our mother's, and right now, I didn't want to keep the flames going. I'm tired of these fractured relationships. I'm content in Eddie's arms, but Eddie's bear must not have liked the comment because he growls at Harper as she takes our mother's place by the island.

Jason, Harper's soon-to-be mate, doesn't appreciate that and follows with a glare so sharp I feel it in my back, and his growls soon fill the kitchen. Eddie is a newcomer, and I honestly am shocked by the growl he let out, but now he snaps his head away from mine and pushes me to stand behind him as he bares his teeth at Jasper.

Harper keeps her distance as Jasper wraps his arms around her. Harper is smart enough not to get close, but not smart enough to stop running her mouth. "Now Dad's going to be stressed, and it's going to make his coughs worse. Only something you would know if you were around. Why does everything fall on me? The big sister—"

I pull away from Eddie, keeping my eyes trained on him. I stare at him and his molten eyes with a small smile on my face.

"I think it's time to go," I say, turning around to face my sister with my hands tangled in Eddie's. "I'm sorry things fall on you, but you need to stop letting them fall on you, Harper. You deserve better." And with that, I lead Eddie out of my childhood home.

THE FACT I'M STAYING IN A HOTEL ROOM INSTEAD of with my parents on this little trip back home is sure to make the rounds in the gossip circles. Waking up in Eddie's arms in a safe zone makes all the gossip I'm sure is spreading worth it. Thoughts of the mating ceremony flood my mind as I turn to face Eddie, who has one arm around me and one hand holding his phone.

We hadn't spoken about dinner last night. I haven't worked up the nerve to mention it, and he hasn't said anything either. I hope he knows how much I appreciated him last night. Milo never fought for me or pretended he even wanted to. He wasn't there with cuddles or whispering sweet nothings in my ear afterward. He was always stoic, staring off into space as if nothing happened, or even worse, like whatever my mother or sister spouted off was... right.

"Ready for today, Buttercup?" he asks as he shuts his phone off and cuddles into me. His eyelashes fluttering against my skin as he tucks his face into my neck. He is well, he is alive, and at least for now, he is mine.

Was our invite revoked after the fight? Or will my family pretend it didn't happen and go on as they normally do? I'm not even sure how I want to proceed. To bite the bullet and enjoy the event or stand my ground? The problem with that is that Harper is my sister, and though we might be fighting now, I want to be a part of her special day. I want to be accepted.

"As ready as I can be," I mumble, snuggling closer to his vanilla scent. "Eddie, you don't have to go—"

"If you're going, I'm going. No questions asked. Now get that cute ass out of bed."

Eddie nearly takes me with him as he moves off the bed to get ready, but I'm not nearly ready to actually get out of bed.

I watch Eddie get ready in a delicious two-piece brown suit instead. I don't have the heart to say we might not be invited anymore. He looks too good to let this outfit go to waste. I would hate to be denied entry to my own sister's ceremony; I couldn't chance him feeling rejected in any capacity, which means I should call the family to make sure we'll still be let in. Grabbing my phone, texts from the group chat come flooding in. Mostly from my mom, but a direct message comes from Harper.

I hope you're awake and getting ready.

The smile that crosses my face makes Eddie pause while buttoning up his black shirt. He crosses the room to grab my ankle and drag me so I'm practically under him, and he's standing over me. His brown eyes peer into mine with that shining smile he always has. "Willow."

"Yes?"

"Go see the outfit I packed for you. Please."

"What am I going to find?"

"Go and find out," he says, landing a kiss on my forehead and stepping away. I want his heat to consume me, but Moon Goddess knows we don't have time.

I guess it's time to get out of bed now. My feet drag along the floor as I leave the incredibly comfortable bed. I close the bathroom door behind me, pulling out my phone to call my sister. I wouldn't find the answers I needed by moping in my hotel bed. The rings go on and on, and just as I am about to give up hope, my sister finally answers. "Where the hell are you?" I hear her whisper-yell into the phone.

"We're still invited?" I ask, biting my lower lip in nervousness.

"Willow, are you serious right now? Get your ass here. I need you for the family photos." A smile breaks out on my face. We are still invited. Rushing from the bathroom, I hang up the phone with the promise to be there in twenty minutes.

"Eddie, we're still on. Like super on!" I excitedly shout as I grab my makeup bag.

"I knew we would be, Buttercup," he yells back as we switch places in getting ready. Thank goddess I could put myself together fast when I needed to. I wet down my hair, refreshing my curls, while running a hand down my face. I'd have to go basic with the makeup, and honestly, it was probably for the best since that's all I know how to do. Blending my blush in I catch a glimpse of the dress hanging on the curtain rod. I wasn't a huge fashionista like Flora, so when Eddie asked to pick my dress out, I was more relieved than anything. The dress is a beautiful silk maxi dress that hugs all my curves. This was one of those dresses I just had to have but never had anywhere to wear it to. This dress is stunning and was collecting dust both in my closet and in my mind. The warm orange color compliments my dark skin, and, gosh, how did he find this? Is this why he picked a brown suit over black?

I step out of the bathroom in my heels. Eddie is sitting on the bed with one leg off the bed and one leg on, his suit jack on but wide open. His glasses sit perfectly on his face, and I blush at the sight of my hot date. He is scrolling on his phone before he looks up at me. I have to admit; I am darn sure excited to be showing him off as my date. "Eddie, you are joyously handsome."

"And you are breathtakingly gorgeous," he replies easily. His eyes drip down my body, pressure following his eyes trail. I'm drawn forward by his eyes alone. No sooner am I tucked between his legs, one still bent to the side of me and the other planted on the ground as he leans up to kiss me. His lips consume mine, and I've got his neck trapped between my hands. I take each breath he slips between our lips. His tobacco and vanilla smell eats me up whole. He leans back, taking me with him before I snap back to reality, pushing away from his chest and standing up straight. We have a mating ceremony to go to. My sister's ceremony is not one I want to miss.

"Mmm, stop. We have a mating ceremony to go," I say, stepping out of his grasp. We have to save our smutty spicy time for later.

"Only if you say so. I'm itching to get another taste," he says, leaning up and trying to capture my lips again.

"Eddie Enchanted! Let's go," I nearly yell, pushing myself to stand out of reach. I pray my beet red blush will fade by the time we get to the venue. There is no way it will pass as makeup blush.

He swoops in behind me on my way down to the hotel lobby. His shadow takes hold of my body. He makes me whole. Beautiful. Enticing. He's made me feel more in the last couple of months than I had in my whole life before, and that thought is scary. The idea of ever being with Milo is horrifying. My sudden realization of Milo's family being at the ceremony crushes me like a grand piano. That sure knocks the blush off my face. In fact, I'm pretty sure I'm pale now.

"Oh my goddess," I mutter as Eddie opens the car door. I stand in the car doorway with my hand pressed against my lips. "I'm bringing a date."

I don't want to admit I'm scared of Milo's family's reaction to Eddie. Would hate be spewed at my sister's ceremony because I'm bringing a date? Should I stay home?

"Whatever horrid thoughts you're having right now aren't changing our plans. We're in this together, no matter what. Now get in the car, Willow." Eddie's voice is low and tight. He sends shock waves through my system, my head shooting up to look at Eddie.

I can't say anything, though. Not yet. My words tangle in my throat, and I can't get a full thought together. I only blink at him before getting into the car.

He reaches over me, pulling my seatbelt on, and I'm

too dazed to stop him. His switch flipped, and I think he knows what I was thinking. He doesn't say much, though. I don't know if my guilt for the hesitation is eating at me and causing me to overthink, but I hate that I hesitated in bringing Eddie. Eddie is—Eddie is mine. Right? He's mine. He's... my mate?

"Don't let the thoughts of others stop you," he grumbles. One hand on the wheel and the other caressing my thigh. I am trying to focus on his hand on me, his strong fingertips slightly digging in. He's right. Of course, he is right, logically. Emotionally, his words are easier to say than they were to do.

"How did you know?" I ask, staring at him as he keeps his eyes on the road.

"Nothing else could possibly ruin your excitement for your sister's mating ceremony. That's how I know." I let out a hum. It's about all I can do right now.

"It's hard," is all I can say, left speechless. "What if... what if you coming as my date causes problems? What if me coming at all creates an issue? I can't ruin her special day."

"That's not in your control. Harper invited you, did she not?"

"Well, yeah."

"Then she wants you to be there. I'm sure she's thought of all the potential conflicts that could arise, especially after last night, but she chose you," he says, like it is so simple. So obvious. Yet an arrow pierces my heart. She chose me. So I should choose myself too.

"Okay," I say as I slide my hand over his on my thigh. More and more, this man shakes the foundation of my center. At the time, I'd thought Milo was a great man, but I connected and communicated with Eddie on a level so deep and so different it shocks my system.

I know I was wrong.

We were wrong.

Milo couldn't have been my mate.

There is no way in this universe that he could have been my mate.

Not when Eddie makes me feel like this.

"Let's go have an amazing time, Buttercup," Eddie says, a smile finally reaching his eyes.

This man is my mate. There is no possible way that he isn't. Eddie Enchanted is my soul mate. He is the one destined for me by the Moon Goddess. He has to be.

"Eddie Enchanted, you're my—" I nearly stumble over my words in the sudden rush to get them out, which doesn't matter because he interrupts me.

"Don't rush it, Buttercup. I'll always be here." He holds out his hand for mine. Did he know what I was going to say? Why did he stop me?

As much as the rejection stings, I let it rest as he pulls into the parking lot of the venue. We step out together, hand in hand, as Harper and Jason walk over to greet us. It's amazing seeing all the guests and the surrounding beautiful forest that would please any bear shifter's soul. There isn't a white aisle for Harper to walk down. Instead, bear shifters have a round table outside big enough to fit an insane amount of guests with the couple of honor in a hole in the middle of the table.

There's a light tap on my shoulder, and I turn around to greet the first guest to break the ice on my attendance.

"Willow, I'm happy you're here," Sherry, one of the many bakers in Kaler City, says. She wears a snake-like smile, and her eyes glint with mischief. I knew eventually I would have to deal with this city's nosy-ass gossips.

"I wouldn't miss it for the world," I reply, a grim smile on my face. I glance at Eddie, who is trying to hold back a laugh by the way his shoulders keep trying to rise up. He slides his arm around my waist, pulling me comfortably into his side. He is here with me, proudly. I blush again and lean my head on his shoulder.

"After everything with Milo, I thought you'd never date again after your mate's death and everything." Sherry's bite is quick, and honestly, I'm thanking my mother's vileness at dinner for preparing me for the nasty citizens of Kaler City.

"You may not know everything like you think you do, Sherry." My mother comes up behind Sherry, causing the woman to jump and gasp with a hand on her chest. Both women glare at each other. "The art of minding our business has done wonders for our skin, don't you think, Willow? Maybe Sherry should try it."

"I'll get going. I have to congratulate the mating couple," Sherry excuses herself, rushing in the opposite direction.

"Isn't she a piece of work?" my mother comments, rolling her eyes. I'm not completely sure how to interact with her after our fight last night. Normally, she leaves me to the wolves, no pun intended, when it comes to the town's gossips. My mother appears to be over our fight, which is nice, of course. I never want my mother to be upset, but she was the offender, not the offended. It is up to me how I wanted to proceed, and to be honest, I'm not sure how I feel. I know I didn't have to forgive her for cruel words, but I feel guilty for holding on to my wounded heart. Always have and probably always will.

"Indeed, she was," Eddie cuts in. He gives my mom a small nod in acknowledgment as I remain still. I see a sharpness in his eyes, and it's the only sign I get of Eddie's dislike, or maybe awareness, of my mother. Is it shameful to have a quiver of happiness at seeing he's on my side? I mean, I should want Eddie to like my mother; in any normal situation that would be expected. But this isn't a normal situation, and I can't help the love that flows into my system as I catch the tiniest sign that he is on my side.

"She wasn't the first and she won't be the last," I mutter while bringing my drink to my lips. I'd dealt with about a dozen other Sherry's and lived with one for nineteen years. I didn't need my mother to step in. Though it was nice to be defended by her. It wasn't something that happened often, and I can appreciate the act. As nasty as it is, I am not ready to forgive her, not that she is even apologizing. "Enjoying the party?"

"Of course, dear. I planned it."

"It's nice to see one of your children mated off, huh?" I joke. Tender emotions of past comments made by the woman in front of me come to the surface, but I shoved them back down. Why bring up old drama now?

"Yes, Harper is happy, and I've come to learn that's all I can ask for," my mother says, glancing at me with an unreadable look. I would love my mom forever and always, but forgiving her was something that would have to be earned, not given.

"Willow, darling?" Wrinkles form around her eyes, showing the smallest amount of stress and maybe even worry.

"Yes?" I say, preparing for the mean comment she's bound to deal to me.

"I acted... foolishly last night. I'm... I apologize for my unkind words. I shouldn't have said them." Her eyes are downcast, and her shoulders are straight. She was never the woman to apologize for anything, yet here she is, giving her daughter her first apology.

"Thank you," I say. I'm not comfortable for much more than a thank you. What do you say to someone who's crushed you since you were a child? I can see she is a changing lady. I am a changing lady too. We were growing and changing, and I can't ask for anything more. But I can't forgive her like I wish I could.

I offer her a small smile before I take Eddie's hand and head towards the thickly wooded part of the forest. Standing on the outskirts of the event, we watch the crowds of people here to celebrate Harper's mating, and in a way, I'm happy she has all these people who celebrate her. As much as I wish to be part of their circle, I know I never will be. As cruel or nasty as small-town people can be, I still grew up with them, and a small part of me wishes I fit in with them.

"How are you doing?" Eddie asks. His presence suddenly covering my back as his body heat and hands wrap around my waist. He cuddles into me with his chin resting on my shoulder. With him here, I can breathe a little.

"I'm okay."

"But something still upsets you," he says, leaning his head on top of mine as we stand huddled together.

"I'm more realizing a loss, but then again, as much as I can try to fit myself in here, I've found a place where I don't have to try so hard. A place where I can be myself. Thank you, Eddie—" I turn around in his arms to face him, my eyes meeting his.

"Thank you for what, Buttercup?"

He interrupts me again. I was going to tell him he was mine, and somehow, I know it like I know how to breathe, yet he stopped me. Once could be an accident, but twice is... twice is definite. He isn't, I don't know, interested? "For being perfect," I say, pulling out of his arms slightly. "Let's go back."

"Willow, I see you've been doing well," a voice I didn't want to hear any time soon says. Mr. Barrow is a man who didn't give anyone a break, not me, not his kids, not even his wife. He's a tall, black bear shifter with the anger of a real brown bear. He's alone, which only makes me wonder if his mate is left mingling with the rest of the guests alone. It wouldn't be a surprise to me if she was.

More importantly, though, are the words that spark from my memory when his face comes into view. When Layla said Milo *and her parents* sold her off to the BSM. It wasn't only Milo who took part in Layla's misery; it was them, too.

My teeth itch as my canines try to come forward. As much as I want to fight this man today, Harper and Jason catch my eye. I can't ruin their day. I don't want to let the crimes committed against Layla go unpunished, though. Was it even my punishment to deal out?

I don't bother saying hello back. Instead, I raise my eyebrows and scowl at the man.

"Impolite, as always, Willow." He rolls his eyes, and it takes me back to all the "family" dinners we used to have when Milo was "alive." The arguments, the storming out, the insincere apology gift the next day; it all is a vicious cycle that they keep living in.

"Is there something we can help you with, Mr. Barrow?" Eddie says. His chest vibrates with a rumble, one I can only feel since I'm practically plastered to his side. I know he's trying to be on his best behavior, but he can only take so much and so can I.

"And of course, you bring a fake date. Are you not better than this? Did Milo mean nothing to you?"

"Let's go, Willow," Eddie says. His body trembles, and his hand is a band of steel around mine.

"Running scared again?" No, Mr. Barrow. No. Why did you say that? I watch Eddie, who's stopped walking and marches right up in Mr. Barrow's face.

"You don't get to disrespect her, not after she fought more for your own son than you did. Not when she gave a home to your daughter after the hell you put her through. Not when she's been nothing but kind to your family, even after all the shit you've pulled."

"Don't you speak to me like that." Mr. Barrow is shaking with anger and he's now yelling.

"Please, the last person I want to be talking to is someone whose kids ran away from him," Eddie says, trying to guide us away from the angry bear. Mr. Barrow goes to swing at Eddie, but I yank Eddie down towards me. Mr. Barrow's fist scrapes my arm, and even though the punch barely hit me, it frickin' hurt. I try to keep my face neutral so that Eddie won't notice that the hit landed on me, but I can't hold back the grimace of pain.

"Swinging on someone's back, Mr. Barrow? Really?" I ask, trying to grip Eddie's suit jacket. It's as if I disappeared because Eddie turns around with a force I've never seen and punches Mr. Barrow, making his head turn. He steps to the side to balance himself, but it doesn't matter because he loses his battle with gravity and hits the floor.

I yell Eddie's name, but he hardly hears me. All the acknowledgment I get is a slight push back, moving me out of the way as he charges Mr. Barrow again.

Eddie laughs, but it's not his soothing laugh, not his laugh that lights up a room. He chuckles darkly as he nods his head as if something is clicking in his mind.

"You fucking touched her! Hell no, let's get this party started for real," he says, taking off his jacket and tossing it on the ground.

Eddie shifts into his bear, ripping his brown suit off entirely in the shift, and so does Mr. Barrow, and they're swinging. Their claws are swiping at each other, but Mr. Barrow is no match for a younger, angrier bear.

Eddie's drawing blood, and I watch as a crowd forms. I see Mrs. Barrow rushing to the front, yelling for Mr. Barrow to stop. My parents, Harper, and Jason, are making their way towards me.

I can't decipher their faces, but I pick up on the fear. My hackles raise, and a sudden whoosh of terror and sadness covers every inch of my body. I move my eyes to Eddie's bear, who is playing with Mr. Barrow now. He circles him like bait with a bearish smile and anger still lingering in his eyes.

Disrespect is a hard limit for shifters, for Alphas and Lunas especially. It's a huge mistake to disrespect someone in an Alpha's presence, let alone to disrespect an Alpha, but Eddie isn't an Alpha. I've never seen him this angry before. I've never seen him angry. He's happy. He's laughing. He's Eddie. But I guess everyone has limits, and I feel horrible for not sensing that Eddie was closer to his limit than I recognized.

I'm not stupid enough to jump between two bear shifters fighting. No one is. All that matters is dominance, and what comes from living in a world ruled by dominance is fighting. It's not completely abnormal for a fight to break out at events, but this, this is different.

It's for me. It's for Layla. It's for the families we lost.

A sick sort of pleasure takes root in my mind, in my bear, and this is just another part of me I don't like. My bear takes great pleasure in being defended, but I, human me, can't take the guilt in my stomach for putting Eddie in a situation where he'd have to protect me.

"Eddie, please, let's go." I can't take it anymore. I need to leave, and I need Eddie to come with me.

I need Eddie to be okay, and I need him to stop fighting before my bear makes her appearance. She getting mad about the blood on his arms from the hits Mr. Barrow landed, and she sure as hell doesn't like the cut stretching across his waist.

My desperation must have reached his ears because he shoves Mr. Barrow away and stalks towards me. Still in bear form, he picks me up in his arms and storms away. I curl around him. He's incredibly strong, and I won't pretend my size twenty-two ass is small.

He shifts, and the skin of his human body rubs against me as he carries me away. I wrap my arms around his neck as he carries me all the way to the car and gently sets me down. He carefully puts my seat belt on before shutting my door. He stops by the trunk to get some clothes, I assume, then storms to his side and gets into the driver's seat.

We ride to the hotel in silence. I don't know what to say, and I'm full of emotions that anything I could say would get choked up in my throat.

When we enter the hotel room, he shuts the door and takes my hand. Sitting on the bed next to each other, the only thing filling the silence is the sound of our harsh breathing.

"I'm sorry, Willow." His voice comes out harder and lower than I've heard it. His hand is shaking, and grips mine tighter, as if I would float away.

"No, I'm the one who is sorry, Eddie. I've dragged you to this ceremony without checking in on you, or—or anything—and I'm sorry."

"Willow, you have nothing to be sorry about. I'm the one who lost control. I'm the one who ruined your sister's mating ceremony and probably your relationship with her, fuck."

"Eddie, I'm not mad, and I'm not worried about Harper. She chose me, remember? I'm worried about you. You need to shift again and heal that scratch, please," I say. I try to stand up to give him room, which he must not have liked because his arm shoots out fast and yanks my body, so I'm on top of him completely. His chest rise and falls under me as his arms wrap around me, and his legs open up to give me more room.

"You should be mad, Willow. I embarrassed you."

"I couldn't be mad at you. I couldn't be embarrassed by you, Eddie. You are the only person here who stuck up for me. You didn't hesitate. You didn't care who was watching. You stood up for me. How could I possibly be mad at you?"

He takes a deep breath in and out. A breath that calms him and me.

"If anything, I'm the one that's sorry," I say, and there's an undeniable smile on my face that I can't get rid of. He's not mad at me.

"Willow, say you're sorry again, and I'm gonna have to fill your mouth with something else." He chuckles, and I see the Eddie I recognize is coming back to me.

"Will I like that something else?" I laugh between the kisses as I trail down his neck and chest. I can't get the words to come out about how turned on I am by him fighting for me, but maybe words aren't the only way to let him know.

"You wanna find out?"

"I do, I really do," I say, getting to the waistband of his shorts. I know he has nothing on underneath, and that gets me wetter than I already am.

Suddenly, a phone ringing ruins the moment. I rest my forehead on his stomach as he lets a strained laugh out. He mutters a curse as I sit up and reach for the phone. My father's name comes up on the screen. I let out a huff and move to answer the darn thing. I remain on top of Eddie, and his grip on my hips doesn't give me much room to move.

"Dad?"

"Willow, are you okay?" My eyebrows scrunch, and the skin around my cheeks get tight. He's wondering if I'm okay? Was this his gateway into a lecture on how I should have seen this coming and done more to prevent it?

"Yes, Dad. Are *you* okay?" I ask, barely holding the surprise in my voice back. I always feel as if I am a little girl with her hand stuck in the cookie jar when it came to my dad. With my mom, we were always on the opposite ends of a battlefield, but with Dad, I constantly strived to be his little girl and had never earned the title. Not at five and not at twenty-five.

"Oh, pumpkin, I'm fine. Harper and your mother are losing their minds, yelling at the Barrows, but we both know those two were itching for a fight." He laughs as a cough comes through the line. "Two peas in a pod, those two are."

"Yeah, two peas in a pod," I mumble. It's one thing to be on the phone with my dad, and another to do so while straddling Eddie's legs. His hand settle on my hips, his thumb rubbing back and forth on my hip comfortably. It's not sexually charged anymore, but it still is off. I move up higher on his stomach, just in case. "We're fine, both us of are okay," I say, only for a lack of things to say. How did one conversate with their dad after so many years?

"Make sure Eddie shifts a few times. Mr. Barrow is old

but he got a few licks on him. No need for pride to get in the way of having smooth skin. Trust me."

"I will," I say, my eyes landing on the shifter under me. He smiles, as I'm sure he can hear both sides of this conversation. My dad says goodbye and hangs up as I toss my phone on the chair next to the bed.

"You have orders from the old and mighty Mr. Buttercup, young man, and I happen to agree with the man I call a father, so you, my kind sir, need to shift and heal."

"I do?" he says, leaning up on his elbows. His face is carrying the same smile I thought I lost, and, gosh, it's good to have him back.

"Yes, you do. Let's go. I'm sure my parents won't mind you shifting on their land."

"Do you want to visit your parent's house now? Are you sure you want to face the angry bears of the Buttercup household?"

"Good question, but if it means you'll heal, then I'm ready to do anything." It's an easy question, and one I didn't need to pause and think about. For Eddie Enchanted, I'm ready to do anything.

"Hold on, someone's calling me." He grabs his phone from his pocket, which is silently vibrating. If another phone rings today, I think I'm going to lose my ever-loving mind. Eddie answers, and his face sets into an immediate frown. Dread bubbles in my gut, and suddenly, my head gets light, and my body gets shaky. He pulls the phone from his ear before putting it on speaker.

"Willow, can you hear me?" Felix's voice comes through, and I'm not sure if it's me or the phone, but my instincts know this isn't going to be good. I answer with a low confirmation, and my eyes stay glued to the phone as if all my answers will come shooting out of it.

"Layla's missing."

Layla's missing?

Layla's missing.

My brows furrow so hard a headache is building, and I can't stop shaking. Am I about to shift? I can't. I know I can't, I won't have any control, and my bear is too emotional to let me see or hear anything. I'll lose precious hours in finding Layla. I grasp my elbows and squeeze in an attempt for control. "Where is Dylan?" I ask. If anyone can find someone, it's him.

"He had an impromptu assignment, but he's on his way. Even then, we can't wait for him," Felix answers.

"How long has she been missing?" Eddie asks as I slide off him, and he moves around the room. He's packing our bags, and I sit, watching him. I can't move. Not yet. My steady control is lost, and I know that Layla missing is probably my fault. I shouldn't have come to this darn wedding. Not with Milo somewhere out there. Was it him? I should have forced her to come. I should have... I don't know. Would they have taken me instead? Was it James? Did he trick us? My eyes shoot up to Eddie's.

"Where is James?" I ask on a whimper.

"We've got him. Come home," Felix says before disconnecting the line.

"Let's go, Willow." Even when one of our own is in danger, he still reaches for me with grace and gently pulls me up from the bed. His hand lands on the small of my back, and thank goodness for that.

Layla is missing. My arms are still shaking, and my bear is pacing inside me. She's getting riled up, and the flames of her anger heating my skin. I only take deep breaths, trying to do everything in my power to keep from shifting in Eddie's car.

MY PHONE SITS IN MY LAP THE WHOLE DRIVE back to Rainfall Avenue. Once the Enchanted Pack house's white front door comes into view, I launch myself out of the car and up the steps of their front porch.

I whip the door open, and my heart stops for the briefest moment. The sight I'm greeted with warms my harshly beating heart and makes my eyes water slightly. Biting the inside of my cheek, I try to hold back the waterworks.

The whole gang's here. Luxe, Flora, Jackson, and the whole Pack are standing around a table in the living room, waiting for us to arrive. They turn to me quickly. Remi, the teenage temporarily adopted vampire, zooms to me and now Eddie, who drops our bags on the floor. Her eyes rush over us, checking us over, lifting our arms as she needs to before crushing us into hugs. I'm surprised, to say the least, since we didn't know each other well, but I welcome her hug, anyway. Maybe she can sense how badly

I need it. Vampires can sense emotions, and I am all over the place.

"When's the last time you heard from Layla?" Jackson asks us immediately as he leans against the table everyone is standing around. With the break in formation, I can see the notes they've accumulated on Layla. Every member had recounted the last time they saw Layla and when they noticed she was missing.

My eyes stay on the board. Felix was at my house yesterday, waiting for her to come home from work when she never came. He called the Pack, and they checked her job, the grocery store, gas station, and both our houses and found nothing. Not a scratch, not a scent, only her car parked on the side of a road.

I gulp, sliding my phone from my pocket. I should call her. I should try. What have I done since finding out she was missing? Absolutely nothing. Sat on my dumb shaking hands for a half-hour in the car. I need to do something. Something needs to happen. My fingers can barely select her name in my contacts, and I miss the call button a few times due to my shaky state. Each ring sets loose any grasp of control I had. Fat tears roll down my face, each one going faster and faster as they roll down my cheek. I stare at the board on the table. I can't look at the Pack right now. I can't show them my shame.

Layla, I'll find you. I'll save you, I promise. Just answer the phone. Please. Please answer the phone.

"I'm away from the phone. Leave a message or, better yet, text me." Beep.

The phone is in my hand one moment, and the next it's flying across the room, where I hoped the wall would smash the useless thing to pieces, but Dylan catches it with one hand. "If she gets the chance to call, she'd call you, Willow. We need your phone."

The silence is deafening, and the ring of silence gets louder as the attention is turned on me.

"I need her, Dylan." My fingers shake as my composure breaks down. I nearly crumble.

"I know." He says it with so much confidence, I can almost breathe normally. But it doesn't feel real. It doesn't feel as if he understands, and if anyone in this room understands what I'm going through, I know it's him. I know it was his mate who went missing when her coworkers kidnapped her. I know this, yet it doesn't feel right. It's as if I'm all alone. That no one is here but me on this island of shame and guilt.

It's my fault.

I shouldn't have left her. I shouldn't have pretended that life was normal when it was anything but.

"I have to find her."

"We will."

"She's my family." I don't know who I'm reminding at this point, but I'm lost.

"We're going to find her, Willow. We do things as a Pack. We are strongest when we all work together, and today, that goal is finding and returning Layla back home. We are going to find Layla," Jackson says with a conviction I wish fazed me.

I turn back towards the table with a nod. We are going to find her, and I'm going to bring her back home.

Eddie's presence swallows me from behind. Towering over me as his arms come around me, caging me in as he leans on the table. He's speaking, but I can't hear him. Not until he leans in and whispers directly into my ear. "Willow, Buttercup, my love, we've got this. I got you, and we'll get her."

Ice chips off the glacier that is my body, and I can move. I wobble back and forth a bit, only noticeable to me and him before I stand straight. He doesn't realize that as long as he is with me, as long as everyone in this room is associated with me, this will keep happening. People will keep getting hurt, and it is because of me.

I wanted to be a main character but not in this kind of story.

"Where's Ghost?" I ask. The sadness deepens in my chest, but anger bubbles there too. What does he know? Was this a part of his plan the whole time? The thoughts run through my mind, but my feet are faster. My vision blurs, and I move by pure instinct. I dip under Eddie's arms and dodge the lame attempts to stop my moving form. Ghost steps from around the corner, but it's his scent that makes me run faster. He gets to stand here with us, free, while Layla is moons knows where. No, this isn't just my fault, it's his, too.

I land a slap across Ghost's face.

"It's James. Ghost is my cover name," he says with his face turned to the side, but his arms still crossed. While I may not have been strong, my bear is, and she's as sad and angry as I am. Layla is mine, she is my family, and she means the world to me, and yet she's not here.

I don't stop at one slap. Wide palms and nails scratching, I land more and more blows. He took her. That damn dog. I bet he's a wolf shifter. He took my Layla. Dogs love to take things. I should've known not to trust him. I scream as I launch my attack. I'm getting stronger as he takes my hits, and it's making me mad he isn't fighting back.

"Where is Layla, you shit" I yell, with no answer in return. His hard eyes stare at me, and his body barely flinches as I land another blow.

"Willow, stop!" Luxe's Alpha voice streams into my ears, and Eddie's hands wrap around my arms as pulls me flush against him. I try to get free, digging my nails into his arms, but it does nothing but make him hold me tighter. His strong arms bands around my body, and his scent only takes a moment to completely surround me. I blink a few times, trying to focus on Ghost, but my mind is pulled away from him and onto the tobacco and vanilla in my air.

My mind is racing, and my bear is flaming mad, yet a tingle in my stomach grows, and the guilt of what I've done forms like boulders. I hit Ghost—I mean James. I attacked James. I stare at James. He's barely ruffled, but that's not the point. He stands strong and nods at me. But that's not enough. Not for me.

"James, I'm... oh my goodness, I'm sorry. I shouldn't have. You should have kicked my butt." He didn't even try to fight back.

"Consider us even for the tea lacing," he says before going to see the board. I watch as he walks past Eddie and me. He purses his lips. Maybe he's helping, maybe he's still working for Milo, but now that I see him, he doesn't appear happy, or even neutral.

He looks mad.

I match my breaths to Eddie's, with his arms still

wrapped tightly around me. There is just one thing that doesn't sit right with me. One thing I should've been focusing on when I was in Kaller City. "Do you know what Milo did?"

"I intended to find out, but I wouldn't keep hurting you or Layla to figure it out."

"What properties does he own? What name would they be under? Are there any abandoned buildings nearby? She could be anywhere. We have next to nothing on this guy," Luxe says, sidestepping me and Eddie. She has a marker in her hands, and she leans over the table to write.

"Why is this important?" River, the youngest member of the Enchanted Pack, asks, running a hand over his short locs. His eyes find Jackson's, knowing if anyone was going to answer him, his Alpha would.

"Milo took Layla. She was a target too," Jackson answers.

She was a target. How could I forget she was a target? How could I have let her out of my sight?

"Where could she be?" I hear River ask. I pinch my eyebrows. I'm more confused now that I'm on the brink of something, and it flushes my cheeks in frustration. We're all staring into space with thoughts not connected enough to say out loud.

"What are we going to do?" I mumble and look towards Eddie. He's got the same saddened expression on his face and has me wrapped tight in his arms as if he's afraid of losing me too.

"I'll find her," James says as he stalks out the door to goodness knows where, leaving no room for questions.

"Jackson?" River asks, for what I'm not sure. What am

I supposed to do with that? *"I'll find her."* Okay, where? What does he know that we don't, and why didn't he bother to share?

"One of us should follow him," I say. "Where do we go from here? He obviously knows where she is, or at least has an idea—"

"Willow, go take a shower," Jackson demands, pointing to the stairs.

"A shower?" Confusion is the top emotion I've experienced in the last twenty-four hours, and it seems even around my most trusted group of people, the emotion continues to choke me.

"Yes, go take a shower, and Eddie, go with her. Take a moment to breathe, then meet us back down here, and Felix—go with James, and the rest of us will work on a Plan B. Go."

I have little experience with an Alpha, even less with Alphas in a crisis, but a shower will not help anything. Our focus should be on Layla. What if—

"We'll be right back." The voice is a whisper that warms me head to toe, and I move instinctively. I don't say anything, and my mind turns off. I'm in the presence of the one man that has stuck by me since day one, and my body knows if anything, I can trust him. We move together. We breathe together. And for a moment, I can pretend we will be together forever.

24

GHOST—JAMES

"Where are we going?" Felix asks as he slides into the front seat of my car. My eyes narrow at him as he buckles his seatbelt. "Safety first, you fucking weirdo. Don't make me ask again."

I shake my head and turn on the car. The Alpha probably ordered him to come along, and I can't blame the guy since they don't know me. Not as much as I know them.

It's not only Layla I've been watching.

"Milo, used to meet in person since technology can be traced; he wasn't the fucking brightest. There's an abandoned apartment building nearby—it's the only place I can think of," I say, peeling out of the driveway.

The building is old as shit and rotting from the inside out. It's on the outskirts of town, and with how far it is, I'm not surprised no one lives here.

I park the car, and we stand outside for only a moment. Only enough for me to say, "You can start at the top. I'll start from the bottom. We used to meet at the on the top floor. You'll most likely find her first. She'll be more comfortable with you than me." The lie rolls off my tongue, and when he nods his head in agreement, I smirk as I make my way to the basement where Milo and I actually used to meet. The guy was so damn obvious. How did he live this long being this stupid? He is rich, I guess that must help a lot.

"Hello, sweetheart," I say as I enter the basement. Layla's eyes are wide, and the gag in her mouth is soaked in spit. Her little muscles strain against her skin. My goddess, she's gorgeous. She's a goddess in distress, and the only thing wrong with this picture is that I didn't cause her distress. The terror wasn't caused by me or in my control, and for that, Milo will have to pay. For a blood sister, he's treated her as a scorned lover, and that fact confused me almost enough to wonder why.

Such a simple job turned into a cluster fuck, and it's all because of one fucking girl. One girl has changed the course of my life, and not only have I rejected a 500k dollar job, but now I'm going after my employer.

Milo tested me. He played right into a game he won't survive. I told that motherfucker to lay a hand on what's mine. I told him to try, and he did. I could smile at the stakes of this game, and I can't believe I got the chance to play. He better hope the Enchanted Pack gets to him before I do. There is no moral code or council that could stop the wrath from coming his way.

Layla Barrow is mine.

It's about damn time for the world to know it.

This fool kept my girl in a damn apartment building. I could give him credit for choosing an abandoned apartment building, but in reality, it's cheesy and way too easy to find. He literally sent me the address—did he think I wouldn't come? Could this dumb fuck be any fucking stupider?

Layla sits gagged and tied to a wooden chair in the middle of the boiler room, surrounded by moldy boxes and random scrap metal pieces. My boots crunch on the little cement rocks that cover the concrete floor as I get closer to my cub. The silence is filled with the sound of water drips and Layla's heavy breathing, and it's a different level of soothing for me. Hearing her breathe may be better than music.

"What? Can't speak, my little cub?" I ask as I shut and lock the door behind me. Her eyes go from scared to pissed, and my pants get tight. She's lovely. She's mine.

She growls, and her shoulders shake as the chain she's wrapped up in gets tighter. "Don't worry, my little cub, I got you."

I untie her gag that's covered in spit and deep bite marks, and in my mind, I'm debating on whether I should keep it. I bring it up to my nose and can smell her toothpaste and snot on the cloth, and, damn, my eyes light up. It's hot and wet, and I love that combination with anything, including Layla. She glares, and I'm more excited than when I walked into the room. I've got the grizzly's full attention finally.

"Aren't you going to untie me, dimwit?" she growls. Her shiny straight hair is mused and messed up with sweat, her curls coming through by her roots.

"Not quite yet, sweetheart," I squat in front of my little cub. "I'm not exactly the good guy."

"I know you're not the good guy, dipshit. You poisoned my sister-in-law. For all I know, you're still working with Milo." She spits at me, and I let the glop land on my pants, smiling at my cub as her lips quirk up in disgust.

"Why did he take you? He wanted you as far away as he could possibly get you. He wouldn't even come into town because you were there," I say, trying to figure out what motivated Milo to kidnap the sister he's supposedly scared of.

"The fucker asked for my forgiveness," she scoffs, more spit landing on my legs, since I'm still hunched in front of her. "He wants to put the past away, since I 'killed everyone already, anyway.'"

"Killed who?" I ask, surprise coloring my face. I didn't know my little cub was a killer.

"My collectors." What? "My owners and their guards who tried to keep us in line. Then it'll be Milo, for selling me off, and then my parents for helping him," she says in a daze. Hopefully, a bloody, glory-filled daze. My little cub has been through more than I knew. That must've been where the fucker got the money to pay me. By selling his little sister.

"Hmm," I say. The Black Shifter Market? He sold her to the BSM and is asking for forgiveness? "How was he able to kidnap you if he's scared of you?"

"He's not a killer. That's why he hired you, and I play the long game."

"You let him kidnap you?" I ask, a smile creeping over my face. What a little shit she is.

"He can hurt me, but he can't kill me, not yet."

"Curiosity killed the cat, you know?"

"Good thing I'm a bear," she says, and I can see the peek of a smile on her lips before the silence reminds her I'm not here to save her, not completely.

"Where is Milo now?"

"We heard your car pull up, and he took off."

"I need something," I say, knowing she isn't going to like my offer but has shit luck to do anything about it.

"I don't know if you couldn't tell from all the fucking stalking your creepy ass has been doing, but I have nothing. Not even a family who gives a flying rat's ass that my brother sold me off to fund staging his death."

"I want in the Enchanted Pack." I want more. I want her, but she won't bite that quickly. I know my little cub is going to fight me to the end on owning her, but I know, by the Moon Goddess herself, this woman is mine.

"What am I supposed to do about that, smart guy?" She says it with a shake of head and furrowed eyebrows as if she really doesn't know.

"Be my mate."

"You've got to be fucking kidding me." She's glaring again. She tilts her head to the side in disbelief and her sass fuels my urge to annoy the shit out of her.

"I'm not."

"What would being my mate do?"

"They are going to ask you to be part of their Pack, and as your mate, that invitation is extended to me too," I say with a smile of my own.

There's a rumble in the building, and the noise scares my little cub, and she trembles. Her little quivers are adorable. I raise my eyebrow in question, and the scathing glare she gives me makes this day the best fucking day of my life.

"Okay."

"Okay?" I ask, surprised.

"Yes, Ghost, you can be my mate. On two conditions," she says. I wonder what the vixen wants, and I'm all ears to what could possibly make her agree to being my soul mate.

"What?"

"One, set me free, and two, give me a year."

"A year for what?" I don't know if I have a year, if my family has a year, but if she'll easily agree, then what could it really hurt?

"A year to convince the Pack we've been seeing each other, and a year to get revenge."

"Revenge," I echo, raising an eyebrow.

"On my fucking brother."

Little did she know, I was already planning on ruining Milo, so all in all, I win.

25

EDDIE

Getting Willow to step away from the meeting downstairs wasn't nearly as hard as I thought it to be, and that worries me more than soothes me. She's yet to utter a word since I've gotten her up to my room and into the bathroom inside. My tongue is dry from not knowing what to say or do. My nerves are shot, and I should be the one to have it figured out, but I'm as lost as she is, and I can't help but be disappointed in my lack of control over the situation.

Pulling out her bag from the trip to Kaler City, she only has one clean outfit left. It's a long skirt with a matching purple tank top, and I pray it's something she's comfortable in. I watch her face as I set it neatly on the bathroom counter, but her face remains unchanged, as if it was set in stone and her eyes are empty.

Steam fills the room as I turn on the shower, and it warms up. It kills me to think that Layla is out there possibly hurt, but it absolutely has obliterated Willow. I help her undress, quickly undressing myself and sliding on a shower cap over her hair as I guide us into the shower. My own braids will just have to frizz at this point.

She stands stock-still in the shower, and I quickly lather soap and clean her and myself. Starting with our faces and working my way down, I quick use our shower. Dried blood and dirt from my fight with Mr. Barrow colors the shower floor. I see her grimace, and I almost sigh in relief. Sadness is better than nothing.

"I'm sorry," she mutters, turning around to face me with her big, sad eyes and down-turned lips.

I land a quick kiss on her lips before switching us around so I can rinse off quickly before putting her back under the water.

"There's nothing to be sorry for," I say as I get us out of the shower and cover her skin with lotion.

"What am I going to do?" she mutters, and something cracks in my heart when I hear her use *I* instead of *we*, but I know it's my fault. My heart plummets as I remember our conversations today, when I was sure she was going to say she thinks I am her fated mate.

I'm wishing now that I would have let her say the words, but I knew I couldn't hear them unless she was 100 percent sure. I couldn't hear her admit the words out loud and let her think there was any possibility that I could walk away for any sort of reason after that.

I couldn't do it, and so I stopped her. I stopped her from potentially creating a monster she'll only be able to get rid of by death.

"You are going to get dressed," I tell her, lifting her foot and rubbing lotion on it, messaging her foot as she maintains her balance by gripping the counter.

"Then what?" she says, and her voice is low and vulnerable that I flinch. I stare at her feet, unable to look anywhere else because if I meet her eyes and see the pain I know is filling them, it might crush me. Her teardrops land on my back as she cries again.

I want to take each tear from her and carry her burdens, but her sister is missing, and as much as I want to, nothing will stop her tears until her sister is back home, safe.

"We'll find her. Felix is with James, Jackson, and the entire Pack are going to help us," I say as I rub her feet.

That gets me a choked sob from Willow, and her hand pushes me away from her feet. I come to stand, stark naked and not touching the love of my life.

We get dressed in silence, and this time, it's not too heavy. We'll figure this out, and we'll save Layla. I take her head in both my hands and kiss her forehead. She's too emotional to think rationally. I'm sure that's why Jackson sent us up here instead of keeping us huddled around the coffee table with everyone else. She's a loose cannon, and no one hates that more than Willow.

She doesn't have to fight things alone anymore. She doesn't have to figure everything out for everyone. This time and every time after this, she has more than willing people who want to help her. She has us.

We go downstairs, and I can hear the discussion, taking this investigation back to its roots. Walking into the living room with Willow right behind me, I see the whiteboard has moved to be propped up against the fireplace mantel in front of the tv with the words "Where's Milo?" written over it.

That's the million-dollar question that we've been wondering since this whole arrangement started. If we find Milo, we find Layla. I can admit, it wasn't my complete focus, and that is one of my regrets right now. Willow is hurt, and Layla is missing. If I would've got my head out of la-la land sooner, we wouldn't be huddled around our table, trying to find any clues of where the hell Layla is. We have no phone trackers, no calls, no ideas about where Layla could be.

"Maybe we can plan something? Like make Milo think we want to hear his side of things. Get him out of hiding?" Willow mutters as she stares at the board.

"How would we reach him, though?" Luxe asks.

"I still have his old number, though he never answers. It doesn't mean he doesn't listen to voicemails?"

"That's about all we got. It's worth giving it a try," Jackson says.

"Any updates with Felix?" Dylan asks.

"He texted the address of where they are at and are searching the building now," Jackson says with a sigh. "I know Felix can handle himself, but, Dylan, could you just—"

"I'll join them in search, just in case. Someone should be with James until we can fully trust he had nothing to do with this," Dylan says, dropping a kiss on Flora's head before storming out of the house.

A ding sounds in the quiet room. All our heads shoot to Willow's phone, where a text from an unknown number pops up on her screen. She slowly exhales as she opens the text, and her shoulders tensing back up under my hand.

Public Place. Come alone.

"Absolutely not," I quip.

"Tell him the grocery store in ten minutes," Jackson directs her, and my eyes shoot to him. Is he serious right now?

"Okay," Willow murmurs as she drafts a reply.

"No, you can't go alone. What if—"

"She won't. We'll be there. We need a place that is constantly busy with tons of scents to mask us being there. You, Willow, me, and Leo will go to the grocery store. Ryder, River, Luxe, and Flora will hold down the fort here in case this is a misdirection," Jackson decides. "Let's move. There's no time to waste."

He doesn't let me argue, and while Layla is a priority to me, so is Willow's safety. Is our only option to use her as bait?

We walk out the door and to my car. The clouds graying and the wind cutting my ears. I don't like this at all.

"Willow, are you going to be okay?" I ask, holding her hand over the car console. She remains quiet, no sight of a smile when I turn on her favorite song. We're back to the Willow before our shower. I can't blame her or even be upset with her cloudy mood, but I can't help but try to make her smile as we drive.

"Let's go," she mumbles once we park at the store. She pulls away from me and gets out of the car.

I'm sure she was holding my hand more for my sake than hers. She needs a moment to breathe, and I can't tell if I am making things worse or better. I sigh as I jump out of the car to catch up with her. I hate the way she watches over her shoulder, and I hate the way her arms wrap around her stomach to protect herself.

She should be carefree. She should be running aimlessly through the aisles without a care in this world because I should be strong enough and reliable enough to protect her. My chest aches. Goddess, my chest hurts, and my head spins at the thought, and here I am, completely useless.

I see Jackson and Leo get out of their cars, too. They will spread out around the store, since we didn't set a specific spot in the store to meet, so we'll be spaced out but close enough to Willow for when Milo shows up.

"Eddie, go," she snaps, but then frowns and crashes into me as she turns around to apologize.

"I don't want to be separated," I talk quickly to prevent the apology from leaving her lips.

"We're in a public place. I'll be fine, go. He won't approach if he sees you, and we're gambling a lot already. What if he picks out your scent?" she asks, trying to walk away. I stay walking behind her, but she abruptly stops again, and I nearly run into her. "Eddie, please."

My eyes pierce hers. She's standing on shaking legs, and her baby hairs are frizzy and sticking up all over the pace. She's stressed—beyond stressed. I'm stressed. But I can't argue with her. I need her, and she needs space from me to bait Milo, the sick bastard. "Okay, but I'm not going far. I'll be in the next aisle over."

"Thank you."

"You don't have to thank me," I say, forcing each foot up and over. Left right, left right, as I make my way to the next aisle.

26

WILLOW

THE BOXES THAT MY TEA COMES IN ARE YELLOW. A happy color that used to brighten my day. I haven't bought a box of tea bags since... the incident. I'm here, looking at tea bags, and Moon Goddess knows what Layla is looking at. Is she being tormented? What would Milo want with her?

Huffing, I trace my fingers over the boxes. My eyes track over the stack of boxes on the display table, finding the little imperfections on each one before finding the one I would have chosen. I can't believe even after Ghost attacked me in my apartment that I would drink from a tea bag I randomly found. Milo and Ghost knew I would drink it, regardless. Am I that predictable?

Am I that stupid?

As I pretend to browse the aisle, memories fill my head. Milo could've never been my mate.

There is only one person who I hated going grocery shopping with. One person who'd follow me around like a lost puppy, yapping my ear off about how long I was taking. Or about how we should try to make something he wouldn't end up eating, or how his parents were getting on his nerves, and how he had to leave early—the only time we had to spend together between work and classes—because his parents were calling him home to fix the TV.

I knew fixing the TV would turn into him staying for dinner without inviting me, which always ran over the time he said he'd be home, and that would be the reason he came home at three in the morning instead of being home at seven in the evening to spend what little time we had together with me.

Milo never treated me like a mate.

"Miss me?" The voice makes me jump out of my skin. I itch and ache in all the worst ways as recognition of the voice seeps into my brain, and I turn towards the voice.

He stands there with his hands in his pockets. Wearing a loose, tropical-patterned shirt and matching shorts. His skin is darker, as if the sun and him have become best friends, and his hair is freshly cut. His eyes are still molten brown. Milo Doug Barrow is standing in front of me.

The natural glow of happiness that used to surround him isn't there anymore. I can see the scar across Milo's face from when Layla said she almost had him. I wonder why he hadn't shifted to heal the mark? I don't care enough to ask, though. Not when I know what he did to Layla. What he could've done to me.

Milo Barrow is not the man I thought he was.

My mind is reeling. He's here. He's breathing. From the outside, I'm sure we appear as old friends with how casual this setting is and how nonchalant he's standing. I can sense Eddie racing towards me, but I flex my fingers, hoping he, Jackson and Leo take the sign to wait. I need to know; I need to hear this from Milo himself.

"It took you a while to figure it out, though." He shrugs as if we're old friends, and he hasn't paid someone thousands to kill me. He smiles like a bachelor's first day on vacation at a villa on a beach somewhere warm and close to the ocean. It makes my skin boil.

My skin tightens around my eyes and breathing is getting more complicated. Heavy? I should feel an immense sense of danger, but all I feel is my bear simmering under my skin, wishing to make her way to the surface. Unfortunately for me, she's not interested in answers. She wants blood.

"You haven't answered my question."

"What question?" I ask, my mind going blank, not believing I'm actually having this conversation right now. I want to reach out, and see if he's real, if my hand would swipe through him like it would a ghost, but I can't bring myself to move.

"Did you miss me?"

"Why do you care? Better yet, why are you back from the dead?"

"Why won't you answer me?" His eyebrows furrow as if he's genuinely confused and angry. I see his jaw lock, and I try to keep my eyes from searching for Eddie. I don't want to reveal the Pack's presence yet.

"You want to hear how I was wrong? That we weren't mates, and that I regret every single moment we spent together, and that I'm glad that you 'died' because I found my true mate? Is that what you want to hear?" I hate to be rude. To be hurtful, but I can't contain my bewilderment. How dare he ask me that? Do I *miss* him? No. Not for a long time.

"No. But I needed it. I thought—I don't know. Wait. I do. I do know. Willow, there's something wrong with me."

"You don't think I know that by now?"

"No, I had it all. I had you, my family, a great job on the way. It was too much."

"Milo, if you don't get to the point, I am going to call my angry, surprisingly violent mate, who will come running after me. You want to know why he'll come running? Because he is my mate, whether or not he knows it. Because he loves me, and he doesn't have to say he loves me—I just know it. Eddie Enchanted is more a man and mate than you'll ever be, and I need you to wrap your point up before either he or I kill you in this grocery store."

"Willow, don't threaten me—I'm trying to tell you I'm sorry."

"So, you admit to paying James tens of thousands of dollars to not kill me, but get close to keep Layla from killing you for selling her to BSM?"

"James?" he asks, and it only rouses my bear to fight harder to get out.

"Ghost!" I nearly shout in frustration. My goddess, was he always this dense?

"Oh, then yeah, I admit to doing that." Is this man crazy?

"Okay," I say, huffing in frustration. I want to walk away, and let the Enchanted Pack swoop in, but I'm not dumb enough to give the man my back.

"Okay? That's all you have to say, Willow? You're not mad or going to yell at me?" He's becoming unstable, and now I truly see the beast I'm dealing with. He's unraveling at the seams, and the real Milo Doug Barrow has arrived to the show.

"I'd have to care to do that, Milo," I say, trying to take an unnoticeable step away from him, but I run into the table behind me, a few boxes tumbling to the floor. That's when I remember that I'm not the only one he's hurt, and that there were no bounds to this man's torment. "I'll let it be water under the bridge if you tell me where Layla is?"

"I don't want to hurt her, but she has to let this go," he says, as if it is the most obvious observation any simpleton could make, but I know better. I know better now than to trust this lying, self-centered piece of trash.

"She should let go of you selling her off to pay for your faked murder when you could've just talked to me for free?" I say, absolute shock covering my skin.

"She was helping her brother be free. She should be happy to have been able to help me."

"Was I so terrible that you couldn't just talk to me?"

"I needed out. I needed to move on. I needed cash, and fast. Then you kept running your mouth, placing doubts all over town. I had to get you to keep quiet. I wasn't murdered. I ran away."

"I see that, Milo," I mutter, trying to think about all that's happened since he faked his murder and ran away. He lost everything, I lost everything, families were broken, and all because of what? "But then you moved to this town, and everything was fine."

"Where is Layla?" I ask again. I don't care about his

breakdown or that I was wrong. I need to know where Layla is. He obviously has her.

"She's so vengeful, and I needed you to protect me from her. She's dangerous, Willow."

"Milo, where is Layla?"

"James has her." I can't process the betrayal, not when I finally got Milo back on track.

"James has her? Has her where?"

"He found her two hours ago. I heard a car pull up, and I had to run. I'm sure he's pissed, but you won't let them kill me, right, Willow?" Okay, James *is* on our side?

"I wouldn't bet on it," I mutter, realizing we never really knew each other. He doesn't know I can be as much of a killer as Layla and James. I didn't know he could betray his own family. He may not realize it, but he's hurt *my* family. My tongue runs over my teeth as if I have chocolate stuck over them, and I'm sure my eyes are glowing as my and my bear's emotions intertwine with mine. I can't quite distinguish this feeling, and I've only ever experienced it one other time, and that was when I killed Cassandra. I crave to have his blood under my claws.

I tilt my head in thought. I could shift right now. I may have to go to the human grocery store from now on, or maybe I could plead my case with the owner, but my bear is fully committed to killing him. I am fully capable of murder. My eyes stay focused on Milo. Every rise of his shoulders in response to every breath he's taking has my fingers fidgeting to get closer. To stop his breathing.

I am a killer too, after all.

"That's not the only reason I agreed to meet Willow, I swear," he says, his worry lines from his forehead disappearing as he smiles. I let my fingers drop, and I hope Eddie and the guys know to swoop in. I shouldn't take Milo on by myself.

"Why are you here, then?" Eddie finally speaks up. He moves to stand in front of me, though I don't think Milo is here to hurt me. I mean, I think he would have been smart enough to do it before Eddie approached us. In fact, I think I want to hurt him more than any threat he could be to me. I see Jackson and Leo flank Milo's sides as if to stop him from running, and I see panic build on Milo's face. His eyes tracking around the aisle searching for an exit as he bends at the knees, getting ready to take off.

I'm not sure where, since we have him surrounded.

"I want Willow back," he says, even though he is preparing to run away... again. How frickin' hilarious. I can't help the giggle that slips from my mouth, both at the admission and the actions that I don't even think he realizes he's doing.

"Are you fucking kidding me?" Eddie says, his shoulders slump a tinge as he refuses to look at me.

"No, not all. Seeing her with you has angered me, and I want her back. I'm here to fight for her hand."

"Milo—" I say, and his name comes out with a lisp since my canines are still out. I wasn't a damsel, and I don't need them duking it out. Even if my bear is getting riled up at the thought, she's more excited about getting her own paws dirty.

"Okay, let's fight," Eddie says, that same look on his face as when he fought Mr. Barrow, but this is different. He's shaking with anger, and I hope he knows there is no real competition between the two. At least not in my eyes.

"Jackson," I yell, and he's grabbing one of Milo's arms as Leo is grabbing the other. I'm not sure what the plan is here, but we can't kill him here.

"I've been waiting to kill this fucker since he fucked with your tea," Eddie says. He shrugs my hand off of him, but I step in front of Eddie, blocking him from getting any closer to Milo.

"By Layla's request, this one is mine," James's voice comes through from behind me. I whip around, now standing protectively in front of Eddie as James gets closer to our little group.

"I was wrong, Willow. I shouldn't have left you. I know now. I'm your mate," Milo says, trying to get closer to me, but James pushes past us to grab him by the neck.

"You're not my mate, Milo. You never were." My words come out like quick fire, but I'm more focused on the shaking of Eddie's shoulders. "Layla, we need to get to Layla."

"She's at the Pack house. She's fine. I made sure," James says.

"Make it hell, James," Jackson says with a sneer. His eyes glow with anger too, and he appears to want the honor of killing Milo himself. Which isn't too surprising because he's an Alpha, and if he views Layla as Pack, that's enough for his protective instinct to take over and for retribution to outweigh familial ties.

"My pleasure."

"Willow! How could you let your mate be treated like this? When did you become so heartless?" Milo shouts as James drags his flailing body away. Milo isn't weak by any means, but he's obviously been relaxing since faking his death, while James has muscles that would scare any sane being.

"Don't you dare call her anything, you piece of shit," Eddie roars as he goes to lunge, but I beat him to it.

"I'd do anything for my mate. I'd deal with anything, fight through hell and earth for my true mate, and that's not you. It can't be. The Moon Goddess isn't as cruel as to pair anyone with you," I say, grabbing Eddie's arm and pulling him to me. Eddie is my true mate, whether or not he accepts me.

"How do you know?" Milo shouts, and he gets the attention of other shoppers. I see some want to come help Milo, but others are rushing through the store to get out. A shifter brawl is never fun from the sidelines.

I do something I shouldn't, but I do it anyway. I grab Milo's wrist and bring my canines forward. His skin rips around my teeth as I bite him. I pierce his skin, drawing blood, but the bloodstream doesn't make it past his wrist as the healing process has already kicked in with his shifter instincts so close to the surface. Eddie's hand slips from around my hips, and James step back, forcing my teeth to rip more of Milo's skin.

My bear definitely enjoys ripping into his skin, but she hated biting him as a mark of mates. She wanted his blood, but not in this way.

"You're already healing, Milo. In a few moments, you'll be completely healed, and my bite will have disappeared. You're not my mate," I say, spitting the blood in my mouth onto the floor, which instantly makes me want to clean it up, but I have bigger things to worry about.

I turn to Eddie, whose eyes are wide and mouth is

dropped open. I know I shouldn't have bitten Milo, and I hope he doesn't take it the wrong way, but now he'll know I'm serious when I say he's my fated mate.

"There's no question whether that monster is my mate or not," I say as my bear retreats and gives me full control. I watch Eddie carefully, trying to evaluate if I messed everything up.

He closes his mouth as a small smile takes over his face. I hear Jackson let out a laugh as the yells of Milo pleading with James to let him go fade into the distance. Eddie roughly grabs my arm and yanks me into a hug I couldn't break even if I wanted to. I sob a sigh of relief as his scent surrounds me, and I finally peace. I hear Jackson and Leo's footsteps leave as Eddie and I stand stuck in the aisle by the display of tea boxes.

"It's over?" I ask. Were all my problems solved just like that?

"Willow?" Eddie says, shock dripping from his voice. His lips pressing against the top of my head, and his hold doesn't loosen even an inch. "You bit him."

"I knew it wouldn't take," I say, and I mean it. I knew there was no possible way my bite would take, and I wish that this would've been more common knowledge among shifters. Maybe Layla and I wouldn't have gone through everything we had if we'd known.

"You bit him," he mutters. He runs a hand calmingly up and down my back, and I'm not sure if it's for me or for him, but I need it all the same.

"It healed, just like your mom's did. Milo's not my mate."

27

WILLOW

I'm not sure what to do now. I'm not sure what reality is and is not. Am I truly free now? Is everything done with? With one look at Eddie, I am ready to go home. I want to disappear with a good book, a hot mug of tea, and blankets with my fan on high.

I need to see Layla. That's what I need to do. With that realization, I suddenly can't get out of the store fast enough.

"Oh my goddess Layla, she's safe. I have to go see her. Let's go," I say as I grab Eddie's arm and rush us out of the store. Mentioning Layla must have brought him out of a daze, because he's rushing as fast as I am now as we dash towards the car. He starts the car, and we break all sorts of laws trying to get back home.

All I can think as we race off is that she's actually okay. Oh my goodness, she's okay.

He pulls into the driveway, and I'm out of the car before he can put it in park. Layla is sitting in one of the rocking chairs on the huge front porch of the Enchanted Pack house. She jumps up when she sees me. Her smile is tight, and her hair is curly from being washed, but I don't wait to wrap the girl in my arms.

"Layla! Oh, Layla, are you okay? Let me see you. Where were you?" I ask as I run my hands over her hair and crush her into a hug again when my inspection is done.

"I'm fine. Nothing crazy happened. James found me."

"How? How did he even know where to look?" I ask her, and she responds with a shrug before being pulled into a hug by Eddie.

"Glad you're okay, kid," Eddie mutters, giving her a squeeze before letting her go.

"Barely younger than you, Eddie." He smiles and teasingly shoves her before stalking over to the house.

"Yeah, whatever," he yells as his Pack greets him before he can even open the door.

I turn to Layla, placing my hands on her shoulders. "I'm sorry, Layla. I shouldn't have let this get this bad and made more of an effort to find and stop Milo. You might want to call James. I think he's really gonna kill him."

"He won't," Layla says, and I'm not sure what makes her so confident in the statement, but I don't question it. She was set on killing him earlier; what made her change her mind and let James take him?

She only smiles with a wink that I'm unsure what's for. Leaving me in a cloud of concussion, she turns on her heel and walks back onto the porch. I sigh and spin towards Eddie, who's already made his way back to me. He only shrugs at Layla's response.

"That's up to her."

"Yeah, I know. I just—I hope she's okay."

"She'll make her way through it, Willow," Eddie says, pulling me into one of his bear hugs. Gosh, I love this man. His scent calms me, and I melt into his arms, snuggling my head against his chest.

"It's over?" I ask, locking my hands behind his back so he can't pull apart from me.

"It's over, Buttercup," he says, resting his chin on my head. "What now?"

"Well, I don't know. I think you know what I want, but, Eddie, what do you want?"

"I want you to go home." My hands fall from around him, and I take a shattering step back.

"What?" I ask. My voice falls, and it comes out in a whisper, but I can't muster much more. He wants me to go home?

"Go home, feed Nola and Sunny, give Layla the space I'm sure she needs," he says.

"Eddie—" Wait, I didn't mean we were over. I meant the situation is over. What does he mean by go home? I am home?

"Go home, Willow." He's smiling, and my heart is tearing apart, layers falling apart bit by bit.

"Okay?" I ask, praying he'll clarify. Praying he will change his mind. I didn't think that we would be over like that. He's my mate—right? He feels what I feel. Oh my goodness, am I wrong again? No, I couldn't possibly be wrong again. I'm not wrong. It's him. I know it's him.

"Okay," he confirms, walking back to his car and pulling off. Leaving me dazed in his front yard.

I'm not sure what to do. I feel like a zombie walking to my car. Which got here how? I don't know, but I'm glad it's here 'cause Eddie left. I turn to Layla, unable to stop the tears welling in my eyes. She appears as confused as I do as she gets in the car, but doesn't say anything. I can hardly comprehend what just happened myself, let alone try to explain to her.

I get to my driveway, and I don't want to get out of the car. Did the Pack hear our conversation? Did Layla? Is that why she didn't ask? My cheeks flush red with disappointment and embarrassment.

I swear he's my mate. I know it like I know how to breathe, yet he walked away from me.

"Let's go," Layla mumbles, opening my car door and walking with me, arm in arm, back to what is supposed to be my home, my safe haven. Yet it isn't the same anymore. The pink kitchen doesn't sparkle with life, and the orange front door doesn't bring me happiness, as it once did.

"Give it some time. Maybe he needed some space," Layla murmurs as she takes me to my room. I forgot about the bag I left in Eddie's room filled with my dirty clothes, but I also know I wouldn't have been able to face anyone in there. Did my mate reject me?

I collapse in my bed, and Layla leaves. I don't know where she goes. Maybe to her room; maybe she thinks that this is all over, and she wants to leave too. Oh my goodness, is she going to leave me too?

I reach for my book off my nightstand, the book Eddie and I were reading together, but all it does is start the race of tears falling from my face. I wallow holding the book to my chest as the tears damage the pages. Each antagonizing minute spent in my room tears my heart deeper. For each minute no one calls or texts me, for each minute that I think about Eddie. My chest constricts, and my heart stops beating for a second as a sob rushes past my lips. For thirty minutes, I cry over my losses, over being alone again.

As I set the damaged book down on my comforter, I curl into a ball when my video doorbell chimes detecting motion at the front door. It's probably Layla leaving without even saying goodbye.

I pull up the feed. I know I'll only hurt my own feelings more by watching Layla leave, but I can't stop myself. Nola makes her way to my bed and curls up in my lap, purring and snuggling, but my heart hurts far too much for her to make me feel better.

I watch the video load. Seeing the turning blue swirl of death before, a man appears on my screen. Oh, what? Did he leave something here at my house? Oh, wait—his game console. He must be here to get his game console. The thought brings me back to before the mating ceremony, just before things started to go bad when we played that game, and I was happy. So happy, even with Milo after me, and now I almost wish he was still after me. So I could still be with Eddie. So Eddie wouldn't have a reason to leave.

I turn on the mic and speak to him, since I have no strength to get up and see him in person. "Leave," I whisper, trying to hold back the sadness I'm sure is pouring out of my pores.

"You owe me a favor, Willow," Eddie says, holding a yellow box of tea bags and a packaged blanket in his arms.

"What are you talking about? I don't owe you anything," I say as I sit up in my bed. Owe him? And is he holding gifts for me? Are they parting gifts? If so, I don't want them. He can keep them just like he has kept my heart.

"Yes, you do, Willow. It was my witch that saved you when you were having an allergic reaction, and in exchange for her saving you, you owe me a favor. I'm cashing it in today."

Favors are unavoidable in the paranormal world. It's worth more than gold and diamonds, and it is an incredible betrayal to not honor them. He's put me in between a rock and a hard place, and I have no idea why.

"Willow, I want to tell you what the favor is in person, please," he begs, and I can feel myself giving in. No, he can't come to my home and make demands. I'm kind, but not a darn rug he can walk all over. I get out of bed, even though I don't want to, and walk to the door, but I don't open it. I slide down the door with my back against it and turn my mic back on.

"You lost that privilege when you asked me to leave. What's the favor, you jerk?" Name calling is way better than when I struck James for thinking he was the one who kidnapped Layla. I'll have to remember that next time I get angry.

"Willow, tell me how you feel about me."

"I know you heard me at the grocery store," I mumble into the mic, rolling my eyes. Is he serious right now?

"You weren't talking to me. You were talking to Milo. Talk to *me* now, Willow. Confess to me."

"I would've if you'd let me at the wedding," I say, still reeling in the rejection. He would've heard it before Layla was kidnapped, before Milo appeared, before I bit Milo; he would've heard me, yet he stopped me.

"I want to hear it in our place, Willow. Not at the grocery store, not at your sister's mating ceremony. Here, just me and you."

"And Layla, she's still here, I think," I say. I'm far too emotional to scent if she is still here. But this is the first time my door camera has gone off since I've been home, and she has way too much stuff to try to go through a window.

"And Layla. Me, you, and Layla. Now on with it, woman!" he says, smiling into the camera. I finally stand and open the door, but I don't step outside.

My eyes focus as I wipe away the tears, and I fully see him, breathing, smiling, with a box of tea and a blanket. I see him, really see him. He's my fated mate, whether or not he accepts it. He stands in a coordinating outfit to mine, and I'm suddenly glad I didn't change. He's wearing a purple T-shirt similar to my skirt. He smiles, and he has his glasses on, which I think he knows I love.

He is everything I could have ever wanted in a mate, and he sent me away.

I take in a deep breath, readying to lay myself bare. "Okay, Eddie Enchanted, you are my fated mate. I was wrong about thinking Milo could ever be my mate. Not just because of things he did to Layla, but because I know he would have never been my mate. Not when I've never felt this explosive wave of emotion every time you look at me. Not when I see and smell and feel all the good in the world showering me every time you're around. Eddie Enchanted, I love you. I love you so much, and you broke my heart," I say with a sob as my hand comes up to cover my mouth as I drop my phone.

"I'm sorry, Buttercup, but I needed you to tell me, face to face, what you were feeling was even a tenth of what I feel. Willow Buttercup, you are my mate, and I thank the Moon Goddess she brought you to me because I know, *I know*, you are mine."

"Kiss me, please," I mutter as I rush towards him. The box of tea and the blanket fall from his hands onto the porch. His lips crush against mine, our teeth almost bumping. Hearing him say I am his mate is everything I need to push forward. Our kiss is explosive, and even when I stand right under the fireworks, I crave more.

"I need you," he mutters as his hands swallow me up. He urges my legs up, and I jump to hook them around him. He walks into the house, leaving the gifts he brought on the porch, and kicks the front door closed with his foot as he us into my bedroom. Dropping me on the bed, both of us breathing heavily as he lifts my hips and yanks my skirt and panties off. Exposing me bare to the harsh wind of my AC.

"I need to see all of you, Buttercup. I need it like I need my next breath," he says, and I'm quick to lean up and get rid of my shirt too.

Completely bare to my mate, my cheeks getting red, my insecurity peeking its head out, but the glow of Eddie's eyes melts that monster away as he's almost frozen in place.

He slides his own shirt off, still dazed by me, fueling my aching cunt with want and need as he unbuckles his belt. That gets me jumping up as my mouth waters from the sight of my mate.

My mate.

I don't need a bite to tell me this man is my mate anymore. I know, I just know, Eddie Enchanted is my fated mate. I crawl forward, placing my hands on his belt, lightly moving his own away. I look up at him through my lashes as his breathing gets quicker, harsher, as my skin brushes his.

He doesn't let me get much farther as he pushes me back down on the bed, nodding his head. "You first, my mate."

I sigh in complete satisfaction as his words reach my ears, and I catch his lips in another kiss. Goodness, this man is everything.

"Absolutely not, Eddie. I need you in every way I can have you," I say, using my bear's strength to flip us over and work his pants down. I let my fingers explore him for a bit. Feeling every crevice of him before I lick my lips and bend down to latch my lips onto his cock. I tease his base with my tongue, watching his face as he closes his eyes for a second, and his chest heaves as if he can't hold back any longer. I flatten my tongue against him and let it drag up his length. Watching his every jolt and twitch as his anticipation builds up makes me feel all the more powerful.

I want him to want me as I want him, and I can see that he does. I go down, wrapping my lips around his head and taking him fully in my mouth. I'm aching darn near as much as he is.

"Christ—Buttercup," he says as his hands tangle in my hair, directing me just how he likes. I put one of my hands at his base, working him there too as I moved up and down his length. His moans filling the room alongside the grumbled moans I let out while still around him. I work slowly, now understanding why he edged me last time. Understanding the joy and pleasure around prolonging the experience. Goodness, I could do this all day. I gag around him, and tears form, but I don't care. I suck him down as far as I can before coming back up and starting all over.

"Baby girl, I'm coming," he says, and I stop, slowly sliding up and off him with a pop, not letting him come.

"How do you like that?"

"Not nearly as much as you're going to like this," he says, tossing me down like a rag doll. He slowly parts my thighs and trails his fingers down to my center. He presses two fingers into me, and his head lolls back as he groans. "Buttercup, you're soaked."

I moan as I arch my back. He twists his fingers to hit just right. Between that and him rubbing my clit with his thumb, I nearly combust, and that's when I know I'm mating Eddie Enchanted.

Tonight.

My teeth ache in my gums, and my fingernails get sharper. I can feel the glow in my eyes.

"Eddie," I whimper. He slips his fingers from me before I can come, and soon his cock is inside me. He gives me one slow starter thrust before the dam of his control breaks.

This is the moment I mate Eddie Enchanted. My canines coming down fully as he pushes in again, a wave of pleasure racing forward, closer, to where I want. He slinks back out and then in again, faster and faster as we both get closer.

"I love you. Oh, damn, I love you so damn much,

Willow," he mutters, kissing me all over my face and neck. I can feel the nip of his canines as he kisses me, and the tiny shocks add to the mounting pleasure.

"I love you, Eddie," I say as my body has had enough, and I lean up to kiss the spot between his neck and shoulder before I fully bite into him. He takes this moment to bite my shoulder, and his teeth sink in, past my skin, marking me as his for life. There is a settling in my soul as our bites recognize one another, finally being completely at ease. That euphoric feeling pushes me over the edge, and we come together as our fates are sealed.

Eddie Enchanted is mine, and I am his.

EPILOGUE
EDDIE

OUR BITES DIDN'T HEAL, AND TODAY IS FINALLY the day. It's our day. The day of Willow's and my mating ceremony. As much as she protested, there was no way I was letting Milo rob her of her having her dream ceremony.

Even if we already have our bite marks, which was only supposed to happen the night of the ceremony, but since when are Willow and I so traditional? We have two pets, for goodness' sake.

I stare into the mirror, watching as the brown suit molds to my shoulders and lays just right across my chest. Sliding my glasses up my nose, I smile even harder than I already am, remembering how feral Willow gets over these damn glasses.

My Buttercup won't be a Buttercup anymore; she will be an Enchanted.

Willow Enchanted.

I like that. Actually, I love that. Since our little

encounter with Milo, she's been free to love me, and I can't help but eat it up every chance I get.

I stand outside watching my Pack members crowd around for our monthly Pack barbecue that's been taken over by my mating ceremony. Many of my Pack members are wolves, and they don't do this whole shebang, but it's nice to see my Pack dressed up in suits, and Flora, Layla, Luxe, and Remi dressed in formal dresses.

There are people everywhere, including my mother and Willow's family. My mom comes up to me as I step outside, closing the sliding door behind me. My heart races as I get excited about officially being Willow's mate. I'm sure my mother can feel my racing heart when her hand reaches my chest. Chuckling, she moves and cups my face between her hands.

"You made it, baby. You did it," she says with tears in her eyes. "You've found your mate."

"Yes, I finally did," I say. I pull her into a hug, secretly hoping her tears don't fall on my suit jacket. Can't kill a guy for wanting to look his best for his mate.

"You may not have got the heat house, but you got the mate, and that's just as beautiful," my mother says as she smiles encouragingly, even though it's not needed.

"I would be satisfied if I only got Willow, but I got my heat house too," I say.

"How?" she says in shock as her smile gets bigger.

"I've gone independent. With Jackson as my investor, I'll be forming my own team, and we'll bring the idea of heat houses to the shifter community." Everything was happening so fast, and I have no idea where Jackson got the money to invest in me, but we're doing this together.

Starting by finalizing the heat house in our backyard. After that we'll advertise to other Packs in the area and once they become normalized, we'll use the profit to build houses for the community, for those without Packs. It's a long road, but I know we'll get there. I'll keep my job at Cloud until we get our first buyer, and then it's off to the races for Jackson and I.

"Baby, I'm so darn proud of you." She marvels.

I soak up the praise as I grab my mother for one more hug before letting her go gush over Jackson's involvement.

I wait by the edge of the back porch, waiting for Willow before we make our rounds to greet guests, when I finally see her. Willow slips out the door I just exited from. She blushes as she walks towards me, and I can't help but trail my eyes down her body.

I have my girl here, next to me. Thank the Moon Goddess.

She's dressed beautifully in a silky orange wrap dress that sits off her shoulders. Wow, she's gorgeous, and she's all mine.

I reach my hand out to my beautiful goddess and twirl her around before crushing her to me, my lips finding hers.

"You ready to greet everyone?"

"Yup," she says shyly as we head to my mother first, since she hasn't wandered off far. She's talking with Jackson about food before we walk up, but she stops mid-sentence and gasps when she sees us.

"True mates. Wow, you are absolutely stunning, dear," she tells Willow, pulling her into a hug.

"Yes, Willow, welcome to the Pack. We're honored to have you."

"Thank you. Thank you both," Willow says as I pull her away. As much as I wanted to put this event on for her, I also can't wait to have my Buttercup all to myself, which means flying through the greetings and dinner.

"I'm glad to not be the only adult female at these things anymore," Flora says, in conversation with Luxe as they walk up. Besides Flora, and now Layla, who reluctantly joined the Pack, the only other female we have is Remi, and who knows how long she'll be around, since I'm sure she'll want to find her real family soon.

"Yeah, well, it seems one by one these men will be snatched up."

"As long as they all are into girls, that's at least five more women. That will even us out," Flora says, looking around as if she can sniff out their mates.

"As long as they are all into women, yes," I confirm, grabbing Willow and me a drink. I sip on orange juice. Willow shakes her iced tea, and only the Moon Goddess knows what's in Flora's cup.

"Yeah, what's the up and up on Ghost—James? Is he still allowed on Pack lands?" Flora whispers, even though everyone here has heightened hearing.

"As a rogue wolf, his invitation on Pack land was limited, and now that Layla and Willow are safe, unless he joins the Pack, which Jackson wasn't willing to do, he had to leave," I explain.

"Layla was okay with that?" Luxe says, raising her eyebrow.

"Why would she care?" I ask. But I know there's something going on there. Hell, anyone could tell from the pure tension between the two that something was going on, but he is too old for her, I'm sure. He's damn sure too fucking dangerous and should stay at least ten miles away from Layla if he values his life.

"They're mates, I thought. That's what he said when he dropped her off here after finding her?"

"What mate would drop their mate off? That doesn't make sense," I say.

"If you guys are going to talk about me, at least go somewhere I can't hear you," Layla pipes up with a roll of her eyes.

"Layla, is James your mate?" Willow asks.

Layla hesitates. The snarky, smart-mouthed girl hesitates, and that rocks me with a chill. There's something more. More than that, I'm sure she isn't willing to tell, but I try anyway. "Did he hurt you? Is he hurting you, Layla?"

"No, the opposite, in fact. I can't get him away from me." She scoffs, staring anywhere but at me.

"Why didn't you tell me? You can always tell me anything, Layla," Willow says, landing a comforting arm on the girl's shoulder, but Layla shrugs it off.

"It wasn't important."

"A mate is important. Why aren't you with him?"

"I deserve to be courted, Willow, that's why. He has to work for my attention regardless of what the Moon Goddess or fate may think."

"All power to you, sister," Flora says and lifts her drink in a cheer before downing it.

Willow stares up at me with furrowed eyebrows. I shake my head. If Layla doesn't want to share what's going on, she's not going to. We'll just have to find out for ourselves.

"Give her space, Eddie," Willow says, as if I was the one who was going to pry. I'm not the only cop around when it comes to Layla.

"As long as you do."

"Hey, I'm not that bad."

"Yeah, till momma bear mode kicks in, and suddenly everyone is mute to the anger."

"Aww, you jealous?" River asks, kicking around a soccer ball with Remi now. They are muddying the bottoms of their nice outfits, but as long as Willow or Willow's mother doesn't notice, they should be fine. I glance over at the Buttercup family, who are huddled around their seats at the table. They smile in our direction but don't offer much more. Even her sister, Harper, and her mate, Jason, made it, and I'm glad they didn't let the tension between us stop them from coming to their daughter's mating ceremony.

I take a glance around, my skin warming at the view of everyone I love all here, together with my fated mate in my arms. I press a kiss to the top of her head as she's talking to her friends. We would build our own memories here, together, and they won't be perfect, but we'll be together, and that is pretty damn close to perfect to me.

ALSO BY JORJOR BATTLE

Stained Perception

Check out the first book in the STAINED SERIES following Willow's best friend Flora and her ex-assassin mate Dylan in their book Stained Perception!

ACKNOWLEDGMENTS

Another one down for the books!

Writing has become so important to me, and being able to share it with everyone is such a blessing and an honor! This book took me even longer to write and publish than my first book, but the time it took was worth it. I've grown in my writing and publishing so much with this book, and I hope to continue to grow with each book I put out.

I'm incredibly grateful for every single person who made this book possible. Thank you to my lovely readers for giving me a chance to entertain you with my book Stained Fate. I hope you have enjoyed Willow and Eddie's story and are excited about Layla and Ghost's story!

Shout out to my family for believing in me through this process. Without their continuous support and listening ear to my random ramblings of ideas and plot holes this book would not be where it is today.

Thank you to my beta readers, Maddi and Cassie. Your help is immensely appreciated, and your feedback elevated my story in ways you may not imagine!

Thank you to the discord chat (The Writing Cave) for endless days and nights of writing with me!

I absolutely cannot forget to thank my amazing editor

at EJL Editing, Maddi, who cleaned up this mess of a book and helped me polish it.

My cover designer over at AS Book Designs was a dream to work with. You really captured the image I wanted for Stained Fate, and I cannot thank you enough! I can't wait to see what we come up with next!

To all my ARC readers who have a less polished version of my baby, thank you for giving her and me the chance to entertain you! Your reviews and words help me find readers who will enjoy this book, and I thank you for that.

I appreciate every single person who has been my side in publishing this book, and I thank you all.

ABOUT THE AUTHOR

Jorjor Battle is a Michiganer pursuing her dreams of becoming a romance author. She'd prefer to fall in love in real life but, for the time being, accepts her unhealthy obsession with love in the forms of books, tv shows, and movies.

Follow her on social media to hear about upcoming projects and all things about being a writer and book lover!
Instagram: readingjorjor
TikTok: readingjorjor
Pinterest: readingjorjor

www.ingramcontent.com/pod-product-compliance
Lightning Source LLC
Chambersburg PA
CBHW022013310726
48972CB00006B/1632